REBEL WING

Rebel Wing

Tracy Banghart

Previously published
February 2014 as Shattered Veil
July 2014 as Rebel Wing by Alloy Entertainment — Powered by Amazon

Cover design @2024 Regina Wamba
Character art @2024 Victoria Alessandri
Map @2024 Jessica Khoury
Author photo © April Anft
Published by Snowy Wings Publishing
www.snowywingspublishing.com

ISBN 978-1-958051-69-6

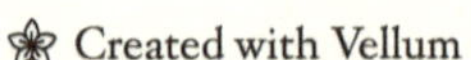 Created with Vellum

To Andy's abs

RUSIANA
Pakan
Spiro
Feln
Revening
Tarik
Me
SAFARA
Bie
Hevensack

vik
Cress
PANTHEA
Pono
lux
ATALANTA

ARIS

ARISTOS

CHAPTER ONE

HIGH ABOVE THE OLIVE GROVES AND BLINDING WHITE ROOFS of the village, Aris danced. She twisted and dove, guiding her wingjet straight out over granite cliffs and the glitter of the ocean. As she did, she imagined its wings were her arms, reaching far out into the blue. Her fingers would knife through a wisp of cloud, and the moisture would linger against her skin, like a kiss.

Her father wouldn't approve of such thoughts. To him, flying was a practical pursuit, for dusting crops or traveling from place to place. Their village was built high on carbonate stilts, so wing-jets were the easiest form of transportation unless you were working the land or hiking down the steep paths leading to the narrow beach below the cliffs. Most everyone here could fly. But no one flew like Aris did.

At least Calix understood what flying meant to her.

She pressed the pedals under her feet and twisted the hand controls, diving in a last tight pirouette before nosing the tiny two-seat wingjet toward home.

A flicker of light caught at the edge of her vision. She glanced out to sea and steered the wingjet in the direction of the movement.

Suddenly, the flash became a speeding wingjet. It hurtled

toward her, its silver sides reflecting the sun. Aris hovered just off shore, the beach a golden crescent beneath her, waiting for the wingjet to change course or slow to land. Instead, it grew larger, advancing quickly. Surely the flyer saw her? Her hands tightened on the controls. She moved farther from the cliff. The other wingjet shifted too, keeping her directly in its path.

Aris nearly waited too long. She jerked the controls down, the force of the other wingjet's passage rattling the bones of her machine as she locked into a downward spiral. Heart beating wildly, she waited until the last second before pulling up and skimming the water. Beneath her, waves rolled from deep blue to white, ruffled by her jet wind.

The other flyer followed, matching her move for move. Her stomach twisted as the wingjet drew up alongside, giving her a clear view of its needle nose and the Atalanta flag decal stretched across its sloping tail. No solar panels curved above its wings like on her wingjet. Instead the whole thing shimmered a silvery gold, the hallmark of new-tech solar material. Aris had only ever seen Military wingjets on news vids, never up close.

What was it doing *here*, so far from the front lines of the war?

Without warning, the jet shot upward, piercing the cloudless sky like a shining arrow. She slowed to watch its progress, waiting for it to disappear. But with a flash of reflected sunlight, it dove again, straight for her.

What is he trying to prove? Her apprehension shifted to annoyance. She darted out from under the jet and flipped through the air to face him. It had to be a *him*. All members of the Military sector were male.

For a moment they hovered in a strange standoff. Then the other wingjet rocketed forward, forcing her into a series of evasive spins and loops. At first Aris dipped and whirled away in anger and frustration. But gradually, his movements lost their aggression and she relaxed into the dance, pushing farther and twisting faster until it was suddenly *her* chasing *him* across the sky. *She*, who flew the most intricate patterns, she who nipped at his jet wind, whooping as she tumbled toward the flashing waves below.

Eventually, the other flyer slowed and headed back to the cliffs, tipping his wings in a "follow me" gesture. She watched him land, her heart still hammering, then followed suit.

As she touched down, the tall, yellow-flowered grass beneath her swept in wild circles. She wrenched the hood-release lever twice before the glass slid back. It always stuck a little—the hazards of a second-hand machine. Not that she was complaining. Her parents had given her the wingjet three months ago for her eighteenth birthday. It was *hers*, and the only thing she owned that she really, truly cared about.

Aris slid both hands through her hair, trying to smooth it down. She'd left it loose and curling, the way Calix liked, but her recent maneuvers had given the heavy auburn waves a reckless disregard for gravity.

The other flyer stood among the flowers, waiting for her. Dressed in full uniform—blunt-toed boots, trim pants, sleek forest-green jacket—the man represented every fear she had for Calix. On the back of his neck was the black rectangular brand that marked him as Military. He could have just as easily appeared in a news vid as in one of Aris's nightmares. Her breath froze in her throat, and her hands went cold.

"That was incredible." The stranger was slight, with a fine-boned face and thin lips turned up in a smile.

"Thanks?" she replied, taken aback by his enthusiasm.

"Really, I mean it. I've never seen anyone go from a right-hook flutter pattern straight into a flat-nosed full spindrop."

With a grin, she said, "I call it the swing zinger."

He laughed. "I'd heard you were good, Aris Haan, but blighting hell, that was *fantastic*."

A whisper of unease unfurled in her belly. "How do you know who I am?"

Instead of answering, he held a hand up as an invitation. "You coming down from there?"

Her weak leg tensed reflexively. Flying was one thing; getting in and out of a wingjet gracefully was quite another. She eyed him warily. "Why don't you answer my question first?"

The man's friendly smile twisted into a guarded expression. "It's not important."

"And how did you know I was here? Is *that* important?" she pushed.

The man shrugged. "I watched you leave your father's grove and followed you so we could speak privately. And so I could see what you can do."

Her mind raced. He'd followed her? How had she not noticed? And more importantly: "Why would you do that?"

"Because I want to offer you a job."

She let out a disbelieving laugh. Not only were women not allowed in the Military sector, they weren't authorized to take *any* job, in any sector, deemed "dangerous." What could he possibly have in mind?

"Tomorrow, at your selection, you'll be invited to join the Environment sector," the man said. "And then what? Work as a duster for your father's groves? There were only two people in your entire year that scored even *close* to you in the aviation trial. That talent would be wasted there."

His words sent ice down her spine. "How do you know I'll be selected for Environment? No one finds out their sectors until the ceremony."

"I know more about you than you can imagine," he interjected. "I know why you won't get down from that wingjet, for one. And I know you'll never fulfill your potential here. It'll eat away at you, settling for this life." He put a hand on the side of her wingjet. "Listen to me—"

"Who are you? Is this some kind of . . . I don't know . . . some sort of trick?"

He raised his chin. "No. And I don't offer this lightly."

"You're Military. You can't be . . . I mean, you can't offer—"

"You have a lot of questions, of course. But I'm not the one to answer them." The man drew a small piece of silco from his pocket and handed it to her. The letters on it were stamped in blood-red ink. "Go to Dianthe. She'll explain everything. You'll find her at this address in Panthea. Tell her Theo sent you."

Aris took the silco, gingerly, as if it might bite her. "You want me to go to Panthea?"

He leaned closer, a new urgency in this voice. "Don't tell anyone where or why you're going. Tell them you got a job in the city, whatever will keep them from asking questions. We'll set it up, however you need. No one can know what you're really doing. It's imperative that you tell no one. Do you understand?"

She studied Theo's face. Understand? He had to be joking. "I don't understand *anything*. What kind of job is it? And why do I have to lie to my family?"

"This is your chance to fly," he said, his eyes serious. "Not that mindless drudgery you do for your father. I mean *real* flying. All across Atalanta. You have no idea how useful you could be to the war effort. How many lives you could save."

She couldn't keep a burst of bitter laughter from escaping. "That kind of flying isn't useful. It's self-indulgent." Her father had told her so often enough.

He made an impatient noise. "I've watched you. I know what your life is like here. Why aren't you jumping at this chance?"

Anger spilled through her. "You don't know anything about me. How dare you spy on me and think you know me? I'm happy here."

"Really? You're happy being a duster and never leaving Lux?" Theo stared up at her, his face set in rigid lines.

"I am." With Calix, she would be.

"You're either stupid or selfish then." He turned away, as if disgusted with her. "This isn't just about you."

Selfish? Stupid? "If you know so much, surely you're aware I'm about to be Promised." She and Calix had already decided. Two years of Promise, then they could choose to marry. And be bound, irrevocably, for the rest of their lives. It's what she'd wanted for as long as she could remember. "He's going to ask me tomorrow, after selection. I can't leave, and there's nothing selfish or stupid about it."

The man turned back to her and scoffed. "A Promise? Don't count on it."

"Excuse me?" Shock painted her words.

"I assume you're referring to Calix Pavlos?"

Her chest tightened. "Tomorrow he'll join the Health sector. He's going to work in his mother's clinic. We—"

Theo slammed a hand against the side of her wingjet, cutting her off. "Have you not watched the news vids? This war will claim us all, one way or another." His thin lips twisted with an emotion she couldn't identify. "Calix *will* be selected for Military, make no mistake."

"You're wrong." A buzzing filled her ears. "We're winning the war. *That's* what the news vids say. Calix isn't going anywhere." This man was her nightmare after all, come to take everything from her. "His family has been part of the Health sector for generations. There's no chance—"

"There is, Aris, and you know it." Theo stepped back, tipping his head up to look her in the eye. "Please. Consider my offer. You could save lives. Maybe even Calix's."

Then, without another word, he climbed into his shining wingjet and sped away.

CHAPTER TWO

PYRALIS NEKOS STUDIED THE ENORMOUS PAINTING OF THE Five Dominions that hung on his office wall. He loved the way Atalanta looked from above, like a brilliant jewel in the center of a gaudy necklace. An emerald caught between the cobalt of the ocean, the golden deserts of Safara, and the diamond ice of Ruslana. To the west, beyond the ocean, Meridia and Castalia formed a shining patchwork of colors, from the white and black of the snow-capped mountain ridges to the pale green of the plains.

Generations ago, before the Peace Accords and creation of the Five Dominions, that vibrancy hadn't existed. War had burnt out all the color, nearly all the life, from the world.

How different would the world look once *this* war ran its course?

Not for the first time, Pyralis caught himself wishing he'd been elected sooner. Every five years, Atalanta's Ward was elected from the five sector leaders. As leader of the Military sector, Pyralis had been elected shortly after Safara declared war, a little less than two years ago. And still, even Military Warded, his dominion struggled.

"The Ward of Ruslana is here," a tech voice chirped into the quiet of the office.

Pyralis tapped the screen embedded in his desk. "Thank you. Send her in." As Atalanta's Ward, he was the most powerful man in this dominion. It was a shame he didn't feel like it.

With a steadying breath, he stood, squared his shoulders, and ushered Galena Vadim into the room. She sat on the padded bench he indicated. His eyes lingered on the smoothness of her blond hair pulled back in a low knot, the way her lashes made feathered shadows against her pale cheeks.

"Thank you for coming," he said.

"How can I refuse when the Ward of Atalanta asks for a meeting?" She settled her hands in her lap, where they laid peacefully, like two small, sleeping birds.

Pyralis sank to the bench beside her, but not close enough that any part of their clothing touched.

"Galena." The name was little more than a sigh.

She stiffened. "Ward Nekos, I insist you share the purpose of this meeting."

He stared at the rich mahogany leather of his sandals. It wasn't hard to guess what she thought of him, why she sat suddenly tense and poised to flee. Her hands were not peaceful now.

"I can no longer deny . . ." he began, the words dragging. Galena made a small noise, as if she meant to speak, but he pushed on, raising a hand to silence her, "that Atalanta will fall. If we are very lucky, we'll be able to hold Safara another two years. But no more."

From the way Galena's pale blue eyes cut to his, he could tell it wasn't what she'd expected him to say. "You mean two years until they reach the Fex River."

"I mean *fall*. I don't expect Ward Balias to stop when he reaches the river."

"That's ridiculous." She stared at the wall of glass across from them, toward the forest that climbed the hills outside of Panthea. "Why don't you renegotiate your trade agreements? Agree to some of his terms? He's just pressuring you for more resources. If he gets what he wants—"

"Oh, he'll get what he wants. Atalanta has been led by Enviro and Tech Wards for generations. Our Military sector has always focused on town infrastructure and internal protections; we're not strong enough to withstand his invasion." An edge of frustration crept into his voice. "Believe me, I've tried to renegotiate trade. I've offered tech to help identify deep water reserves, architectural plans for water treatment facilities. Balias doesn't want any of it. Says he *must* have direct access to the river, which I'll never willingly provide. Our dominion's agriculture and Panthea's entire water supply depend on the Fex. There's no way to give him access without risking my dominion's resources. And he knows it. I believe the river is a convenient excuse for a larger power play."

"What's your evidence? Merely that he refuses to negotiate?"

"Isn't that damning enough?" Pyralis twisted to look at her, wishing she would meet his eyes. "My spies tell me Ward Balias's designs extend far beyond Atalanta. Ruslana and the other dominions are still too strong for him to attack, but once he has access to our resources, our—"

Her head snapped up. "What reason could he possibly have to attack Ruslana? Or the others?"

Pyralis stood and strode to the wall of glass, where sunlight embraced him like a consuming fire. "Safara has been Military Warded for years, building their strength. Why? Why not elect an Environment or Technology Ward and find a solution to the water issue, if it's so concerning? This war is not really about the river. Which begs the question: What does he really want? What *is* it about?"

"And you think . . ." Galena's voice was sour with disbelief, but a question hung in the air.

"I don't know." Pyralis sighed impatiently, turning to look at her. A stray beam of light caressed her cheek. "But I don't trust him. And we are failing."

Galena paced the open floor between the door and his desk. "What will you do? Select more for Military?"

"We've increased our recruiting efforts. The number of

volunteers has been higher this year, but not as high as we need. We'll have to select more from this year's class, yes. I've also reallocated Commerce sector funding to Military, but it won't be enough."

Galena paused a few feet from him. For the first time she met his eyes. "Why are you telling me this now? Why not wait for the World Council?"

"Meridia and Castalia have no stake in containing Safara; they share no borders and rely heavily on Safaran energy. But you . . ." He cleared his throat. "Ruslana . . . you'll suffer, too, as our resources are eaten by the war. If Safaran troops continue to raze our fields, we'll have no crops to export. No timber, if our forests continue to burn. And, if Ward Balias is indeed aiming to conquer Atalanta, I don't imagine he'll stop there. It's in your best interest to help us stand in this war."

For a long time Galena said nothing. She moved to the window. Pyralis watched as she bit the corner of her lip, a habitual gesture he recognized even after so many years. It meant she was thinking, chewing over the problem in her mind like a tough piece of meat. He took a step closer, almost placing a hand on the small of her back, almost leaning close enough to catch the hint of roses in her perfume. But he caught himself, just in time.

When she finally spoke, she didn't look away from the window. "I can't support you outright. We need peace along our border with Safara. But there are other ways, other things Ruslana can do. Perhaps."

It was a diplomatic answer at best. She said nothing more, but by the determined set of her chin, Pyralis knew she'd offer what help she could. He desperately hoped it would be enough.

So far, he'd been able to keep the truth of Atalanta's precarious position from the news vids, but tomorrow, at the selection ceremony, the people would know. Although it was customary to select more citizens to join the Ward's sector, this year's imbalance would be extreme. Nearly a third of the graduating young men would be stamped with black Military brands.

"Thank you, Ward Vadim," he said softly. "I am in your debt."

At that Galena turned and faced him. "You owe me nothing. This is not about you or me. Do not suppose, for a second, that I will be doing this for you."

She stalked toward the door.

Before Pyralis could stop himself, he grabbed her wrist, drawing her to a halt.

"Galena, please." This time he couldn't hide it, the regret. It weighed down his words, ran in lines of pain to where his fingers brushed her skin.

She pulled her arm from his grasp. "No, Pyralis. You don't get to touch me."

In the twin flames of her ice-blue eyes, he could see her true meaning. What was broken between them would ever remain so.

Bowing, he said, "I understand, Ward Vadim. Atalanta is grateful for your support."

He didn't raise his head as she left; he couldn't. Quite suddenly, he could hardly bear its weight.

CHAPTER THREE

Lux's selection ceremony was held in the airy, vaulted main hall of the Council Building. The room—indeed, the entire building—was a marvel, the most imposing structure in all of Lux, built through a partnership of Technology and Environment engineers many generations ago. It was made of gleaming, polished wood, with massive columns of sparkling golden stone that supported the arched ceiling. Vast expanses of glass let in sunlight along with a view of the cloudless blue sky and the endless green of the groves.

Aris searched the crowded room for Calix, trying to keep calm, but it was difficult to smile and joke with her classmates. She was wound so tightly she could barely breathe, her eyes red from trying to wipe away her nightmares.

It's a lie, she told herself. *Everything Theo said was a lie, it has to be.*

"Oh holy, I'm so nervous I could die!" The voice hurtled toward her, along with a small, determined body. Warm arms and a starberry-scented cloud of dark curls engulfed her.

Sputtering, Aris drew back. "Echo, your hair is a menace."

Echo giggled and tugged on Aris's arm. "Can you believe it? Our selection day. *Finally*. Phae's been Commerce for *ages*. I hope I get Commerce, too. I want to work in an art gallery, hopefully in Panthea. More men to choose from." She tossed her mass of hair and winked at a nervous-looking boy beside her. His brown eyes widened. Echo smiled and leaned toward him, opening her mouth—to speak, probably, but to Aris it looked like she was about to swallow him whole.

"Have you seen Calix?" Aris asked, worry edging her words.

Echo shook her head, abandoning her conquest for the moment. "Not yet. Didn't you come together?"

"We said we'd meet here." Now she wished they had met beforehand. Her parents had wanted to have a special breakfast, just the three of them. But even her mother's buttery, spiced peshka couldn't dislodge the stone in her stomach.

In a daze, she left Echo and continued her search through the milling crowd. Finally she saw him, standing at the edge of a group of boys. When he caught her looking, Calix smiled.

Her heart skipped and raced ahead, as if it could burst from her chest and beat her to him. She forced herself to take slow, steady steps. It had been six years since the fever, but she was still unsteady on her feet, especially when she was nervous or tired. Now was *not* the time to risk a fall.

He didn't wait for her; in two long strides he was at her side, meeting her in the middle of the room. "Finally!" he said. "I've been looking for you."

"Same." She tried to smile.

He pressed his lips softly against hers. When he drew away, his brow furrowed with concern. "You look pale. Are you well?"

She nodded, her voice caught in her throat. For a moment, she considered telling him what she feared. But he'd try to reassure her, and right now she didn't want that. She just wanted to look at him, touch him, and confirm his presence. His reality. *Their* reality.

She'd never tire of his face, darkened by the summer afternoons they spent walking along the beach together. His nose was a little crooked, his calm green eyes bordered by two straight sweeps of brow. She loved the way his untidy brown hair curled softly, like a shadow, against his cheek.

"I love you," she said, wishing for a lifetime together to show him how much.

He put his arm around her, drawing her close. "I love you, too, Hummingbird."

It had been her nickname for years. When he'd first called her it, she had asked, "Why do I have to be a hummingbird?" with an exasperated eye roll. "Why not an eagle, or a fanax, maybe? Something a little more intimidating?"

He had smiled down at her. "Nothing is more agile than a hummingbird. When you're flying, the way you flit in and out of the groves . . . you're better than a fanax. Being small and nimble is your greatest asset."

Now, as the wide vid screen bloomed into color on the wall, Aris felt very small. She tried not to cling too tightly to his side.

On the vid, Ward Nekos sat in a sleek white chair, his wife, Bett, and his advisors standing behind him. As the leader of Atalanta, it was his task to begin each year's ceremony with a speech. Today his brown eyes looked flat, and his lips curved stiffly, as if his face were a mask. His hair showed more gray than Aris remembered from past news vids.

"Welcome to this year's selection." He paused for the inevitable cheers. "In each of Atalanta's villages and cities, there are young, hopeful faces like yours. You have all worked hard in your lessons and distinguished yourselves with your ready minds, your willingness to help others, and your enthusiastic support of Atalanta.

"Today, in the tradition of the Five Dominions, you will be invited to join the Health, Commerce, Technology, Environment, or Military sector based on the areas of study in which you have excelled. In these dark days of war with Safara, your hope, ingenuity, and diligence will mean the difference between success and failure. A dominion is only as strong as its citizens, and by this measure, Atalanta is strong indeed."

Aris wished the Ward had sounded more confident when he'd said *strong*.

Applause filled the pause as he drew breath. "To all of those brave young men who wish to volunteer for Military sector, you have my respect and thanks. We need your strength, your heart, and your perseverance to overcome the challenges of this difficult time."

A shiver shook Aris. Even Calix's arm around her couldn't protect her from the chill of Ward Nekos's words.

He ended his speech with a smile. "I offer you my congratulations on this important day. Blessings and best wishes."

The vid went black and the room filled with more applause as the curtains opened, spilling sunlight across the people packed into the room. In the center, those participating in the ceremony milled in small, tight groups, whispering and laughing with their friends. Their families sat on long benches at the back of the room, colorful in their best clothes.

And below the giant vid screen, officials stood behind five tables, one for each sector. In a matter of seconds, the vid would brighten once again, with a listing of all the students graduating and the sectors for which they'd been selected. Then they would all line up to receive their sector-specific brands—a key for Technology, a twisted green vine for Environment, two stylized wings for Health, a blue barcode for Commerce, and that harsh black rectangle for Military.

Aris turned to Calix and wrapped her hands around his waist. "Your father's friend," she said, "the one who works for the Council. He said you'd be selected for Health, right?"

"Right." Calix dipped to press a gentle kiss to her forehead. "There's no need to worry. I'll join the Health sector, and tonight we'll Promise. This is it. This is when it all begins." No fear clouded his gaze. He smiled down at her, confident that their lives would proceed as planned.

She tightened her arms around him, pressing closer, as if this one embrace could somehow cleave them to their hopes, to each other, and bind them to the path of their shared future.

But her hands kept shaking. *Oh holy, please let Theo be wrong.*

A hush fell as the massive screen blinked white. Aris's throat closed. When the names appeared, she didn't waste time looking for hers. Her eyes darted across the letters, all meaningless, until she saw it.

Calix Pavlos.

And there, beside his name . . .

Military.

Her legs wobbled and her vision blurred with tears. *No.*

CHAPTER FOUR

Despite the war, the World Council was held in Atlanta as planned. Panthea's soaring, needle-thin glass capitol building gleamed in all the news vids, as reporters and the people of Atalanta speculated on whether this year's Council would put an end to the conflict with Safara. No one was allowed in the building, no vids were released from within the opulent Council chambers, just terse statements read by Panthea's mayor. This was protocol to protect the political process.

It was also to hide the fact that this year, the Council was not held in the capitol building, but deep below it.

Seated at a round table in the firebomb-resistant room, Galena Vadim remained quiet as the four other Wards argued. Their voices fought like an angry flock of birds above the wood-pecker tapping of the mediator's gavel.

Besides Galena, the only other woman in attendance was Sera, the Ward of Castalia. Thick gray hair was piled atop her head, bound with heavy gold ropes in the traditional Castalian style. Her cobalt and cream robes were bleached pale by the bright solar light that illuminated the room.

"While I sympathize with the plight of Atalanta," she was saying, "Castalia has traded peacefully with Safara since before Ward Balias was elected. In good faith, I can't support a move that would jeopardize the mutually beneficial relationship that exists between our dominions."

"And you're up for election this year, are you not?" Hal, Meridia's Ward returned, his golden eyes gleaming beneath heavy dark brows. He wasn't supporting sanctions either, but he never missed an opportunity to needle his southern neighbor.

"Now, you know perfectly well that has nothing—"

Bang, bang, bang! The mediator, a tired, sallow man in white ceremonial robes, interrupted Sera's retort with the pounding of his gavel.

"With all due respect," Galena interjected in the brief silence, "we cannot, *in good faith*, let Ward Balias run unchecked either." She cut her eyes to Balias. "Atalanta is a peaceful dominion, a target *only* because of its abundance of natural resources and position along Safara's border. Ruslana, at least, feels it necessary to strongly urge, by imposing the sanctions I suggested, that Ward Balias and his army stand down."

Ward Balias's brown eyes glittered as he met Galena's gaze across the table. He was young for a Ward, younger than the rest of them, with sandy blond hair and a broad face worn to leather by the hot Safaran sun. Military trained and hard-muscled from years in the field, his whip-thin body fit awkwardly into the finely patterned tunic he wore.

"Ward Vadim," he said, the long-suffering weariness of his voice at odds with his bright eyes, "perhaps I have not yet fully presented my case. The people of Safara are dying from the lack of clean water. Our irrigation has failed. Our crops have withered. My people are starving. The current trade agreements with your dominions do not offer enough resources." He jerked his head toward Pyralis. "Ward Nekos has refused to renegotiate our agreement each of the last three years we've met at this World Council. He has refused to allow life-saving access to the Fex River for my people."

Pyralis slammed his fist on the table. "You know well that the trade agreements you offered were in no way advantageous for the people of Atalanta! They were barely—"

"And war *is* advantageous for them, Nekos?" Ward Balias said, one brown eyebrow raised. The insult of using Pyralis's name without his title shocked the room to silence.

Galena glanced at Pyralis. His dominion was under siege, his soldiers dying at the hands of Safaran assassins, and yet his weary eyes softened when they met her gaze. She frowned. Streaks of gray lined his temples. The stress of war had dug grooves along his forehead and the edges of his mouth. He looked different. Older.

There was a part of her, a mean, bitter part, that wanted to let his dominion burn.

She glanced down at her hands, as the bickering of the other Wards clamored around her once again. But she couldn't— wouldn't—let Atalanta fall.

A glass of water rested on the table before her, beads of condensation clouding its surface. She drew it to her lips and took a sip. If they'd just work together, if Sera would just *listen*—

The thought slid into blind panic as she suddenly wobbled in her chair, clutching her throat. Pyralis's face blurred, then disappeared as a wave of darkness crashed over her. The glass slipped from her nerveless fingers and shattered on the floor, and then there was nothing but the black.

Chapter Five

It was just before midnight, a week after Calix had been selected for Military. Aris lay in bed, listening to the rain pound against the roof. Usually the sound soothed her, helped her slide into soft-focus dreams. But tonight, each ding was a knife driving into her chest. All she could think about was how different everything would be if it rained like this in Safara. If the desert didn't suck its people dry.

Finally, Calix tapped a fingernail on the window. Aris slipped silently into the waterlogged night and straight into his arms. The time for casual greetings, for words, had passed. She threw herself against him, her hands snaking into his hair. His mouth found hers in the rain and the dark as he pressed her against the side of the house.

She ran her hands along his cheeks, his ears, his closed eyes, touching, memorizing. The slickness of his wet hair beneath her fingers, the sensation of his strong arms around her, the warmth that pooled in her belly when he pulled her closer, running his hands down her back. She found the hem of his Military-issue jacket and slid her hands underneath, paying attention to the smooth heat of his skin, vowing she'd remember the way his flat stomach felt against her fingers.

"Hummingbird," he whispered against her mouth. She shook

her head and kissed him harder. She wasn't ready for this moment to be over. Not when they had so few left.

His hands tightened on her waist. Finally, he pulled away. "Let's get out of this rain," he said, his voice hoarse.

He took her hand and led her down the glowing walkway, suspended high above the ground. Her bare feet slid along the wet surface but he kept her steady. When they reached the steep, rocky path that lead down to the beach, he insisted on carrying her, so her weak leg wouldn't send her tumbling. He moved as swiftly and sure-footedly as the village donkeys, and soon enough they were ducking into their cave, a secret place they'd found years ago.

"I can't believe you leave tomorrow," Aris whispered as they sank to the cool sand. "It's all happening too fast." Her voice broke.

He sighed, wrapping an arm around her. "I know. I wish I didn't have to leave so soon. Or at all."

"You'll write me as soon as you get to the training grounds?"

He squeezed her gently. "Of course. My digitablet is already packed. You can't worry, though, if it takes a little while. I don't know when I'll have free time, if they'll let us comm up right away. There might be rules. But as soon as I can, you know I will."

"I don't want you to go." Such a useless thing to say.

"I don't want to leave you." He kissed her forehead.

"Please, Calix. Let's Promise. We can do it right now, just the two of us." The words were out before she could call them back. When he'd told her the night of the ceremony that he didn't think they should Promise after all, she'd barely protested. She'd still been reeling from all the shocks of that day. But now . . . now the thought of him leaving without a Promise was a gaping cavern tearing open her chest.

"I want to, Aris." Calix dug his toes into the sand, his eyes downcast. "But we said we'd wait. The point of a Promise is to be together, learn everything we can about each other."

"We already know everything about each other." She drew

his hand into her lap. It was soft, with a patch of thicker skin along his right middle finger, from holding countless mediguns.

Calix rubbed his other hand down her back. "My field mender clinic is close to where the fighting is. I probably won't even get leave for nine months or even a year. And who knows when I'll be able to come home for good? That's no way to prepare for a marriage."

"It doesn't matter," her eyes burned with unshed tears. "Distance won't change how we feel. I'm Promised to you. I *am*."

He let out a mournful sigh. "I don't want you to feel trapped."

"Our love isn't a trap." It was the only thing, besides flying, that actually made her feel *free*. She leaned her head against his chest. "I have loved you every day that I can remember, and I will love you all the days I have left in this life. We should Promise right now. Tonight." She raised her head to meet his eyes, so he could see the truth. *Her* truth. "I'll be waiting for you either way."

"I'm sorry, Aris. You know I can't." His voice was low and rough, like he was trying not to cry. "Not when I won't be here. Not when we can't be together. It wouldn't be right."

Holy, why did he always have to follow the rules? His sense of justice and fairness was something she loved about him, but right now she wanted him to be passionate, impulsive. She wanted *him*.

"It isn't fair." The words came out plaintive and needy. She hated them. She hated the burning hole in her chest that made her say them. But it was too late to take them back.

Calix's arm tightened around her. "I wish we had more time. I don't want to leave you."

She leaned up to kiss his temple, sliding her fingers into his soft, shadowy hair. "Tell me you want to be with me," she murmured.

He nodded and when he spoke, his breath was warm against her skin. "Yes, Aris. I want you."

She turned and pressed closer, until she was sitting on his lap.

Cradling his face in her hands, Aris kissed him with all the longing and fear she felt. She unzipped his jacket and pushed it off his shoulders. Underneath he wore a slippery shirt that fit him like a second skin. It was made of a slick, new-tech fabric impervious to the elements. She yanked on it, but she couldn't rip it if she tried. He raised his arms and let her pull it over his head. She wanted to throw the shirt in the ocean, bury it in the sand so he couldn't find it, so he couldn't leave. As if a missing shirt could keep him.

His hands slipped under her tunic, his fingers warm and gentle on her bare skin. She pressed closer, willing him to hold her tighter. He was always like that: careful, as if worried she could be easily hurt.

"I'm not a doll," she whispered against his neck, trailing kisses along his collarbone. "You can't break me."

His arms tightened until she nearly lost her breath. She tipped her head to kiss him. His tongue snuck between her lips as he ran his hands down her sides, brushing the curves of her breasts, and she arched against him. Desire rolled in slow, heavy waves from her cheeks down low into her belly.

For a while, Aris didn't think. She lived in the heated space between their bodies, in the slick warmth of Calix's mouth. Every thought, fear, memory faded, and the world was reduced to the wildness of the ocean throwing itself to shore, the fathomless swish of rain against sand. To the hardness of the rocks that enclosed them, the hardness of his body beneath her.

The ripples of desire flashed hot beneath her skin. She didn't want to wait. Not for a Promise. Not for him to come home.

Tonight. Now. What if they never got another chance? She moved to unfasten his belt.

As soon as he realized what she was doing, he grabbed her hands and stopped her. For a long moment they sat without speaking, their quick breathing a counterpoint to the distant crash of waves. Eventually she slid off his lap and curled up against his side.

"You said you wanted me." She felt no bitterness or rancor as she said the words. Only sadness. Longing.

"I do," Calix replied. "*So much*. You can't even imagine." She could feel the tremble in his hands on her back. "But . . ."

"But it would be wrong." She sighed.

He ducked his head, staring at their legs, pressed close together. Almost as if convincing himself, he repeated, "But it would be wrong."

"No one would know." The way she felt when he kissed her— like she soared, her body full of air and sunlight.

He didn't answer right away, as if considering, then he regret- fully shook his head. "*We* would know."

Maybe that should have mattered to her.

For a long time they sat in silence, pressed close, listening to the lapping waves.

When the gray light of dawn eased up from the horizon, Aris laid a hand on his chest, over his heart. "I love you, Calix. We'll make this work, no matter what happens. You know that, right?"

"I know, Aris." He kissed the top of her head. They both stared out of the cave entrance at the endless, weeping rain. "I know."

CHAPTER SIX

As soon as Aris slipped through the doorway of The Toad, Echo pounced on her.

"Aris!" The petite girl threw her arms around Aris, enveloping them both in her hair. The crystals on her slinky silver dress pricked Aris's bare arms. "I didn't know you were coming!"

Aris tried to catch her breath. "I hadn't planned to. I just . . ." *I just was tired of replaying Calix's last kiss in my mind. His last "I love you" as he said goodbye. I was tired of sitting alone in my room crying.* "You know. I thought it'd be good to get out."

"We've all been so worried about you." Echo pulled back, studying her in the dim light. "Was this morning totally wretched? How are you doing? You look *terrible*."

A rueful smile lifted the edges of Aris's mouth. "Thanks so much."

Echo rolled her eyes. "You know what I mean. But seriously, are you okay?"

Aris's smile faded. "Watching Calix get on that transjet was the worst moment of my life. So yeah, wretched about covers it."

"Well, don't worry, doll. You'll be your old self in no time. Have you seen the men here tonight? Watch out, Calix!" Echo winked, but her face fell into a pout when Aris didn't smile. "I was only trying to cheer you up. Don't look at me like that."

Aris sighed.

Echo pointed to the far side of the dark, cave-like room. "Rakk and Phae are over there. I was just getting us some drinks. What do you want?"

"Just a pineapple fross, please. Do you need help?"

"Nah. Go sit down." With another stifling hug, Echo was gone, her dress sparkling in the dim light. Heads turned to watch her from all around the bar. Aris sighed in envy, not at the looks Echo got, but at the way she moved: smooth and liquid as the lines of paint in the art she hoped to sell in galleries all over Atalanta. Being around Echo made Aris feel even more clumsy and awkward than usual. Her only consolation: Echo was a terrible flyer. Aris could pilot a wingjet just as gracefully as Echo could move. Maybe even better than she could paint.

Aris made her way to a table wedged in a dark, smoky back corner, where Phae and Rakk were sitting with their heads together. When they saw her, they waved.

A faint curl of bakka smoke drifted between them, filling her nose with its nutty, spicy scent. It reminded her of the last time she'd been at The Toad, with Calix. She blinked, eyes stinging.

"On your own now, aren't you," Phae said, standing up to give Aris a hug. Her dark skin glowed velvety and smooth against her red dress.

Aris slid onto an empty stool, grateful for the sympathy in Phae's eyes. "I can't believe he's really gone."

Phae patted her hand. The motion set her thick wooden bracelets rattling against her wrist, revealing glimpses of her Commerce brand. Aris glanced at the vines twining up her own arm. The Environment sector's ivy was the largest of the five sector brands. But it was also the nicest, according to her friends. Phae often wore bangles to hide the small blue barcode on her wrist.

"I'm sure you'll hear from Calix soon," Phae said. "Rakk had time to comm up almost as soon as he arrived at training."

Rakk nodded. "It won't be long. Don't worry."

Aris tried to meet his gaze, but her eyes kept drifting to the red, ridged scar that covered the side of his head and neck. Much of his ear and the hair around the scar was gone. He was still handsome—rich brown eyes, full lips, thick dark hair—but the gruesome scar overshadowed his features.

The thought that Calix could be in danger, could suffer like Rakk had, made Aris's stomach clench and her heart race.

"Maybe the war will end soon," Phae added, trying to sound reassuring. "You never know. Calix might not be gone that long."

Just then, Echo appeared with four frosted, wide-mouthed glasses. She tossed her gravity-defying hair as she placed them on the table. "Am I the only one who thinks she needs to *forget* about Calix?" Echo's words fell into the loud bar like an anvil.

Aris reeled back. "What did you just say?"

"Echo!" Phae said disapprovingly.

"What?" Shooting a quelling look at Phae, she reached for Aris's hand. "Doll, I'm sorry. I know you don't want to hear this, but I just have to say it. Calix didn't Promise to you. He didn't give you *anything*. He's gone, and who knows when he'll be back? I'm worried you're going to put your whole life on hold for him."

Aris yanked her hand free, pressing it against the knotted, variegated wood of the table. "Calix believes in following the rules, and that means Promising when we can actually be together. We decided to wait because it was the right thing to do, not because he didn't ask!" Okay, so that wasn't entirely true. But it might as well have been.

Rakk stood and slipped around Phae, his hands on her shoulders. "I think I'll have a smoke. Pardon me." He made his way to the bakka bar without another word.

Phae turned her reproachful frown on Aris. "Why'd you have to say that?"

"I'm sorry!" Aris raised her hands. "I wasn't commenting on *your* Promise, I was just—"

"Let it be, Phae. I'm sure he just wanted a smoke. You're too sensitive." Echo leaned against the table, cutting her eyes to a group of men a few tables over who were openly staring at her.

"Now *I'm* too sensitive?" Phae asked. "This isn't about me!

You were the one who said Aris should just *forget* Calix, like that would ever happen! She follows him around like a blighting puppy, and you think—"

"That's enough." Aris got to her feet, ignoring the weakness in her legs. "You think whatever you like about us. It has been a very, *very* long day, and I don't have the energy to argue."

Phae held up a hand. "I'm sorry, wait—"

Aris turned away. The air was suddenly thick, the bakka smoke choking. She pushed toward the door, knocking into tables and shadowy figures indiscriminately, desperate for fresh air and the sky's embrace.

Travelers often suffered vertigo when visiting Lux; the milky walkways that connected the buildings, built high on carbonate stilts, were translucent, and the impenetrable chest-high walls transparent. Aris had lived in Lux all her life. Tonight she was dizzy, but not because she could see shadowy trees below her feet.

Rakk emerged from the darkness of the bar. "Aris," he said. "Wait for a second."

"Tell Phae I'm sorry." She glanced toward her wingjet on the landing pad. "I just can't handle it right now, okay?"

"It's not that. I know you don't feel like talking. I get it." He scuffed a boot on the glowing pathway. "It's just . . . for what it's worth, I respect what you and Calix are doing. Waiting, I mean."

Aris raised a brow in surprise. "But you didn't wait."

"Yeah, I know." He lifted a hand as if to run it through his hair, but when his fingers touched the scarred skin at his temple, he dropped his arm to his side. "The thing is . . . I wish we had."

Aris's mind balked. "But—"

"Look at me." Rakk gestured to his face, grimacing. "This is not what Phae signed up for."

"Phae *loves* you," Aris replied forcefully.

He sighed. "I know she does. And I love her. That's why I didn't break the Promise." He leaned against the translucent wall. "But I would have done things differently if I'd known. You and Calix are smart to wait. Anything could happen. Sometimes

I think about . . . if my sectormate hadn't shoved me out of the way just before the firebomb blew, Phae'd be mourning me right now instead of planning our wedding."

Aris's stomach dropped. He'd never spoken about what happened. "Did your sectormate—"

"He lost his leg." Rakk looked down. "He just about died trying to protect me."

You could save lives. Maybe even Calix's. Theo's words echoed in Aris's mind.

"Thanks, Rakk." Aris gave him a hug.

"Good luck." He released her and made his way back inside.

Aris scrambled into her wingjet and let the familiar start-up sequence calm her shaking hands. She drew the jet into a hover, then shot straight into the air, moisture streaking the glass dome as she moved through a patch of cloud. Tears burned her cheeks.

She couldn't stay here, knowing Calix was out there risking his life. Not when she had a chance to help. She thought about what she would say to her parents, her friends . . . when she would leave. Smiling grimly through her tears, she planned her escape.

CHAPTER SEVEN

THE DARKNESS SPUN, ENDLESS SHADOWS TWISTING THROUGH A featureless night. A whispered word and a murmured command cut through the haze like strands of silver woven in black velvet. Galena Vadim didn't recognize the voices, couldn't understand the words.

No . . . cover her . . . in here . . .

When she blinked, the world transmuted from gray to brilliant white. Too bright. She closed her eyes, opened them a slit until they could adjust. The ceiling above her glowed.

She blinked again, catching whispers of black and brown at the corners of her eyes.

Where am I?

For a moment she thought she might still be at the World Council, crumpled on the cold floor, but her body had already begun to register the cushion of a mattress beneath it.

The brown shadows gradually resolved themselves into a huge, hulking man leaning over her, his shaved head gleaming mahogany in the harsh light. Startled by his presence, she tried to draw back, but the bone-white sheets tucked tight to her collarbone restrained her.

She opened her mouth to scream.

"There's no need for that," the man said. He loomed closer and placed something cold and metallic against her neck.

"What happened? Where am I?" Galena asked, and in so doing realized she had very little voice with which to scream.

"You are ill, Ward. You shouldn't speak. And don't try to move."

Ill? As her eyes adjusted to the light, Galena saw that the man wore a sleek white mender's tunic, a tight undersheath, and white pants. An official ID was clearly visible on a chain around his neck. She relaxed slightly. She must be in a clinic.

"Where is Dima?" Even if Galena were still in Atalanta, her personal mender would have come to supervise her care. As Ruslana's premier mender, Dima was responsible for the health of the dominion's highest officials. Galena squinted at the man's ID. "Elom?"

"Dima isn't here," he replied, moving the cold thing to a place just above her collarbone, against her skin. "Take a deep breath, please."

She did as he asked. In the quiet of the room, a machine beeped softly, in time with her heartbeat. Gradually, the beeping slowed.

"Why isn't Dima here? Where am I?" The words scratched her throat as she voiced them, as if clawing their way out.

"See for yourself." He stepped away long enough to retrieve a small digitablet, which he propped up on her lap. When he tapped the monitor on the wall beside her, the top half of the bed slid smoothly upward, until she was sitting. She was still trapped by the sheets, even her arms held immobile.

"Can you free my arms?" Galena's vision remained a little hazy; small black dots huddled in her periphery, the darkness waiting for its chance to claim her again.

Elom settled a large hand on her shoulder. "It's best if you don't move, Ward. Please relax." He pressed a button on the digitablet. The screen shimmered to life and showed a news report, dated four days after her last memory. She couldn't tell if the footage was live.

A woman in a sleek gray dress gazed into the camera. "There is still no word on Ward Vadim's condition. The newly elected Ward of Ruslana fell ill during last week's World Council, after announcing that Ruslana had imposed sanctions on Safara. A vote on whether the other dominions would follow suit was abandoned when Vadim lost consciousness. She was rushed to a local Atalantan clinic, where she's been ever since." The woman gestured to a graceful, glass-walled building behind her. "We're awaiting confirmation that Vadim has regained consciousness and will make a recovery; her menders have not spoken with the press since shortly after she was admitted."

Elom tapped the digitablet screen, cutting off the reporter's voice. The room was silent, save for the faint beeping that echoed her heartbeat. The tall man stared down at her; his dark eyes held all the condescension of royalty, but his broken, pugnacious nose spoke a rougher language.

"My husband?"

"No visitors yet." Elom turned away.

Galena cleared her throat, and the world tilted, the black specks swirling up to blur her view of Elom's broad shoulders. She waited until her vision steadied, horrified at her own weakness. "So I am in an Atalantan clinic? And you are my mender?"

Elom nodded.

"Tell me then, Elom," she croaked. "What illness do I have? What is wrong with me?"

Elom didn't answer. When he returned to her side, she flinched without meaning to.

"You said no visitors. Why?" she asked. "Am I contagious?"

Elom didn't respond.

Beneath the restraining sheets, she squeezed her hands into fists. She still felt weak, fuzzy-headed, but not particularly ill. She cast her thoughts back . . . had she been feeling poorly the day of the Council?

She'd been nervous, yes. The night before the first meeting she'd paced more than she'd slept, gone over her argument for sanctions, and reread the reports her spies in Safara had provided her. That morning, she'd been tired when she'd brushed her hair back into a sleek knot and drawn on her heavy, ice-blue robes. But by the time the meeting had begun, the fire of anger at the other Wards' ignorance had fueled her.

She'd heard of diseases that struck quickly, painlessly . . . death sentences for which there were no cures. Was that the reason Elom didn't reply? Was he trying to spare her the knowledge a little longer?

"I would like to invite that reporter to my room," she tried again, "so I can provide a statement now that I'm awake. Surely something can be arranged?"

Elom ignored her, touching her forehead with something shockingly cold and slick; in a short time he had placed small discs all over her body.

He turned to the monitor beside her bed. "Don't move."

She tried to watch him from the corner of her eye, but the strain made her head ache. In quick succession, she felt a little *fizz* under her skin where each electrode touched her.

The strangeness of the procedure made her notice other oddities: the lack of windows in her room, the silence outside the door. Where were her advisors? Assistant menders? If only for the sake of appearances, her husband would visit her, wouldn't he? But . . . Elom had said no visitors.

Was she *dying*?

Had anyone told her son?

A shiver of panic skittered down Galena's spine. "Please, Elom," she whispered, "tell me the truth. *What is wrong with me?*"

Elom clicked his tongue as he watched the monitor. Why didn't he answer her? He had to have heard . . .

The lack of movement, the sense of confinement . . . she could stand it no longer. She struggled, working her hands up along her belly and bent her knees, a little at a time, in an effort to loosen the tight fabric. If she could just get *free*. . . .

Finally, she fought against the sheets until both arms protruded above the fabric. Without thinking, she peeled off an electrode and held it toward him.

"What are these for?"

He turned to her. "You mustn't touch those, Ward." He took the small metal disk from her hand, affixing it to the hollow place just above her collarbone. He said nothing more, blank eyes passing over her as if examining a specimen of some sort, not a person. Not as if he was her mender, concerned for her health and comfort.

The panic shifted, intensified.

She was Ward of her dominion. She should *not* be alone in this room with a stranger.

Her heart pounded faster within her chest, as if it, too, were anxious to escape. She could hear the faint beeping of the machine speed up, frightening her even more. Close to hyperventilating, she forced words out around the tightness in her chest. "I must insist that you tell me immediately what is going on. I want to speak," she panted, ". . . to . . . my personal . . . mender. And I want you *out* of here." She tore another electrode from her arm and threw it at him but missed; it clanked against the white carbonate floor. She tried to catch her breath, rising in panic as she fought to sit up. "Tell me what is going on!"

Too late she noticed the medigun in the large man's hands. Too late she felt the sting and cool fire slide into her veins. Through a green-tinged haze, she watched her fingers flap helplessly toward Elom's impassive face. And then, with a strangled gasp she'd intended as a scream . . . nothing.

CHAPTER EIGHT

ARIS'S MOTHER HUGGED HER TIGHTLY, AS IF SHE MIGHT REFUSE to let Aris abandon the small stone courtyard and smooth white walls of their home. Aris had no doubt her mother *would* refuse to let her leave, if she knew where she was actually going.

"It's all happening so *quickly*," Krissa said, heaving a sigh that blew wisps of faded auburn hair away from her cheeks. The scents of basilis and browned butter wafted from the folds of her work apron, the memory of well-prepared food the only perfume she had ever worn. Krissa sighed again, as if her heart were breaking.

Aris pulled free from the embrace but held onto her mother's hands, their warmth contrasting with the icy chill of her own.

"This is what you want, isn't it? Your daughter, working in Panthea?" She focused her gaze on the slate floor to keep the lie from spilling into her eyes.

"I always wished I could have worked in Panthea. Such a vibrant city—" Krissa said.

Aris's father grunted. Krissa glanced to him and back. She added, "But, uh, if this is about Calix, doll, maybe you should give it a little more thought?"

"It *is* about Calix," Aris replied, because that, at least, was the truth. "Without him, I can't stay here." Her throat burned with sudden, unshed tears. "That chaise, where Father's sitting. That's where Calix first told me he loved me, after Phae's selection party. And here, where we're standing, this is where he told me we couldn't Promise because he was being sent to *war*. He *was* Lux to me, and now, without him here, I—"

Her father stood up and raised a hand, cutting her off. "You belong here, dusting the groves as we planned. It's your job."

A few tears escaped despite her best efforts. "I can't! Don't you get that?"

He shook his head, anger lighting his eyes. "You want us to say it isn't fair? Well, you're right. It isn't fair. We shouldn't be in this war. Calix should never have been drafted. But that doesn't make it okay to abandon your responsibilities."

"And just saying there shouldn't be a war doesn't make it go away or bring Calix back, does it? It doesn't fix Rakk's face," Aris said, voice rising. "There's a whole world outside of Lux that doesn't care about me or you or your stupid groves." She stepped back and tripped over the spindly leg of the table, catching herself on the back of a chair.

Her father reached a hand out to steady her. "Those 'stupid' groves put food on your table." He dropped her arm. "Look at you. You're not strong enough to be on your own."

As if her tripping was all the evidence he needed.

"I'm doing this, Father," Aris said. "You can't stop me."

"No." He shook his head. "You can't make a decision like this without consulting us."

She raised her chin. "I can and I have. I'm an adult now. I'm taking this placement, and that's the end of it."

"Don't listen to your father. He's just sad you're leaving us. We're proud of you." Krissa brushed away a tear and grasped Aris's shoulders, fingers digging into the muscles. "Be sure to stand up straight. You *know* your limp is more obvious when you slouch. And don't forget your lovely Commerce smile when you meet your new colleagues."

"*Mother*." Aris shrugged away. "I'm not Commerce. No one cares about my smile."

Krissa clasped her hands together by her heart. "This new placement of yours may as well be a Commerce job. A receptionist for the Central Enviro Office . . . It's so *glamorous*."

Aris couldn't meet her eyes. It stung, how easy it was for her mother to believe she'd give up flying to be a receptionist in Panthea. But she was grateful, too; it meant she'd told the right lie. She didn't know what Theo—or the Dianthe woman—would do to back up her story. And that was all she had right now—stories. She didn't even know what she was really signing up for. But she knew what she wanted. And this was her best chance to get it.

"I love you both. I'll write as often as I can, but I may not able to visit . . . for a while. I'll miss you." She wanted to hug her father, let him hold her like a child this one last time, but his eyes were still mutinous. Instead she leaned up and quickly kissed his cheek.

"Next time you write Calix, give him my love." Krissa squeezed her hand. "You'll make it through this separation, my doll. You *will*."

Aris smiled. When Calix left, he'd kissed her and whispered that he loved her. Then he'd walked away without looking back.

She found, as she turned to leave her parents, that she was strong enough to do the same.

THE PUBLIC TRANSJET smelled of sour milk and old sandals. Aris found a seat by a window and tried not to breathe too deeply as the hatch closed. She strapped herself in, wishing desperately she were the one flying the great beast of a wingjet, instead of trapped in its bowels. Next to her, a man in a somber black tunic leaned his head back and closed his eyes.

She turned to the small round window. A green carpet of trees slid past, dotted with clusters of bright white houses. Smaller wingjets, made tiny by distance, zipped beneath them in a chaotic dance of varying flight paths and altitudes. Soon

Panthea rose along the horizon, winking silver and sky-reflected blue. From a great distance, the tall buildings and curving archways of the metroline gleamed.

The transjet landed with a jolt at the wingjet port just outside the city. Panthea did not allow air traffic; all residents and visitors had to travel by land, in terrans or by the metroline, a system of sleek solar-powered trams that crisscrossed the city.

Aris grabbed her bag and shuffled forward, penned in on all sides by the heat of bodies. At last, the gentleman in front of her disembarked and she stumbled out onto the landing pad, gulping fresh air. As she headed toward the far end of the port, she concentrated on taking smooth, even steps and standing up straight, her mother's remonstration still echoing in her ears.

A group of terran drivers clustered before their sleek, low-slung vehicles, calling to the steady flow of people hurrying toward the metroline platform.

As she approached them, their voices clawed at her, loud and raucous. She clutched her bag to her chest, a poor shield against the onslaught. She opened her mouth, glancing toward a female driver. The woman was only slightly less intimidating, with her short, spiky black hair and leather pantsuit. Before Aris could speak, one of the men hustled her to his vehicle, sliding the door closed behind her and asking for her destination, his voice barking the words.

"Five Cleo, the River," she said. The city was divided into sectors based on proximity to the region's geographical features —the river, mountains, a watershed plain.

"That'll be ten crona. You got money, kid?" He glared at her from the front seat. His doughy cheeks drooped to meet heavy jowls, and his unnaturally red lips were pursed, looking more flower-like than he probably intended.

She wanted to ask why he'd been so eager to have her as a passenger if he thought she was a kid with no money, but the words stuck in her throat, so she dug into her bag for her crona-card instead and swiped it across the monitor.

As the terran zipped through the streets of Panthea, she sank into the worn seat, wishing it didn't smell so strongly of meat pies and bakka smoke. The city always gave her vertigo in a way Lux never could. The endless black and silver buildings needling the sky above her, the constant flow of people and traffic along straight, flat streets, the way the air hung, trapped, so far from the freedom of open sky. The quick, darting movements of the terran didn't help.

She breathed deeply, trying to imagine Calix sitting beside her. He'd tuck her beneath his arm, safe and protected, and tell her stories to make her laugh, his dimples appearing when he smiled.

Even as a child he'd been like that, gentle and concerned. A mender at heart, like the rest of his family, he'd come with his mother when Aris had gotten the fever, put cool hands on her forehead and smiled sweetly at her as she burned. She'd always remember the way he looked, his brown hair blurring into the darkness behind him, shadows rippling across his face as if he were underwater.

The driver slowed to round a corner just as a woman in a fiery orange dress carrying a basket of fabric emerged from a store. A man selling meat sticks from a dilapidated cart heckled her, his harsh voice penetrating the quiet interior of the terran as they swept past.

Aris swallowed back the lump in her throat and tapped the screen embedded in the glass partition in front of her.

A news vid blinked on. "The Ward of Ruslana is expected to recover, though for now she's remaining in quarantine." The male reporter, an older man with a bulbous nose and an overly solicitous expression, added, "The Ward's husband has been demanding to see her, but Atalantan menders are taking no chances exposing anyone to the dangerous bacterium. Ward Nekos released this statement—"

The terran squealed to a stop and the vid went black. "Five Cleo, the River," the driver said.

Aris pressed the panel on the door, and it slid open with a

screech. Mumbling her thanks, she stumbled out onto the pavement, arms tangled in her bag's straps.

Trying to catch her breath, she stared up at 5 Cleo, the River. The building was so impossibly tall that its tip was lost within a wisp of cloud. Black and silver panels alternated with huge expanses of glass, reflecting pale blue sky and the shining building across the street. Aris lurched up the obsidian ramp to the entrance, hooking her bag over her shoulder. The imposing chrome door was unlocked but heavy; she had to pull with both hands to open it.

A blast of cool air stung her face. The room she stepped into was round with twisted white columns and lush, wide-leafed trees that grew up from beneath the marble floor. Though small in diameter, the space continued upward, so high she couldn't see the ceiling. Sunlight filtered down through the well-manicured trees, throwing much of the room into shadow.

A throat clearing to her left made her jump.

Standing behind a curved desk along the rounded wall was a very short, very old man with two white wings of hair that swept from each ear across the shining surface of his head. When she approached the desk, he smiled, displaying a bright set of false teeth. "How may I help you?" he asked in cultured Pantheon tones. His voice echoed in the vaulted room.

"I'm here to see Dianthe," she said, so softly her words stayed tethered to their small space.

"Who shall I tell her is calling?"

"Aris Haan. From Lux." She smoothed a hand down her pale blue dress, hoping the back hadn't wrinkled too much. She should have changed her shoes, she thought suddenly, glimpsing her bulky thick-soled flying boots. Everyone in Lux was used to her stomping around in them, but this was Panthea. Here women wore delicate shoes that floated on needle-thin heels and matched their clothes perfectly. In her boots, Aris looked exactly like the ignorant grove girl she was.

Of course, if she tried to wear Panthea-style shoes she'd fall, which would be even worse.

"Floor two-four-three," the man said, startling her again. "Room Three."

"Do you mean floor two *hundred* forty-three?" *Two hundred floors?* Lux might be a village suspended in air, but the buildings themselves were two, maybe three stories at most, even the Council Building.

"Yes, Miss."

When she didn't move, he helpfully pointed to the opposite side of the room, where a glass lift waited.

She thanked him and moved slowly to the narrow box. It was embarrassing that she, a flyer, a child of Lux, was so uncomfortable with the Panthean city heights, but she couldn't keep her hands from shaking. How her mother could ever think *this* was the place for her . . .

With a deep breath, she climbed into the lift and pressed two-four-three on the monitor against the back wall. The doors swished shut and she was hurtled upward, smoothly but so fast her ears popped.

Even with the speed of the lift, it still took a long time to get to the right floor.

When the doors finally opened, she staggered out of the small glass box into a narrow hallway with a muted purple tile floor. The walls were pale and satin-lined, broken at intervals by the dark rectangles of wooden doors. It reminded her uncomfortably of a photo she'd seen once on her digitablet, of the opulent boxes in which Meridians supposedly buried their dead.

She wiped her hands on her dress, hoping she wasn't leaving wet spots, and walked to the first door on the left, which was labeled with a discreet chrome 1. Farther down the hall, she found Dianthe's door.

Aris closed her eyes and thought of Calix—his warm green eyes, the soft, shadowy darkness of his hair. She made herself remember his boyish smile, the pain close and brilliant in her chest. She was doing this for him.

She opened her eyes and knocked. The door slid open. In the doorway stood a woman so tall her head grazed the frame, and so thin Aris felt sure she could see the glow of light through her. Her skin was pink as the inside of a shell and her eyes black.

Even as she noticed these details, Aris couldn't take her eyes from the twisting, blood-red tattoo that encircled the woman's shaved head. Along her cheek, just below the key-shaped Tech brand on her temple, the snake's crimson mouth was wide open, spitting black flame.

Aris's stomach dropped.

"Dianthe?"

Chapter Nine

"Too small," the woman snapped, black eyes narrowed as she looked Aris up and down.

Aris's boots felt like they were melting into the floor, and she worried her knees might soon follow. *No.* She couldn't let Dianthe see her fear. She straightened her shoulders and said, with as much attitude as she could manage, "I've never had complaints before."

Dianthe ignored her, continuing her inspection. "Your chin will do. Let me see you walk." She stood aside, gesturing a graceful hand toward the room.

She wants to see me walk? What does that have to do with flying?

"Now." Dianthe spoke low in her throat, with the rough timbre of a northerner, and her voice held all the fire of a cattle prod.

Aris slipped quickly into the bright, cavernous room, careful as she slid by not to touch Dianthe, who was wearing an ivory tunic over wide-legged, flowing pants of the same color. Aris feared she'd dirty the shimmering fabric just by brushing against it.

As she walked, she took neat, careful steps. The room she entered was sparsely furnished: a black table scattered with sheets of silco and myriad liquid-filled bottles, a large monitor on one white wall, several black, unpadded benches, and, in the center of the room, an enormous wingback chair with heavy purple brocade and carved wooden legs.

Despite the garish chair, the room felt barren. Cold, even with sunlight pouring through the far wall, which was entirely made of glass and provided a beautiful, though vertigo-inducing, view of the city.

"Stop!" Dianthe barked when Aris reached the bench nearest the giant chair. "You have a limp," she accused, sweeping in a circle to examine Aris from all sides.

Aris raised her chin. "My limp has nothing to do with how well I fly."

"Ah, so you're a flyer." Dianthe waved a hand. "Of course you are. From Lux, aren't you?"

"I'm not just a flyer from Lux," she returned, trying to hide her desperation with an indignant scowl. "I'm the *best* flyer in Lux. Maybe in all of Atalanta." They were the words of a braggart, and reckless, but they were better than the words she couldn't say: *please don't send me home*.

Dianthe arched her pale eyebrows, the serpent undulating along her forehead. "That's quite a claim."

"Put me in a wingjet and I'll prove it. Just ask your friend Theo." Aris crossed her arms over her chest, trapping her trembling fingers against her sides.

Dianthe narrowed her eyes. "*You're* the one Theo recruited?"

You are strong. You can do this. "Yes," Aris said, her voice steady. "He begged me to come here. Said I was wasting my talents in Lux. My *gift*." She paused. The crimson snake really was disconcerting, but she refused to look away. "He said you needed me. Maybe he doesn't care so much about silly things like how tall I am or how I walk."

Dianthe skewered her with a hard glare and said nothing.

Warmth bloomed across Aris's cheeks, but she kept her chin up. She couldn't let Dianthe see how intimidated she was. How desperate. If this didn't work, if she was sent away, back to Lux . .
.

No Calix.

At last, Dianthe shrugged, her tunic rippling with the movement. "If you truly are the flyer you claim to be, I might have a place for you within the organization."

Aris was about to speak when the woman turned, exposing a black rectangle on the back of her neck. The Military brand. *That's not possible.*

Dianthe folded her thin body gracefully into the cushions of the chair. Its exaggerated proportions made hers look more normal. "Sit," she ordered, pointing to the nearest bench.

Dazed, Aris sat. "Why do you have a Military brand? You can't be Military, you're a woman."

"What exactly *did* Theo tell you?" Dianthe asked.

Aris swallowed. "He offered me a job doing some flying to help with the war, but he didn't, uh . . ."

"Explain how?"

Aris shook her head. "Just that it was important and I was needed. And I couldn't tell anyone where I was going if I came to see you."

Dianthe brushed her fingers over her bald head. "And now that you're here, can't you guess?"

Aris shook her head again, slowly.

"Women aren't allowed *openly* in the Military. But there are women nonetheless. I help them pass for men, so they can fight the Safaran invasion."

Aris's eyes widened. Women fought in the war? "But why would they do that?"

Dianthe raised a hand in a gesture of impatience. "Why does anyone fight a war? To protect a way of life, to find or support a loved one. To avenge those lost. Or maybe because it's a calling. Because someone has to. Because there's a line no enemy should be allowed to cross." The way she said it, her voice tight and the words tripping over themselves to be heard . . . it was clear Dianthe had a reason for becoming a soldier, for fighting in this war.

Aris shivered at the fire in the tall woman's expression. "But . . . but what about the laws? How can the government allow it?"

"*Allow* it? Shouldn't *women* decide what they'll allow for their own bodies, not a government acting out an antiquated, unnecessary law?" Dianthe's black eyes glittered. "Safara is a powerful enemy. It would be imprudent to turn our backs on some of the most talented flyers and marksmen in Atalanta just because they're women."

Aris could hold Dianthe's gaze no longer. She'd never thought about the ban on women in the Military, never thought she'd be in a position to care. "So what Theo was offering—what you're offering—is a chance to join the Military sector and fight in the war?"

Dianthe stood and walked to the black table against the wall. Several metal chairs were tucked under it, but the clutter of bottles and paperwork strewn across its surface suggested it hadn't been used for a meal in a while. She poured herself a glass of pale green liquid, leaned a hip against the table, and swirled the liquid around and around.

The silence pressed on Aris's nerves.

"I'm offering you the chance to become a Military flyer," Dianthe said finally. "No active combat. But you'll still have to do physical training. First a month with me, and then regularly with your unit. The Military sector requires a certain level of conditioning. If you can't meet those requirements, I'll have to send you home."

Aris was suddenly very happy to be sitting down. Theo hadn't said anything about physical conditioning requirements. How could she possibly meet them?

Even her parents thought she could barely function. Her father loved to remind her of all the activities she was unsuited to—including a desk job in Panthea, apparently—and her mother never missed an opportunity to grab her shoulders and tell her how much worse her limp was when she slouched.

Dianthe watched her, sipping her drink. She didn't pour a

second glass, though Aris wished she would; her throat felt drier than the deserts of Safara.

"There's someone I need to find," Aris said loudly, trying to forget her parents' lack of confidence in her physical strength. Trying to ignore the tremble in her knees that suggested they might be right. "If I do this, I want to be placed in his unit. Or at his stationpoint, at least. I want to work with him."

Dianthe's expression gave away nothing. "Who is 'he'?"

"Calix Pavlos. He's training to be a field mender. He just had selection a week ago, like me, only he was selected for Military." Even now, the thought of him so close to danger made her chest burn.

The room swelled with silence and sunlight. Aris held her breath.

Dianthe tapped a finger against her glass. "I make no guarantees."

No guarantees? *No guarantees* wasn't good enough. If she was going to do this—if she was going to take this massive, ridiculous, *what-was-she-thinking* leap—she *had* to be with Calix.

Aris stood up on legs that only quivered a little and crossed her arms over her chest. "You need me. Theo said so. I'll be placed with Calix or not at all. These are my terms."

Dianthe's eyes flashed, venomous. "*Your* terms."

Aris stood her ground, caught in the cage of Dianthe's stare.

The woman barked a harsh laugh. "You foolish girl. We are losing this war, did you know that? Do you think any of us can afford ultimatums?" She slammed her glass on the table. "Is that what Theo promised you? A chance to play at love on the battlefield?"

Aris sucked in a ragged breath.

Without waiting for an answer, Dianthe continued. "This is no game. I disguise you as a man, train you, and get you documents so you can pass as a volunteer for the Military sector. And then you join a regular unit and train with them. A regular unit, get it? With weapons, and war, and danger."

Aris stared at Dianthe's blood-red snake tattoo as she stalked the room, feeling like a small, defenseless animal at the mercy of that serpent's strike. She shivered. "You said no combat."

"That doesn't mean it won't be dangerous. You'll be a soldier, first and foremost. And you don't get to tell your family or friends where you are or what you're really doing. If the government discovers you're a woman, you'll be sent to prison for impersonating a soldier. And if you get shot"—she cocked her head to the side—"you'll be dead."

Each word hung like the afterimage of lightning in Aris's mind, sinking slowly into her awareness.

"This cannot be about Calix. Do you understand?" Dianthe, still scowling, studied her.

Aris bit her lip, shamed. Because it *was* about him, even now, no matter what Dianthe said. She would fight wars for Calix. In little more than a whisper, she asked, "Are we really losing? The news vids . . ." Her voice trailed off. The news vids still dealt in small victories. Hope.

Dianthe suddenly looked tired. Even the snake seemed to droop a little as she let out a breath. "The situation is . . . dire. If the Ward of Ruslana had succeeded in persuading the other dominions to impose sanctions on Safara, maybe that would have helped us secure our border. But . . ."

"But Ward Vadim fell ill," Aris said, stomach leaden, "and there was no vote on sanctions."

"Exactly. And wasn't *that* convenient." Dianthe looked up. "Every single man—and woman—willing to stand up and fight for this dominion can be certain they are making a difference. Including you, Aris." She drained the rest of her drink and set it back on the table. "Theo was right. We do need you. *If* you can pass the physical training."

Taking her heart, and her courage, in her hands, Aris murmured, "And Calix?"

Dianthe sighed, sounding oddly defeated. "I'll see what I can do."

It wasn't the guarantee Aris wanted. But something told her Dianthe could make it happen. "Okay. So what now?"

Dianthe led her to the first of three closed doors along the left wall of the apartment. A small circular pad beside the door glowed faintly. "This will be your room. Once you've unpacked your things, change into your exercise uniform. It's on the bed. "

"Exercise uniform?" Aris passed the handle of her bag from one hand to the other. It was light; she'd brought little with her from home.

"To begin your training," Dianthe said, walking away.

Aris's heart gave a sudden lurch. "But don't you want to see me fly?"

Dianthe turned back to stare at her. "Physical training first. If you make it through that, *then* I'll see you fly."

"But . . ." How would she make it on the physical training alone? Her one skill was flying; without that, she had nothing.

At the obvious terror in Aris's eyes, Dianthe raised her hands. "I told you, this only works if you can pass the physical tests."

For an instant, Aris considered walking away. There was still time . . . and her father would be pleased. Maybe she could. . . .

No. She tightened her hand on the bag. *You're doing this for Calix. You can do anything for him.* "I'll be right out."

Aris pressed the glowing pad on the wall and the bedroom door slid open. The room had no windows, just a narrow bed, one small trunk for her clothes, and a doorway that led to a tiny washroom. She dropped her bag onto the floor beside the bed, and changed into the tight black pants and sleeveless tunic of her exercise uniform.

When Aris walked back into the main room, Dianthe was waiting.

"What happens now?" Aris tried to sound professional. Like someone to be taken seriously. Like someone who wasn't about to collapse in fear.

Dianthe led her to another door. Aris's stomach sank when it slid open, revealing a collection of frightening machines that gleamed silver in the daylight pouring through the glass wall.

"Each member of Military is expected to run three miles

every day. You'll run one mile today, two tomorrow. And three each day after that. If I feel it necessary," Dianthe said, "you'll run more." She pointed to a dark strip of flooring along the far wall.

Aris didn't move. The first task was *running*? "You can't expect . . . I mean. . . ." She hadn't run more than a few yards since the fever, when she was twelve years old. There was no way she could do this. Pulse pounding in her throat, she turned her gaze to Dianthe's impassive face. "But I don't run." She barely stopped herself from saying *I can't*.

Dianthe's expression didn't change. "You know the arrangement. You run, or you leave."

Aris gingerly threaded her way through the equipment to the black strip of flooring, which gave slightly as she stepped onto it. Without warning it moved and she fell, the thud of elbow and hip meeting floor echoing in the quiet room.

Wincing, she tried to sit up, still unbalanced and awkward.

"Again," Dianthe said.

This time when the floor began to move, Aris was ready. Or readier. As she walked, Dianthe tapped a panel on the wall. Gradually, the floor slid faster and faster until she was jogging. The pace was what anyone other than Aris might call leisurely, but she could already feel weakness in her knees and a tingling ache in the backs of her thighs.

"This is too slow," Dianthe said, "but it will do." She paused. "For today."

Aris heard the hiss of a door closing and then she was alone. *You just have to make it through a month. Then she'll see you fly, and she will have no choice to keep you.* The words pounded in her head to the rhythm of her feet. But within minutes, her legs were trembling and her lungs were on fire.

A month? Who was she kidding? She wasn't going to last a day.

Chapter Ten

ARIS AWOKE THE NEXT MORNING TO COMPLETE DARKNESS FOR the first time in her life. She felt the lack of Lux's constant glow like the loss of a childhood friend. She'd always imagined that when she left home, she would be with Calix, not in a tiny, impersonal room in the heart of Panthea by herself.

When she turned on her digitablet, she checked her comms and noted with a start that she had a message from Calix. With trembling fingers, she touched the screen and opened the letter.

Aris, you don't know how happy I am to finally sit down and write to you. Only ten days apart and it feels like a lifetime. I keep telling myself it'll get easier, but I still dream about you all the time. Sometimes I think about our last night together and wish I'd broken the rules. I'm sorry. I shouldn't say that. I'm so tired I can hardly think. The training has been a lot harder than I expected. In addition to our mender duties, we have to do combat drills and physical conditioning. You'd laugh if you saw me . . . I'm a terrible fighter. I miss you so much, Hummingbird. Tell Rakk and Phae I say hi. And give my mother a hug, will you, if you see her? Please write soon. I need to know you're surviving. I love you. - Calix

Aris couldn't do as he asked and say hello to anyone, or hug his mother. Instead she wrote that she had left Lux. Her story about the Central Enviro Office wouldn't make much sense to him, especially given Panthea's no-fly rules, but there was no help for it. Dianthe had told her she couldn't hint at the truth over comms in case they were monitored. She'd have to wait until they were face to face to tell Calix what she'd done.

"Let's go, Aris!" Dianthe's voice shattered the silence. Two sharp knocks on the bedroom door followed.

"I'll be right out." Aris switched off her digitablet and dragged herself from the small, hard bed. Calix's first comm should have come as a relief. An affirmation. But he sounded so lost. She wished she could tell him she was coming, that they'd bear the burden of their new lives together.

When she walked into the main room, Dianthe was at the door saying goodbye to someone in the hallway. Aris waited, grateful for any small reprieve from the torture.

Dianthe closed the door and turned to study her. "How's the leg?"

About to fall off. "Fine."

"Good." Dianthe pursed her lips, as if pinching back a smile. As if she knew Aris was lying and could see every single aching muscle she was trying to hide. She led Aris into the room with the moving floor and strapped her into a frightening machine meant to work her leg muscles. Aris began the exercise, biting back a groan as her legs burst into pain.

"So," Dianthe said while she watched her work, "What happened?"

"What . . . do you mean?" *Breathe. Don't forget to breathe.* What Aris *wanted* to do was scream. Her thighs were already burning.

"Your leg. The limp."

She paused, trying to concentrate on the question, but Dianthe barked, "Don't stop. Five more."

This time Aris couldn't hold back the groan. Half-breathless from exertion, she mumbled, "When I was a child I got sick, so sick my parents thought I'd die. I couldn't walk for months afterwards, and the pain of relearning made me scream." *Just the way I feel now.*

"Ten more, then you're done with this," Dianthe interjected. "And talk using shorter sentences. Be straight. To the point. Think about the way men speak."

"Not all men . . . speak . . . like that." Aris pushed her legs against the machine as she said it, her face burning with the effort. Her father spoke long and eloquently, often using his hands for illustration. He told wonderful stories.

"But *you* will," Dianthe said, interrupting Aris's regrets. "You'll talk and act like a typical male. This isn't about expressing yourself or the variety of human experience. It's about conformity. You will disappear into the soldiers' ranks. You will *not* stand out. Do you understand?"

Aris nodded.

Dianthe grabbed Aris's knee, adjusting her leg to improve her form. "So, you were ill and had to relearn how to walk. That's it? The end of the story?"

The machine hissed into silence as Aris finished her last leg press. "Calix, the field mender I'll be placed with, helped me. Saved me, really. I couldn't have done it otherwise, without him taking care of me. He wouldn't let me give up."

"How romantic." Dianthe's sarcasm was palpable.

Aris straightened her legs, stretching out the sore muscles, and ignored the barb. "And my father wouldn't either. He taught me to fly when I was too weak to walk. I've been flying ever since." Holy, what she'd give to be flying now. "Flying was my way out of the pain. It was my freedom."

Dianthe didn't respond for a moment, and Aris wondered if she'd actually gotten through to the woman. But then Dianthe said, "Too much emotion. Keep that to yourself, Haan. Men don't discuss their feelings."

Aris sighed. "You did ask."

Dianthe spun on her heel and walked to the panel that controlled the moving floor. "Break's over. Give me a two-mile run, and I'll make breakfast. Push yourself and you might just outrun that limp. There's nothing wrong with your leg. It's only weakness holding you back."

This time, as Aris hauled herself to her feet, she didn't even try to bite back her agonized groan. *Two miles before breakfast?* That much exercise before eating would surely kill her.

At least, then, there'd be no more running. Her lip twitched with the suggestion of a grin. Then the floor started to move and the pain followed.

You are doing this to be with Calix, she told herself with each step. *To make him proud. You will not give up. You cannot go back to Lux.*

And somehow, by the grace of the Gods, she made it exactly two miles before she collapsed in a heap on the floor.

CHAPTER ELEVEN

"So what's it to be today, toast or custard?" Galena asked.

It had taken her less than a week to notice how much Elom hated that he had to feed her. It was the only small triumph she'd found, needling him each morning when he brought her breakfast.

He dropped the tray on the counter with a rattle.

"We can always go back to fluids," he replied, twisting her hand painfully as he disengaged the metal bands holding her arms immobile against the bed railings. She massaged her wrists and wished she could rub away the faint red crimps where the restraints dug into her skin as she slept.

"It's dangerous, you know," she said as she sat up, "tying me to the bed at night. I'm not a young woman. One of these mornings you might have to do worse than bring me breakfast."

He grunted. "You have three minutes." He tapped the monitor, setting up the day's testing.

Galena slid off the bed and pursed her lips as her bare feet touched the cold floor. She walked to the small washroom with her spine straight and tried to hold on to the illusion of Elom as her servant, bringing her food, washing her sheets.

Once inside the washroom door, she slammed it shut and

sagged against the wall. She wanted to scream, pound against the door, break through the walls with her bare hands. She wanted to tear Elom apart.

It hadn't taken long for her to realize he'd lied about her location; wherever she really was, it wasn't an Atalantan clinic. There were no other menders attending her, and she'd had no contact with the outside world.

Galena had come to hate the moment, each morning, when she slid into consciousness. Because each time she finally opened her eyes, what she saw was the same: the restraints on her wrists; the gleam of Elom's bald head looming above her; the look of condescension marring his features. Because each morning, she woke to the knowledge that he controlled everything—what she ate, what she did, even when she could use the washroom.

"Two minutes!"

His voice made her jump. She tightened her hands into fists and stepped slowly away from the wall. As she completed her morning routine, she imagined him standing before the Council in chains, the disdain in his eyes turning to fear.

She splashed cold water on her face—there was nothing but cold water here, even in the shower—then leaned against the sink. Again, as she did each morning, she dissected the room with her eyes, looking for a weapon, some way to escape. There were no air vents, no towel bars she could rip from the wall. There were no light panels that she could tear down to use as a bludgeon, or exposed wires to start a fire, just a high-tech ceiling that glowed. The small shower had no curtain; she couldn't even try to hang herself, if she got desperate enough.

When Elom pounded on the door, she emerged, knowing he would open the door and drag her out if she didn't.

"Eat," he said.

She took the tray and moved to the one hard chair—bolted to the floor, of course. The dishes and flatware were flimsy, useless as weapons. She took a sip of the metallic-tasting orange juice and shuddered.

"What *is* this? Poison?" She knew it didn't make sense to

provoke him, that it would do no good. But it was all she had.

He didn't respond, just pressed the cold electrodes against her skin, sliding his hands beneath the flowing white tunic he'd given her to wear. The feel of his hands on her would have frightened her, if his face didn't always hold so much disgust.

"Wishing I were twenty years younger?"

"You know," he said mildly, straightening, "I could do this just as easily if you were missing a finger. Or two."

Galena kept her features still, but her hand shook as it brought the tasteless toast to her mouth. She forced it down, even though the hum of the electrodes made her stomach churn. He wouldn't feed her again until late in the day. If she didn't eat, it made no difference to him.

"Time for the news?" she asked, as she held her tray up to Elom.

He jerked it from her hand. "Walk first."

With a sigh, she stood and walked around the room. Though the space was small, it was her only exercise so she tried to make it count.

Finally, he told her to stop. When she was seated, he set the digitablet in her hands. Today's news report showed Pyralis, his wife Bett standing behind him.

"I wish Ward Vadim all the best as she continues her recovery," he said, staring earnestly into the camera. The grooves in his face were even deeper than she remembered. For just a second, as she watched Bett reach for him when he'd finished speaking, she felt the pain of losing him all over again.

The pretty reporter summarized the rest of Pyralis's speech and reminded the world of Galena's illness. As Galena watched her point to the Atalantan clinic, she wanted to scream at her, "I'm not sick! I'm not *there*! Find me! Save me, please!" but of course she never said the words out loud. What good would it do?

When the vid was over, Elom grabbed the digitablet and fastened her restraints. Then he left, taking every scrap of light with him.

CHAPTER TWELVE

FOR A SPLIT SECOND, AS ARIS STRETCHED HER FEET TO THE edge of the bed and arched her back, she was happy. She'd been dreaming of the beach, of Calix standing in front of their cave, holding a white candle. The sun was setting, swirling the water with gold and crimson. He held the candle out to her, mouth open to say the words—

Then her legs seized up, her arms screamed, and the truth bloomed in her stomach, red and burning like an exploding firebomb.

Calix was gone from Lux, and she was in Panthea. Alone.

Desperate for some connection to him, she pulled her digitablet onto the bed with her, tapping the screen to begin a comm session.

No messages from Calix. Her heart sank. But there was one from her mother, asking how the new job was going. She dragged her finger across the screen. Instead of responding, she opened a new comm to Calix.

I've been dreaming about you. The last few weeks have been the worst of my life. I miss you so much, I feel like I'm drowning all the time. The new job is a distraction, but I'd still rather be with you. Good luck with your training. I know you'll get the hang of it. You

*were always so fast in the races at school. Write me soon. I love
you. ~Aris*

Aris had made it nearly a week, but she was scared she might
not last much longer. Every muscle in her body screamed, each
new exercise or run made her want to beg for mercy. It felt like
learning to walk after the fever all over again—the pain, the
gasping breath as the effort threatened to topple her, the fear
that she'd never learn, that she'd fail and be a shell of herself
forever.

She wanted the freedom of flight so much she had dreams of
stealing a wingjet and leaving, flying forever over rolling green
blankets of forest, the sparkle of an ocean horizon just out of
reach.

But she wanted Calix more.

She dragged herself out of bed, put on her exercise uniform,
and went to meet Dianthe. As soon as she moved into the hall,
the woman stomped her foot. "Not like that. Widen your
stance," she ordered, crossing the room to join Aris. "Shoulders
back."

Dianthe grabbed Aris's shoulders in nearly the same way her
mother did. Aris might have felt nostalgic, but for Dianthe's
next words, "As a man, you must keep your body straight and
solid. Weight even on both legs. You start favoring that left leg
of yours and I'll send you home."

Aris moved so her feet were hip-width apart and squared her
shoulders, trying to channel the way Calix stood. It was so
strange, learning how to move like a man. She still couldn't
imagine how she'd fool anyone. There was nothing she could do
about her height, her curves, or her facial features.

"Better." Dianthe let go of her shoulders. "Aristos."

"Aristos?"

Dianthe gave her a considering stare. "That's your name. Get
used to it. From this point forward, all of your identification,
electronic and otherwise, will be under the name Aristos Haan.
And for all the world, you'll be male. Come with me."

"How does the disguise actually work?" Aris asked, following her across the large living room and into the kitchen. "You haven't said."

Dianthe stopped before the far wall. On it hung an enormous photo of the three eastern dominions: Atalanta, Safara, and Ruslana. "As a matter of fact, I'm about to show you."

She pressed a finger to the photo, right in the heart of Atalanta, where a silver shimmer indicated Panthea. There was a hissing noise, and the wall slid away.

"A secret room?" Aris asked, eyes wide.

"Clandestine affairs cannot be conducted out in the open, can they?" Dianthe said, with a little smile.

The room was small and windowless, with a panel of monitors and equipment along one wall. In the center, a large white chair was bolted to the floor. The air was cold and had a faint bitter scent, like disinfectant and metal filings.

Aris couldn't help it. She laughed.

Dianthe looked at her, brows raised.

"Sorry. It's just . . . I thought we'd already done the torture part." She swallowed back another nervous giggle as she followed Dianthe into the room.

The tall woman drew a handful of silver disks from a tray on a table against the wall. "With these I'm going to map your body. I'll also record your voice," she said, holding up another strange instrument. "And then, with the data, I'll create a holographic second skin, called a diatous veil. It'll smooth your curves, give you a less delicate nose." She studied Aris's face. "I'll adjust your cheekbones," she continued, tracing Aris's skin with a long, feather-light finger, "And give you a more pronounced Adam's apple. A voice modulator connected to the veil will lower your voice."

"Does it hurt?" Aris asked, eying the gleaming disks in Dianthe's hand.

"Not particularly." Dianthe returned the electrodes to the tray. "The data collection is painless, and the veil itself is only an image." She glanced back. "You have to be careful though. If someone touches you, they'll feel your real shape. When you're wearing body armor it won't be a problem, but you'll have to learn to keep your distance in training and during meals. We'll practice."

Aris nodded. It terrified her, the thought of being surrounded by strange men. Trying to hide among them as if she belonged.

"And you mustn't, under any circumstances," Dianthe continued, "remove your clothing in front of others. The diatous veil is not entirely correct, anatomically speaking."

A blush swarmed up Aris's cheeks. "There's no way I'll have my own room. Where will I change clothes?"

Dianthe settled her hands on her hips. "The network is extensive. You'll be paired with another disguised female as your sectormate. The two of you will go through training together, bunk together. You'll be responsible for keeping each others' secret."

"There are that many of us?" Aris asked, in wonder. Would she be able to tell the difference?

"There are enough."

"So I am Aristos Haan." Aris rolled it on her tongue, trying to fit it around her real name, smoothing it out so it sounded natural in her mind. *This might actually work.* She smiled.

"Alright, *Aristos*," Dianthe said, emphasizing the name. "Sit." She gave Aris a little push into the chair.

"We're starting the body mapping now?" Anything to have a break from the endless running and sparring.

"Yes," Dianthe said. "After we shave your head."

Aris felt as if someone had punched her in the stomach. "After we do *what*?"

CHAPTER THIRTEEN

"Stop that," Dianthe snapped that night.

Aris started and realized she'd been running her hand along her shaved head again.

"Sorry." She couldn't get used to the smoothness, the curve of her skull so exposed. Calix had always loved her hair; it was long and thick, dark as the earth in which the olive trees grew. He was always running his hands through it, tucking it behind her ears.

What would he think when he saw her, looking like any other soldier in Military? Would he mind that she cut her hair?

Would he even recognize her?

She took another bite of the roasted vegetable stew Dianthe had made for them and tried to keep her free hand tethered to the table.

"It feels weird, you know? Having no hair, I mean," she said. "Doesn't it feel strange to you?"

"I'm used to it." Dianthe didn't look up from her bowl.

"How long have you trained women like this? Are you a real Atalantan soldier, too?"

Dianthe took the time to swallow her spoonful of stew before answering. "I was selected for Technology. The Ward at the time—this was years ago—tasked the company I worked for with developing a device to disguise a body's shape and appearance."

"So you invented the technology?" Aris asked, impressed.

"I helped." Dianthe didn't look up from her bowl.

"But if you're in Tech sector, why do you have a Military brand?"

"About ten years ago, Military wanted to experiment with allowing women into the sector. But they didn't want anyone to know." Dianthe took a sip from her glass. "They bought the technology and brought me in to oversee the project. In a way, I volunteered. Just like you."

Aris's jaw dropped. "So this whole thing is sanctioned by the dominion? Then why can't women—"

"The program no longer exists as far as the dominion is concerned," Dianthe interrupted. "There are no women in Military, Aris. We're all just ghosts." Her lips contracted to a thin line; it was obvious she'd said all she was willing to.

Aris turned her eyes to the window, where the city lights twinkled like stars in the darkness. As in her village, electricity here was solar-powered, but in Lux the pathways from house to house glowed cool and milky, like the moon. Here the light was sharp-edged, sparkling.

"Are there other women out there, in Military? In other dominions, I mean?" Aris didn't turn her gaze from the window.

"Atalanta has never shared the diatous veil technology," Dianthe replied. "If there are women in the other Military sectors, they're in disguise, like us. But by the traditional methods."

Aris glanced at her, eyebrows raised in question.

"Breast binding, body language. Luck."

It would be difficult enough with the diatous veil; Aris couldn't imagine trying to pass as a man without it. "So what do you do about your Military brand when you go out? Don't people give you strange looks?"

"When I go out in public, I do it as you will. In disguise."

Aris suppressed a shudder. "So you never really get to be yourself? Ever? That's so sad."

"It's the sacrifice I made to do this job. And it's the choice *you've* made as well," Dianthe pointed out.

"But when I go home, you can remove the Military brand, right?"

Dianthe's eyes narrowed. "No, I can't. I don't have the tech. Only a few high-ranking officials have access. After all, volunteering for Military and getting a second brand is fairly commonplace. Removing a brand is something they only do to criminals." In a harsh movement, she shoved her empty bowl across the table. "*If* you abandon your job and go home, it'll be your responsibility to hide the brand. A tattoo, something big and black on the back of your neck, would be best."

"A tattoo?" The brands might not hurt, but getting a tattoo definitely would. Aris swallowed hard. "Couldn't I just grow my hair out? Hide it that way?"

Dianthe stood abruptly. "Do you not remember a word I said? I *told* you. Out there," she gestured to the glittering city, "you are breaking the law. If anyone sees your Military brand, if a well-meaning shopgirl brushes your hair out of the way in helping you try on a new necklace, they have to report you."

Dianthe grabbed her bowl and took it to the kitchen, reappearing in the doorway before Aris had time to move. "Even when you're out, you'll always worry that someone will expose you. You'll always be looking over your shoulder. And you'll never be able to tell anyone what you did."

Aris ran a hand across her bald head. "Why can't the holographic thing project the brand itself? Why do I have to get one at all?"

Dianthe crossed her arms over her chest. "The diatous veil will sense and adjust to your clothing or lack thereof. If there's an extensive mark of some kind on your skin, it will reproduce that. If you had a scar, you would retain the scar even while the device is active. It will add or redistribute shape and bulk, but pigment, no."

Aris followed Dianthe through the doorway into the kitchen, carrying the remaining dishes, trying not to limp. She kept waiting for the pain to lessen, for her muscles to adjust to the abuse. "Can I ask you one more question?"

Dianthe grunted as she placed the dishes one at a time in a slit in the row of cupboards. She pressed a button and seconds later the dish slid back out, clean.

Aris took the noise as permission. "If Military ended your program, why are you still doing this? Why aren't you working on some other invention or, I don't know, retired? You must have made a lot of money."

For a long time Dianthe didn't speak, and Aris was sure she'd offended her again. But when the older woman turned, her black eyes shimmered, as if with tears. She cleared her throat. "I do this because I believe a woman should have the right to fight and die for her dominion, just like any man," she said softly. "There's no reason for our leaders to ban women from making this choice. So I help them make it anyway. Even if it means giving up who they are. Even if it means joining Military as ghosts." The blank eyes of Dianthe's snake tattoo glared at Aris. "This is not and never will be only about finding a loved one, or avenging those lost. Even for you, Aristos."

She slammed the last clean dish onto the counter. The noise echoed through the room. "I hope you're prepared to live with your choice."

CHAPTER FOURTEEN

"And this goes with the coral dress, the one with the gold belt that I showed you before the red one, remember?" His wife, Bett, held up yet another necklace, this one a long strand of colorful beads.

He tried to focus. "The red one, yes. . . ."

"I don't have any shoes that color, so of course I had to go to Peregrine's," she went on. "They had the loveliest sandals . . . wait, where did they go?" She bent to rifle through the baskets of shoes and clothes and jewelry. "You know, I had nothing to wear to the Sector Ball next month and this will be just perfect—"

"Bett, please," Pyralis begged.

She glanced up. "But I haven't even showed you the dress I got for—"

"Desist, I beg you!" He couldn't keep the exasperation from his voice. "This is the third time you've gone to Panthea in as many days. What is one more dress now, when we're in crisis?"

Bett dropped the necklace. It hit the floor, tinkling like a hundred small, discordant bells. Hands on her hips, she suddenly became a study of angles—sharp elbows, pointed chin, narrowed eyes—beneath her fall of heavy black hair. "We're always in crisis. I see the vids, Pyralis. I see the burned corpses

66

of our villages, the faces of our lost soldiers each and every night."

It always threw him, how quickly she could go from flighty to deadly serious.

She stalked to a spot behind his chair and dug her strong fingers almost savagely into his shoulders, kneading the tight muscles. "How can I not, as the Ward's wife?"

"Not now." Pyralis leaned forward, away from her hands. He couldn't concentrate with her here, flitting every which way like an insistent, buzzing honey bee.

Bett stayed where she was and gripped the back of the chair instead. "And if I want to lose myself for an afternoon? Do you think the worry, the fear just falls away? There is no escape, for me, from the horrors of this war. Not with you carrying them every day for the last three years."

He sighed. "It's so extravagant, when so many are suffering. What message does it send to the people? There must be something . . . you used to speak to the children in school. Why not that?"

She moved to face him, her eyes hard. "Don't tell me how to cope, when *you* will listen to no one, will let no one help you. So many times I've tried to talk to you about your plans, so many times I've tried to help . . . Believe me, I didn't work all those years in struggling Tech companies to improve my *shopping* skills. I have insight to offer, by Gods! But you never listen. You won't even *look* at me." She gathered her baskets of bright cloth and shimmering jewels.

Shamed, he reached for her, his hand floating for a moment between them. But he let it fall when she didn't see it, when she didn't turn around. "I'm sorry, Bett. It has been a long day."

"A long day, a long week, a long year . . . I know."

"Please—" he started, half-rising. He would pull her into his arms, let her hold him. Do his best to forget the rest of the world, if only for a moment—

"Ward Nekos." Kellan, Pyralis's assistant, strode into the room. "Oh. I'm sorry. I didn't realize you were occupied."

"He isn't," Bett snapped. "I'm leaving."

Pyralis let her go. Kellan was holding a red digitablet, which meant it was secure tech and not something Pyralis could delay. His assistant's short ginger hair stuck up every which way, as if he'd run his hands through it . . . or tried to pull it out. His hair often looked like that these days.

"The reports?" Pyralis stood and gripped the back of his chair.

Kellan nodded. He placed the digitablet in its docking station in the center of the desk and tapped the edge of the screen; the huge monitor affixed to the opposing wall blinked on.

Together, the men studied a series of images: flame-engulfed villages, the ruins of Atalantan wingcraft. In one, a fleet of Safaran wingjets sat on a landing pad with the remains of bombed Atalantan wingjets all around them.

"Where is that?" Pyralis asked, pointing to the photo.

"Bieza, a village just inside Atalanta's southwest border. They took over the regional landing pad."

Pyralis rubbed a hand over his chin. "And how far into Mittaka?" The fighting was the worst in this hilly, wooded region between Safara's border and the Fex River.

"This week, three miles."

Pyralis let out a deep, heavy breath. "Are we still holding to the north?"

Kellan tapped the digitablet and the monitor went black. "For now."

"Has Ruslana chosen an acting Ward yet?" Pyralis stalked to the window. Headaches were a daily nuisance now, the blades of tension that ran from the base of his neck to his skull seemingly permanent. Each night Bett tried to work the knots out, tried to ease the tightness, but she'd only had success in strengthening the muscles of her fingers. Pyralis's pain remained.

"They are still determined to wait until Ward Vadim can resume her role. Her advisors and the head of their Technology sector have shouldered some of the responsibility, but no one is talking foreign policy right now. They're just trying to keep Ruslana running smoothly."

"So their trade with Safara?"

"Still halted, as of now. Ward Vadim had stopped water shipments before the World Council; they've left her policies in place."

Pyralis stared into the forest, at the army of trees pressing close. "Thank the Gods for that."

Without those sanctions, without the miniscule amount of hope they provided, there would be little left to do but watch as his country shattered.

CHAPTER FIFTEEN

Calix, I'm sorry I didn't write sooner. The new job has been more of a challenge than I expected. But no matter how busy I am, I still think about you every moment. It's different, living in the city. I miss the ocean, and Mother's cooking. She's happy I'm here, but I still haven't heard from Father.

The worst part, aside from missing you, is not being able to fly. I knew it would be hard, but it's so much worse than I imagined. It feels like half my soul is with you, and half is soaring above, without me. There's so little of me left.

I've found one thing that helps. I pretend you're a mender, Health-selected, living in Panthea, and we're here together. There is nothing I want more than that. Than I want you. Stay safe. I love you. - Your hummingbird

ARIS PRESSED THE BUTTON TO SEND AND STUFFED THE digitablet into her bag. Calix couldn't understand what she was saying to him in the white space, the silence around her words, the small details she wove through the lie that had become her life. She so wanted to tell him what she was really doing. She wanted to tell *someone* what was actually happening to her.

Every morning for the past two weeks, Dianthe had hooked Aris up to the slick silver disks, mapping her body and voice. She drilled Aris for hours in walking like a man and hand-to-hand combat, which gave Aris new bruises every day. In the afternoons, Dianthe made her run and strapped her to the frightening silver exercise equipment to strengthen her arms and legs.

Now Aris's legs didn't just tremble; they spasmed and buckled beneath her. She'd fallen so many times her skin resembled starberry jam more than it did human flesh.

Still, Dianthe didn't send her away.

But she wasn't kind either.

"You think that hurts?" she taunted as Aris attempted a push-up, arms shaking with the effort. "You have no idea how bad it will get."

When Aris fell during a sprint: "Why don't you drag yourself home to your mother and let her coddle you. Is that what you want?"

And, as she heaved herself into another sit-up: "Don't think that one's going to count, not with your arms in the air like that. Again!"

At each insult, Aris would nod, snot and tears and sometimes blood streaking her face, and Dianthe would laugh. Worst of all were those moments when Dianthe twisted Aris's own history against her. "Feel a fever coming on, sick girl?" one day, and "You want to give up? Your precious Calix not enough?" the next.

Just when Aris was ready to walk away, when Calix and the flying and getting out of Lux didn't seem worth it, the "can you *really* be this pathetic?" would burrow under her skin and make her burn to prove Dianthe wrong. To prove them all wrong—her father, her mother, and most of all herself, she who wanted to cry, "Yes, Dianthe! You're right! This is too hard. Send me home."

So she'd pull herself up, bloody and numb with pain, and keep going.

ONE AFTERNOON, during the third week, Dianthe skipped the run and led Aris to the secret room instead. She asked her to sit, then held a thick silver medigun to Aris's throat. "This is your voice modulator," she said, as she engaged the gun.

"Ow!" Aris flinched at the sudden sting as the tiny chip was shot under her skin, where it lodged against her voicebox. "You could have warned me it would hurt."

"Why?" Dianthe said, dabbing at the spot with a piece of gauze. "Was that worse than me kicking you in the head this morning?"

"Good point." Aris ran her fingers lightly over the sore spot at the base of her throat; the lump made by the modulator was nearly imperceptible. "I don't sound any different."

Dianthe helped her up from the sleek white chair, pushing her toward the full-length mirror at the back of the lab. "Of course not. It only works when the veil is activated."

Aris stared at herself in the mirror. Her black exercise clothes hung off her; she'd lost weight in the last couple of weeks. Across one cheekbone, she sported a purplish yellow bruise, and a scabbed-over scratch marred her temple. The newly shaved skin that curved along her head was paler than her face, her cheeks still tan from all the time she'd spent on the beach in Lux.

"You ready?" Dianthe met Aris's eyes in the mirror. "This won't hurt, but it will feel . . . odd."

Aris took a steadying breath and nodded. Without another word, Dianthe pressed the clear, rectangular diatous veil against the back of Aris's neck, where her Military brand would go.

An electric tingle radiated outward, up the back of Aris's skull and down her arms, sizzling along her spine and legs. It felt like millions of tiny bugs scurrying across her skin. She nearly succumbed to the impulse to scream and bat at the invisible creatures. But as soon as the tingle reached her fingertips, it faded to a subtle hum beneath her skin. Which was still plenty disconcerting.

Even more unsettling was how Aris's face changed in the

mirror. Instantly, her narrow jaw became defined and square. Her cheekbones suddenly rounded. Her nose widened, a blunt stub at the tip. Only her blue eyes were the same, though now they looked even more like her father's.

With the activation of the veil, Aris disappeared. And Aristos was born.

She rubbed the back of her neck gingerly, fingers catching against the subtle hardness of the diatous veil. In the mirror, Aristos did the same, his muscles engaging as she moved. *You are Aristos Haan, the fiercest Flyer in Atalanta. Your enemies tremble when they hear your name.* She narrowed her eyes and turned her lips down in what was meant to be a threatening scowl. The expression just made Aristos look ill.

Aris leaned closer to the mirror, touching her skin with an experimental finger. The place where cheek and fingertip met shimmered, just a little, like heat on a wingjet pad in the middle of summer. It was subtle; if you weren't looking closely, you'd miss it.

"See? No touching," Dianthe said. "No rubbing or scratching your face in public. And I wouldn't cross your arms too tightly, either."

Aris looked down at her arms. They were still marked with bruises but larger than her real arms would ever be. Another glance in the mirror showed that she wasn't any taller, but her shoulders looked broader and the proportion of her hips to waist had shifted to a more boyish shape.

"This is . . . this is blighting insane." Aris clapped her hand over her mouth automatically, her eyes widening in shock. "My voice! It really is lower."

Dianthe nodded, a satisfied look crossing her face.

Aris stared at herself in the mirror for another long moment. She genuinely did look like a man.

Now all she had to do was act like one.

CHAPTER SIXTEEN

Aris – I can tell how much you miss flying. It's making you miserable, isn't it? Have you gone home to visit your parents yet? Maybe you need a break. Or, I don't know, maybe Panthea isn't the place for you. You should go back to your family. Your wingjet. I'm sure she—they all—miss you. You sound so tired. It makes me worry for you.

Adjusting to the new stationpoint has taken some time, but I did something today. I saved someone. There's a soldier here who's alive because of me. It's a consolation, knowing I'm really helping, when I miss you so much I can barely breathe. I hope you'll find it a consolation, too. I love you. – Calix

ARIS SIGHED AS SHE POWERED DOWN HER DIGITAB. IT WAS A comfort knowing Calix missed her as much as she missed him, but his worry over her was less welcome. She didn't want to cause him added stress.

After washing her face and pulling on her exercise uniform, she strode into the main room, where Dianthe was waiting.

They began with yet another sparring session. "Get your left arm up!" Dianthe yelled as she drew one impossibly long leg into a kick.

Aris ducked, too slowly, and collected another bruise on her shoulder. Her breath hissed through clenched teeth at the pain.

She had a pounding headache from the diatous veil's constant hum and a building knot of frustration in her chest. As she lurched to the side, trying to avoid Dianthe's fists, she panted, "I don't . . . know why . . . this is necessary. I'm a *flyer*, by Gods!" This couldn't be what Calix was going through in his field mender training. It had to be some kind of special torture, just for her. To make her a *man*.

"What do you think this is, the peace brigade? Block!" Dianthe sprang forward, lithe and precise as a striking snake. "What happens if you crash in enemy territory? How will you defend yourself?"

Aris grunted as another blow connected with her shoulder. She threw a weak jab. "If I crash, I'll be dead."

"That's all you've got?" Dianthe taunted. "My ninety-year-old uncle could throw a better punch than that."

Aris jabbed again and, tripping, went down hard on one knee. Her legs barely held her as she staggered to her feet. Why couldn't Dianthe let the insults *rest*? Wasn't the pain and lack of sleep and endless training enough?

"Come on, you weakling, attack!" The woman lunged at Aris, holding nothing back.

And just like that, Aris could take no more. "*I am not a weakling!*" she screamed, the words pushing her anger through the pain with a burst of desperate strength. She blocked Dianthe's blow and threw her fist as hard as she could into the woman's belly. And, for the first time, she connected.

With a thud, Dianthe went down, sucking at the air like a dying fish.

Shocked, Aris's knees buckled. "Holy hell," she gasped, "I'm so sorry. Are you okay?"

Dianthe coughed, the grating noise sliding into a gruff laugh. With a little groan, she scooted up against the glass wall, suspended over the silent city. For a minute she sat there, catching her breath. Then, "Haan, let me ask you something," she said, her voice hoarse.

Aris looked down at her bruised, swollen hands, bracing for another insult. "Yeah?"

"Didn't *anyone* in Lux treat you like a normal person?"

Surprised, Aris glanced up and met her eyes. "What do you mean?"

Dianthe raised an eyebrow. "I *mean* . . . after this fever of yours, did anyone in your village ever treat you like a capable human being? Someone they didn't constantly need to take care of?"

Aris leaned back on her hands and frowned. "But I'm not capable, am I," she said bitterly. "Look at me." She gestured to her bruises and shaking legs.

Dianthe laughed again and stood, holding out a hand to help her up. "You're doing just fine. Worse than some, better than others." She smiled. "Better than I expected."

"Really?" Aris stood, frozen, as Dianthe left the room. Surely she'd heard wrong. There was no way, after all of her falling and weakness and, yes, tears, that she was doing "just fine." It wasn't possible—

"Come on, Haan," Dianthe called over her shoulder. "I want to see you fly."

Dianthe gave Aris a pair of men's pants and a gray tunic but let her wear her own flying boots. After Aris washed up and changed, spurred on by her excitement to *finally* fly, she headed back to the main room, only to find a tall, thin man in Dianthe's place. The woman's disguise was uncanny; her tattoo still blazed crimson and black, but her facial features had changed: a subtle widening of her chin, heavier brow bones, less pronounced lips.

"Wow." Aris stared.

"While we're out, watch the men around you, the way they stand. How they interact with one another. Pay attention to how they assert themselves in a crowd." As they walked down the hall to the lift, Dianthe added, "It's important that you blend in. Do not draw attention to yourself."

Without thinking, Aris pointed to Dianthe's snake tattoo. "And that doesn't draw attention?"

"It does. That's exactly the point. My tattoo is a distraction, drawing the eye so no one questions anything else. You don't have that luxury." Dianthe stepped into the lift and pressed the button for the lobby, staring straight ahead. Quieter, almost as if to herself, she added, "The tattoo is something that's mine, whether I'm wearing the veil or not. It's the part of me I always get to show the world."

Clenching her hands tight at her sides, Aris considered this as the lift plummeted downward.

When they reached the ground, they disembarked without a word. Their boots thudded across the shining lobby floor, and her head pounded in time to the diatous veil's constant hum. Aris watched Dianthe from the corner of her eye; the woman didn't change her gait or posture much, but little adjustments—the thrust of her chin, the minimal movement of her hips—made a big difference. If Aris hadn't known the truth, she never would have guessed Dianthe's secret.

As they emerged onto the street, Aris squinted in the bright sun. Already the city shimmered with early summer heat. The air swirled with the scent of cooking meat from a cart a few yards away, and the enticing smell of fresh bread wafted from the open doors of a bakery across the street.

Aris tried to take long, confident strides, but she still struggled to keep up with the taller woman. Her limp wasn't as obvious now, after weeks of physical training, but she could still feel a fine tremor in her weak leg.

Sleek black and silver terrans zipped past them, like a school of shining, well-organized fish. The sidewalks slowly filled as well-dressed men and women emerged from the tall buildings in search of their midday meal. Aris caught herself staring at her boots, just as a husky man in a white mender's tunic jostled her.

He gave her a hard look. She blanched, frozen. Could he tell? What if he—

The man kept walking, the moment of panic over in an instant.

"Keep up," Dianthe growled. She paused when they reached a steep latticework of stairs leading up to a metroline platform. "You're too stiff," she murmured. "Relax."

If only it were that easy, Aris thought, her nervous gaze flitting from man to man among the crowd. She watched the way they moved, really studied them for the first time in her life. Unfortunately, noticing their differences was one thing, putting them into practice was quite another. She followed Dianthe up the stairs to the platform, biting back a groan as her sore muscles protested.

The metroline ride to Panthea's main airfield, just outside the city, required one transfer from the River line to the Watershed line. Most of the seats were full, but the trains weren't packed as tightly as they would be at the end of the workday.

At one point, Dianthe dug her sharp elbow into Aris's side. Glancing up, Aris saw a young woman standing in the middle of the aisle, gripping a loop of silver chain that hung from the ceiling. Her body swayed gently, her head drooping from her long neck like a flower nodding on its stem. Much of her dark brown hair had pulled free from its braid. Dianthe elbowed Aris again.

Aris shot to her feet. "Would, uh, would you like to sit down?" Her voice came out low and gruff. She'd almost gotten used to it. Almost. At least the sound didn't make her flinch anymore.

The girl looked up. "Oh, thank you." She sank into Aris's seat with a sigh. "I'm just coming off a night shift at the central emergency clinic. It was a busy night. I'm about ready to collapse."

She tilted her chin up with a sleepy smile, waiting for Aris—Aristos—to reply. The words stuck in Aris's throat. What would a man say? Would he be sympathetic? Understanding? Try to cheer her with a dinner invitation or something? When Aris didn't reply, the open, cheerful expression on the girl's face faded. Heat blazed along Aris's cheeks.

At last, Aris mumbled, "Yeah. Sounds like a rough night."

The girl's gaze fell to her lap, her head dropping forward again like that delicate, bobbing flower she resembled. "Yes, it was."

Next to her, Dianthe sighed. Aris stared out the glass panel along the side of the train. She actually felt *bad* that she hadn't made conversation. But what could she have said? Done? Awkwardness clogged her throat. Outside, gleaming buildings alternated with a bright blue sky as the train zipped toward the outskirts of the city. In the distance, to the west, green-swathed mountains rose, disappearing in a haze of wispy clouds. In the space of one deep, cleansing breath, Aris's discomfort melted away. She smiled.

It was a beautiful day to fly.

Chapter Seventeen

"So," Dianthe said later that night.

Aris sat on a bench, leaning back against the glass wall, eyes half-closed. It didn't matter what Dianthe said, or how much her muscles burned at even that small movement. In her mind, she was still soaring above the lush forest outside of Panthea. She was still enclosed in the familiar, comforting cabin of a wingjet, and the whole bright sky was glowing all around her.

"You were right. You can fly." Dianthe didn't quite sound impressed, but she wasn't yelling either.

"I passed your test, then." Aris settled her hands in her lap; in the dim light, she couldn't even see the bruises. It was the happiest she'd been in days, maybe even since Calix left. Flying did that to her. Made the rest of the world—the pain—fall away.

"You aren't going to be able to disappear into the ranks, with flying like that," Dianthe said, almost to herself.

"Is that a problem?" Aris asked. But she wasn't really worried. Dianthe wouldn't send her home now, not after everything. Not after seeing what she could do.

The woman tapped at the digitablet in her hands. "Not a problem, exactly. . . ." she murmured. For a while neither of them spoke, the only sound the quiet *tap tap* of Dianthe's finger against the tablet's screen.

Aris closed her eyes and tried to imagine Calix's face when he saw her for the first time. He'd be surprised, of course. Maybe even shocked. A Military stationpoint would be the last place he'd expect to see her. His eyes would narrow in confusion, the way they did in school when something didn't make sense to him. But then, when she explained everything—that she'd been recruited, that they'd be working together—he'd smile wide, dimples appearing as if by magic.

It would be exciting, the way they'd have to sneak moments together, share secret looks. She'd be in disguise, of course. They wouldn't be able to Promise, except unofficially, secretly. And when the war was over, or their tours ended . . . there'd be no more questions. No more obstacles. They would be together for the rest of their lives.

"Where will we be?" she asked, still half in her daydream.

Dianthe didn't look up from the digitablet. "What do you mean?"

"Calix and me. Where will we be stationed?" To the west, along the Safaran border where the fighting was the worst? Or by the shores of the Fex River, where large numbers of soldiers were massing to protect Atalanta's resources?

At this, Dianthe paused, finger frozen above the digitablet. The snake on her forehead kinked. "There's a new search and rescue unit forming," she said, finally, with a strange little sigh. "Report date is next week. You'll join this unit as a flyer."

"Search and rescue?"

"S and R is responsible for finding and retrieving stranded or injured soldiers."

"That's where Calix is? In this unit?" There was something in Dianthe's face, the way her lips twisted slightly at the corners . . . Aris's stomach tightened, and the peace she'd been feeling leached away. She sat up straight. Seconds marched on in slow, agonizing silence.

"Not exactly," Dianthe said at last. "Field menders aren't embedded with S and R."

"Then why . . ." Aris couldn't continue. Her heart pounded as if trying to tear its way from her chest. "You said you'd put us together. I told you—I'm doing this to find him. You can't . . ." Every sore muscle and bruise pulled painfully beneath her skin. All of this and it was for nothing?

"Relax," Dianthe said forcefully, setting the digitablet on the bench beside her. "Aris!" She reached out and grabbed Aris's arms. "*Relax.*"

Aris tried to yank herself away but Dianthe's grip was too strong.

"You're too good, Aris. Your flying is *too good.* I can't just tuck you away in some mender stationpoint. It *has* to be this unit. But —*but*—you'll still see Calix. Do you hear me?" Dianthe gave her a little shake. "Stop acting like a child. I told you that all I could do was *try* to put you with Calix. You chose to stay anyway. Now just listen to me."

The words were starting to penetrate. With a gasp, Aris heaved air into her lungs, and some of the tension in her shoulders ebbed. "I'm sorry," she whispered. "I'm listening."

Dianthe released her arms and sat back. She looked more frustrated than annoyed . . . and maybe even a little apologetic. "S and R units bring the wounded they rescue to field mender stationpoints. You'll have many opportunities to see him. I promise. Each and every mission, you'll deliver your injured soldiers to his unit. Every time you fly, you'll see him. It's the best I can do."

Aris leaned back against the wall. Disappointment still pounded in her temples with the strength of a hammer, but her breathing had evened out. *It's okay. You'll still get to see him. You'll rescue injured soldiers and bring them to him to save.*

There was something romantic about the prospect. They'd both be working to their strengths, and he'd be proud of her, doing so much to be with him. Doing so much for Atalanta.

"This is really the only way?" she asked one more time, just to be sure.

Dianthe sighed. "Theo was right about you, Haan. You *do*

have a gift. I can't let it go to waste. This isn't about your mender friend, it's about saving lives. Don't you understand that?"

Aris nodded, because that's what Dianthe expected. Dianthe wanted her to be the hero, the hardened flyer doing her part to win the war. But she wasn't a hero. She was a romantic. A foolish one, probably, giving up everything for the boy she loved.

But you're a flyer too, a voice whispered deep inside.

"Now it's your turn," Dianthe said. "Are you still in? If this isn't enough for you, now is your time to leave. After you join your unit, it will be much harder to walk away."

Aris turned to look out over the silent, sparkling city. When her father had taught her to fly, he hadn't expected her to take to it so strongly. She knew this because he'd told her as much. He wanted her to be serious and concentrate on her schooling. Focus on being a duster for his groves. The fancy flying, the dips and twists and turns . . . it had never been important to anyone but her. And maybe Calix, who knew how much she loved being in the sky.

But now . . . Theo had called it a gift. And Dianthe, the most intimidating person Aris had ever met, was telling her she was good. She made it sound like Aris wasn't just a silly girl but a person with power. Someone who was really *needed*. Aris had always been the one needing someone else. All her life, her friends, her family, and Calix had taken care of her. And now, Dianthe was asking *Aris* to be the strong one. Those injured soldiers the S and R unit rescued . . . they'd be counting on her.

Even if she didn't see Calix everyday, how could she walk away now?

"I'm in," Aris said, the decisiveness in her own voice surprising her.

"Good. Then it's time." Dianthe led her to the secret room. She stood Aris before the mirror, removed her veil, and pushed a cold metal bar against the back of her neck.

"What was that?" Aris asked, staring at the woman's reflection.

"Your Military brand." Dianthe set the branding tech on a nearby counter and returned the veil to its place on Aris's neck, on top of the black rectangle. "The last piece of the Aristos puzzle. Now your disguise is complete."

CHAPTER EIGHTEEN

WHEN SHE AWOKE ON THE DAY SHE'D REPORT TO HER UNIT, Aris stared at the ceiling and admitted the truth, if only to herself. She'd thought she would fail. Fail to pass the training. Fail to find Calix.

In just an hour, she'd board a transjet to her stationpoint, and there'd be no going back. She wouldn't be able to hide behind Aris the weakling anymore. She would have to become Aristos the flyer. And if she slipped up, even once, everything would be lost.

Stop that, she commanded.

Powering up her digitablet, she found a comm from Calix waiting for her.

I miss you so much, Hummingbird. Sometimes, after lights out, when I'm lying in my tecon alone and the wind is punching the sides so hard the fabric touches my face—it's always windy here, by the way—sometimes I imagine you curled up beside me, and we're in a tecon on the beach, and I can smell the salt and sand and feel your hair against my face.

Most days, though, they work us so hard I fall into my bedroll and am asleep before I've thought to close my eyes. I don't dream. I think maybe, for a few hours, I'm so worn out I just die. I'm so glad

*you're safe and happy back in Panthea, though it's hard to imagine
you there. I love you. ~ Calix*

She wrote a quick response. Who knew how long it would be
before she'd have a chance to write him again?

*Calix, I imagine us on the beach together all the time. Usually
standing with our feet in the water, or hiding away in our cave.
We're always alone, as if we're the only two people left in the world.
I crave quiet and isolation these days, after the bustle of Panthea.
When you come home, we'll spend a whole night on the beach, like
when you left, only this time it'll be to celebrate your return. Time to
go to work. I miss you. Love, Aris.*

It was a good comm: only one lie. Dianthe offered her plenty
of quiet and isolation. But if Aris was really working in a normal
office down in the city, the chaos and crunch of people would be
one of the hardest parts for her to deal with.

With care, she pulled on her Military uniform and walked to
the washroom. She stared at the mirror, Aristos's eyes staring
back, trying to remember the feeling of Calix's arms around her,
the warmth of his breath against her neck. She bent and
splashed cool water on her face. Soon, she wouldn't have to
remember. Soon, she'd be in his arms once more.

She grabbed her bag. Dianthe had given her two uniforms,
nightwear and underclothes, two pairs of boots, and a small
stack of thin, high-tech shirts like the one Calix had worn. She
had some toiletries, her women's things, which were hidden in a
boot, and her digitablet. Nothing of her home or who she'd been
before.

When she emerged from her bedroom, Dianthe was
standing against the window with a man Aris had never seen
before.

". . . and she's still in quarantine?" she was asking, so low Aris
could hardly hear her. "Will the sanctions hold?"

The man shrugged. He was shorter than Dianthe but just as

thin, with the same brand and shaved head as every member of the Military sector. As Aris.

"Ruslana hasn't appointed an acting Ward yet, so the policy hasn't changed," the man replied. "Word is she'll be out of quarantine soon. Her husband is still causing trouble though . . . shouting 'conspiracy' to anyone who will listen."

"And who is listening?" Dianthe asked.

The man lowered his voice. "Not many. Yet."

"Have they found her son?"

As the man shook his head, Dianthe looked up and caught Aris's eye. She turned back to smile at her visitor. "Thank you. I'll be in touch." And with that she shuttled him out the door. He didn't acknowledge Aris, never even glancing her way.

Aris followed Dianthe to the table and watched the woman pour herself a drink. "Were you talking about the Ward of Ruslana?" Aris asked. "Do you think she's in trouble?" The sound of her low, gruff tone barely fazed her now.

Dianthe turned to her with a strange, sad smile. "We're all in trouble, Aristos. Safara is a powerful enemy."

"But you were saying, about Ward Vadim . . ."

Dianthe's voice hardened to its usual growl. "You're expected at the hub in an hour. It's time for you to go. Do you have your things?"

Aris nodded toward the bag she'd left by the door and fought the sudden urge to throw up. A month of training wasn't enough. *I'm not ready*. Her body was still battered and sore, and there was no way anyone would believe she was really a man. She couldn't do this. What was she *thinking*?

Dianthe grabbed her shoulders, stared her straight in the eye, and scowled. "Stop it," she said. "When you question whether you can do this, you question me. I know what I'm doing."

"You really believe I can do this?" Aris murmured, trying to keep her chin up.

The woman squeezed Aris's shoulders a little harder, fingers digging into the already sore muscles. "Yes, I do. Do you know why?"

"Because I can fly?"

"Because no matter how far I pushed you, no matter how much pain you were in, you never walked away." Dianthe gave her a little shake and pat that bordered on affectionate as she released her. "*And* because you can fly."

They walked together to the door, and when Aris turned back to say goodbye, Dianthe waved a dismissive hand, but there was pride in her eyes. "Get out of here. And don't disappoint me, Aristos."

CHAPTER NINETEEN

IT WAS TWILIGHT WHEN THE MILITARY TRANSJET LANDED AT Spiro, a small stationpoint located in a dry, desert-like valley surrounded by forest a few miles from the Fex River. Aris collected her bag and filed down the ramp with about twenty men. She kept her shoulders back and took long strides, but she still could feel the burn of a blush on her cheeks. Every moment since Dianthe had dropped her at the Military hub, she'd been waiting for someone to take a good look at her and expose her deception. But so far, everyone's eyes had just slid past her, accepting her for who she appeared to be.

Aris shifted her bag to her other shoulder as she followed the rest of the soldiers. Before her sprawled a collection of rounded buildings, a bubbled line of blisters along the dusty, sun-bleached skin of the plain. In the fading light the buildings reflected the shadowy silhouettes of the approaching men. Aris could tell by the way the windowless walls glittered, just slightly, that the material itself was solar, like Theo's wingjet.

She shivered, pulling her arms tight to her sides. This far north, the warmth of the day seeped away quickly with the setting sun.

A tinted glass door in the nearest domed building hissed open as the line of men straggled forward. By the time Aris and the rest of the soldiers had been ushered into the building, the massive transjet had taken off once more.

Aris followed the line of soldiers down a long corridor to a large room with a padded floor, low ceiling, and mirrored walls. It smelled faintly of old sweat and onions. She fought the urge to wrinkle her nose.

"Specialists!" a voice shouted, "Two rows, tallest in back. Now!"

She shuffled through the milling soldiers to a place up front. The men around her all shared the same short hair or shaved heads, trim green uniforms, and stern expressions. She tried to look serious too, instead of scared, and she tightened the muscles of her legs to keep her knees from trembling.

When the muffled thud of feet and the whisper of moving fabric finally stopped, five officers took their places before the group of soldiers.

In the center of the line, one of the officers stepped forward. He was of average height, heavy-legged, with a series of blood-red scars that crisscrossed his neck. He looked at them all like he could easily—and happily—squash them under his boot. His steely gaze reminded her of Dianthe's. "My name is Commander Nyx," he said, "and you will address me as Commander Nyx or sir, only. Is that clear?"

Together the unit shouted, "Yes, sir." Aris mouthed the words, the breath to voice them locked in her throat.

"As a member of this search and rescue unit, you will be responsible for putting yourselves in great personal danger to save or extract those who have no other recourse." His voice echoed in the silent room. "You will rescue your stranded comrades, non-Military Atalantans who have been captured or otherwise put in harm's way, and even take into custody enemy forces. You will learn to assess danger, make life or death deci-sions, and, above all, protect and support the members of your unit."

Aris stared at the officer, transfixed. Even with all of

Dianthe's lectures, Aris's new role as *soldier* hadn't actually felt real. Until now. She swallowed.

Commander Nyx continued, gesturing to his right. "This is our Operations Officer, Major Vidar, my second in command. He will be in charge of your training." Major Vidar needed no scar to hold her gaze, though he had one, a knife-thin pink line that ran from his left temple to the edge of his lip, hitching his mouth into a permanent sneer. He was younger than she might have expected for someone of his rank—maybe twenty-one or twenty-two—and tall, with the palest skin she'd ever seen. In the brightness of the training room, his eyes glowed a shockingly clear blue.

He must be from the North. His coloring and the sharp edges of his jaw and nose reminded her vaguely of her father, though her father's features were softer, well padded and grooved with age.

"Lieutenant Wolfe will lead flyer training," Commander Nyx said, nodding to the man on his left. Wolfe was pale like Major Vidar, but taller and thinner, with a large, narrow nose and air of disdain that was palpable, even from a distance. On the Major's other side, Commander Nyx introduced Lieutenant Daakon, the gunner expert. He was wide rather than tall, and dark-skinned, a solid shadow next to Major Vidar.

"And finally, Lieutenant Talon, our retriever," Commander concluded. As Lieutenant Talon nodded, his hand swung slightly away from his side. He was missing two fingers. Aris's fingers clenched automatically, in sympathy.

"Lieutenant Daakon will give you your room assignments. You will be bunking with your sectormate. I expect you to work together and support each other at all times. Is that clear?" Commander Nyx barked.

"Yes, sir!"

"Lights out in twenty minutes. Tomorrow we'll begin combat training and conduct your physical evaluations." With that, he nodded and swept from the room, Major Vidar and Lieutenant Wolfe following.

"As I call your name," Lieutenant Talon said, tapping the

screen of a small digitablet with his maimed hand, "please step forward and pick up your room number from Lieutenant Daakon. Barracks are to the left, down the second corridor on the right. When you've received your number, you are dismissed. You'll find your bags just outside the door." He paused for a second, then called, "Specialist Galec."

A short, freckled man with ginger eyebrows stepped forward. Lieutenant Daakon handed him a small passcard before calling another name. The longer Aris stood there, the more the room shrank around her, filled with the rustling and breathing of strangers. A sudden, inexplicable homesickness slammed into her stomach like a battering ram.

Finally, her name was called. "Aristos Haan."

When she moved, the muscles of her legs protested. She couldn't meet Lieutenant Daakon's eyes when he handed her the card. "Room 2410," he said. "Welcome to Spiro." His voice wasn't quite as gruff as Commander Nyx's. But when she glanced up, his eyes were already turned to the next soldier stepping forward to collect his key.

Aris stumbled into the hall and tried to remember the directions to the barracks, her bag banging against her sore leg. Once she found her room, it didn't take long to unpack. Her clothes went into a cubby on the wall, her empty bag into a chrome trunk at the foot of her cot. There was another cot and collection of cubbies on the other wall, and a narrow doorway led to a small washroom that she and her sectormate would share. She hoped Dianthe had been right about pairing her with another woman; there'd be no way to hide the truth in such close quarters.

Just then the door hissed open.

A tall, olive-skinned man stalked into the room and threw his bag onto the other cot. He had the Tech brand—a small key— emblazoned on his temple. His dark brows drew together over narrowed brown eyes.

"What you staring at?" the man growled.

Aris blinked, startled. "I'm sorry. I—"

"The tech brand's a beast, yeah? I wish they'd just remove our old brands when we volunteer." He—*she*, Aris reminded herself—stabbed a finger to her temple as if shooting herself.

"Um. Yeah." Aris bit her lip. *This* woman would have no trouble maintaining her disguise. Even knowing what she really was, Aris couldn't see past the tall, terrifying man standing before her.

"I'm Dysis Latza." She bent to yank the neatly folded towel from the foot of her cot. When Aris didn't say anything, Dysis glanced back at her, eyebrows raised. "And you are?"

"Oh, I'm, um, Aristos Haan," she said, the words tumbling over themselves. *Come on, you've got to do better than that*. Dianthe would be ashamed.

Without another word, Dysis removed her jacket and shirt. Her flat chest was bound in a thick, bandage-like bra. The diatous veil made them look male, but their real breasts were still there beneath the disguise and had to be kept secure.

She twisted away from Aris and began to remove her pants. "If you want to shower, you better hurry. Only ten more minutes before lights out."

Aris drew in a breath. She was still frozen in the middle of the room.

Dysis put her hands behind her head, touching the edges of the black brand on the back of her neck; in the bright light of their room it glittered slightly. When the veil released, the small, clear rectangle fell into her hand.

She turned back around, sighing. Now that Dysis was a *she*, her nose was thinner, cheekbones more pronounced, and her lips fuller. Aris tried not to stare.

"I hate the way it hums. I can't seem to get used to it." Without the veil, Dysis's voice was still deep, low and smoky like the singers that performed at The Toad.

"You coming?" the girl asked, impatience creeping into her voice.

"Of course." Aris stopped fiddling with her jacket and removed it. It was stupid to be self-conscious anyway, after weeks of Dianthe sticking electrodes all over her body while she was dressed only in her underclothes.

Dysis disappeared into the washroom. A second later, the sound of running water filtered into the room.

Aris removed the rest of her clothes and wrapped herself in the towel at the foot of her bed, then she gingerly reached up to release her own veil. She breathed deeply. She didn't like the hum either. It made her feel oddly disconnected from her own skin, shivery and disjointed.

In the washroom, there was a little cubicle with a toilet and sink on one side of the room and two frosted shower stalls on the other. She hung her towel on the hook outside the second stall and slipped inside, pressing a panel on the wall to turn on the water.

"So what's your position?" Dysis asked.

"Flyer." Aris's hands slipped along her bald head. "You?"

"Gunner."

"I hope we start specialty training soon." The warm water pounded against Aris's shoulders, and she tried to relax.

"It'll probably be a week or two. We'll have to do the physical evaluations and combat training first. Probably weapons training, too."

"Oh Gods, two weeks? Really?" Two weeks of walking on quicksand, terrified each step could be the one to sink her? She wanted so much to feel the caress of sky, the freefall in her stomach as she spun and twisted through the air. Flying was her solid ground.

"It's no bother for me. As long as I get to shoot something, I don't care if it's the big guns or the small," Dysis said.

How could Dysis be so casual about it? The thought of shooting a solagun—or any weapon, really—made Aris's stomach churn. As a flyer, she hoped she wouldn't be asked to carry one. Dianthe hadn't mentioned weapons training.

"Have you done this sort of thing before?" Aris asked.

"Nah. This is my first assignment," Dysis replied.

"What'd you do before you joined?"

"Taught mechanics to the children in my village." Dysis's voice took on a hard edge.

"You went from children to weaponry? What made you choose this?"

There was a thud and the water in the other girl's shower stopped. "That's kind of personal, don't you think?"

Clearly it *was* personal to Dysis. Very personal.

"You're looking for someone, too?" Aris said, hurrying to finish rinsing off. At last, here was someone who would understand the longing that had brought her here. The desperation.

A pause. "Who are you looking for?"

"His name is Calix," Aris replied eagerly. "We were going to Promise, but he was selected for Military and sent to be a field mender. I joined so we could work together. I'll rescue people, and then he'll make them well."

Dysis's glass shower door banged against the wall. She muttered angrily to herself, something that sounded like, ". . . so stupid . . . ."

Aris bristled. "Did you just call me stupid?" she demanded, turning off her own shower.

Dysis stared at her over the top of the shower door, unselfconscious and angry. "You came all this way for some lovesick suicide mission? Yeah, I'd say that's stupid."

Aris matched her glare. "And your lovesick suicide mission? Who is *he*?"

Dysis ripped her towel from its hook and wrapped it around her body so tightly the edges dug into her skin. She didn't say anything, letting the challenge build in the steam-filled air. Finally, lips twisting bitterly, she growled, "Well, he's not a little mender puppy, safe in his little mender cage."

"What's *that* supposed to mean?" Aris grabbed the top of the shower door with both hands. "How can you stand there, *mocking* me, when you're here to do the very same thing?"

"It's not the same thing! I'm not looking for someone who's safe and sound at a stationpoint somewhere. For all I know, my brother's dead!" Dysis's voice echoed in the small room.

Aris shivered, suddenly freezing. She grabbed her own towel and dried off. *Brother?* She hadn't expected that. "Are any of us really safe and sound?" she asked gruffly, but her anger was ebbing.

"Safety is relative. I bet you hear from your little mender all the time. I haven't heard from Jax in almost six months."

"Six months?" Aris didn't want to admit she'd gotten a comm from Calix that morning.

"Yeah, six months. I'm here because our damn dominion hasn't gotten around to finding him yet." Worry overtook the anger in her voice. She kept her mouth pinched and her eyes narrowed, but her mask had slipped.

Aris softened. "Do you know what happened to him?"

"He was captured," Dysis snapped, her words like hard stones falling loudly in the silence. "No one knows where he is or if he's even alive."

Dysis acted as if she were an injured animal, protecting herself by lashing out. Aris forced her eyes to remain blank. She knew pity would only rile Dysis up more. But Gods, she wished she'd kept her mouth shut. "I'm so sorry."

"Yeah, well, our parents died when we were young, so he's all I have. I refuse to let him just disappear." Dysis's voice went low and dangerous. "I'll find him. No matter what it takes, or who I have to kill."

A shiver kicked up Aris's spine.

They moved back to the bedroom and slipped on the loose olive-green pants and tunics Military issued as night clothes.

Aris cleared her throat, swallowing against the perpetual lump made by the voice modulator. "We're both stupid, you know," she said wryly. "Doing this, coming here for them."

Dysis raised a brow and looked ready to argue, but Aris continued. "It's okay, though. Because in the meantime, while we're looking . . ." she paused, thinking of Dianthe. "We're going to save a lot of people."

Dysis broke into a sudden, only mildly bitter laugh. "You're a real romantic, aren't you?"

Aris smiled and shrugged. "Just ask my friends back home. Practically the moment Calix was selected, they were telling me to move on, ring around. Thought I was silly for not letting go." Except for Phae, who had Rakk and understood. Aris wondered what she'd think now. "But I *am* a romantic," she said. "I don't care what anyone says. I want to believe things will work out. I'll be with Calix. You'll find your brother—"

"We'll win this war." Dysis voice was quiet, her face serious. No hint of bitterness or sarcasm. In that moment, the look they shared forged them as sectormates—friends—as surely as any two soldiers in any dominion, in any time. In any war.

"Yeah," Aris echoed softly. "We'll win the war."

Dysis gave herself a little shake and laughed. "We better finish up. Lights out any minute now." They clicked their veils into place, and with a nearly imperceptible shimmer, their curves smoothed and faces hardened. As if on cue, the room plunged into darkness, a faint glow along the floor of the washroom the only hint of light.

In the dark, they felt their way to their cots. Aris sighed as she sank onto the hard bed. She was exhausted. And tomorrow, with the physical trials and combat training, it would be even worse.

"Goodnight, Dysis," she whispered into the darkness.

"Goodnight, Aristos."

That night Aris dreamed, as she so often did, of flying. Only this time, Calix had been captured. She flew over the endless deserts of Safara seeking him until, in a great flash of light, she was shot down and the earth rushed toward her, a terrifying golden blur.

CHAPTER TWENTY

WHEN THE LIGHTS FLASHED ON THE NEXT MORNING, ARIS dragged herself off her bed and slowly pulled on her uniform. Smoothing her shirt, she thought of Calix and their last night on the beach, as she always did when her fingers touched the sleek fabric. She buttoned up the fitted jacket, making sure the collar was folded precisely, so her Military brand was visible. The diatous veil hidden in the stamp was solar powered; it needed little sunlight to fill its reserves.

Dysis was silent as they dressed. "Nervous?" she asked.

Aris shrugged. "I know I won't be any good at the physical stuff. It's flying I'm good at. I just need to survive the next few days and I'll probably be okay." Her gravelly voice sounded unconcerned, but her stomach jumped and twisted.

"Yeah, I'm nervous, too," Dysis said, and then she opened the door.

In the cafeteria, Dysis and Aris got their food and sat at the end of a long, empty table. Soon, a short, barrel-chested soldier paused beside them. A closely cropped layer of ginger fuzz clung to the curve of his skull, and tiny wrinkles radiated from the corners of his eyes. "Mind if I join you?"

"Of course. Yeah." Aris said, trying to keep up her nonchalant act.

The man held out a hand. "I'm Tavis Galec, but you might as well call me Galec. Everyone does."

Aris shook his hand, remembering to squeeze tightly and give a firm grip. Dianthe had explained that the slenderness of her fingers would be less noticeable if she gave short, strong handshakes. "Aristos Haan."

Dysis half-stood and held out her hand as well. "Dysis Latza. We're sectormates."

Another man, narrow-shouldered with an impressive potbelly, plopped down beside Aris. "I'm Otto," he said, then got to work on his plate of gelatinous eggs.

Galec sat beside Dysis. He did a double take when he noticed the key-shaped brand stamped into her temple. "You're a volunteer, eh?" Approval filled his voice.

She nodded. "Both of us. Couldn't let you old men do all the fighting."

Otto rolled his eyes. "Green ears. Don't worry, we'll show you a thing or two. You'll wish you had our experience soon enough."

Galec sighed. "To be eighteen again. The stupid things I would've tried."

"Have you been with this unit for long?" Aris asked, hoping her voice came out politely curious rather than insecure and uncertain.

Galec shook his head. "We're both new to S and R. I got rotated from a combat unit near Bieza."

Dysis gave a low whistle, a new respect filling her eyes. "Is it as bad as they say?"

"Nah," Galec said, all amusement dropping from his face. "It's worse."

* * *

After breakfast, Lieutenant Daakon assembled the unit, nearly fifty soldiers, outside in tight formation on a dusty training ground. As the sun beat down on her bald head, Aris took her place in the front row. She glanced to the clear blue arc of sky above and wished she could be up there, tipping her wings to the tiny ribbons of cloud that hung along the horizon.

The hiss of a door interrupted her thoughts. From the domed, shimmering building beside the training ground, Major Vidar, Lieutenant Wolfe, and Lieutenant Talon approached. Without a word, they formed a line along the edge of the clearing. When they were in position, Lieutenant Daakon gestured a brown hand to a pile of mats stacked next to him.

"Pair up with your sectormates and grab a mat," he said. "Spread out. Make sure you leave enough room."

Before Aris had time to move, Dysis was there, dropping a mat on the dirt between them.

"Alright, let's see what you green ears picked up at basic," Daakon continued, once everyone had paired off. "Kicking and punching are okay. No face blows or biting. Go to it."

Aris put her fists up, but she was too nervous to bounce on the balls of her feet as Dianthe had taught her. It didn't make a blighting bit of difference that she knew Dysis was really a woman; all she saw in that moment was a tall man with fierce eyes and large fists coming toward her.

She blocked Dysis's first punch, barely.

Dipping her head, Aris weaved to the side. If this fight were a dance between wingjets, a thrust and parry of silver wings—

Crack!

The top of Dysis's foot made contact with her ribs. Aris tried to retaliate, jabbing upward, but Dysis deflected her fist easily, spinning behind her. Another blow to the ribs.

Aris focused on dodging her sectormate's blows and not falling down, ignoring the grunts and thuds of the other fighters. Dysis was going easy on her, she could tell, but it still filled her with panic every time a large fist flew toward her. She'd gotten better under Dianthe's tutelage, but she wasn't nearly fast enough to make it an evenly matched fight.

Aris groaned as she attempted yet another kick, high enough but still too slow to be effective. Dysis ducked and swept her other leg, sending Aris tumbling to the ground.

She stayed there, belly up on the mat, panting, until a dark shadow blocked out the clear, blue sky. "What's your name, Specialist?" Lieutenant Daakon asked. She couldn't read the expression in his eyes.

Aris scrambled to her feet so fast she got a head rush. "Aristos Haan, sir."

The officer studied her, one heavy brow raised. "Just had your selection ceremony, did you?"

"I volunteered." She cleared her throat against the rising panic. "Uh, sir," she added quickly, drawing back her jacket to reveal the twining vines of the Enviro brand on her arm.

"Where'd you train?" He glanced down at the digitablet in his hands, presumably consulting his soldier roster.

Oh holy. He's suspicious. He knows. In her gruff new voice, barely above a whisper, she said, "Pono," the name of the training stationpoint Dianthe had made her memorize.

He nodded thoughtfully, swiping his finger across the digitab. Behind Aris, Dysis was still breathing hard from their fight. She didn't say anything. Aris wondered if she was also frozen in fear.

Lieutenant Daakon's silence went on and on, eaten up by the sounds of the rest of the unit sparring. Finally, he looked up. Little black dots appeared before Aris's eyes; with a belated gasp, she realized she'd been holding her breath.

"Watch how you expend you energy, Specialist," he said. "You're putting too much effort into avoidance. Focus on *your* fists connecting, not as much on Specialist—?"

"Latza," Dysis supplied.

"—Specialist Latza's blows," Lieutenant Daakon said. "Understand me?"

Aris nodded.

Lieutenant Daakon turned his attention to Dysis. "You have a fluid fighting style, nice variety of movement. Well done."

Dysis bowed her head. "Thank you, sir."

As Daakon walked to the next pair of soldiers, Aris swayed on liquid knees. Dysis whispered, "Thought that was it."

"Me, too." Aris was certain she still wore a wide-eyed look of terror.

"Enough!" A strong voice carried over the thwacks and grunts of the other fighters.

With a secret sigh of relief, Aris lowered her fists.

Major Vidar paced in front of the field of soldiers, his suitably short golden hair practically glowing in the harsh sun. "This afternoon, you'll be issued a solagun. We begin weapons training tomorrow."

Her stomach sank. So much for hoping she wouldn't have to use one.

"In the meantime, as you practice sparring, I want you to pay close attention to your partner. Every look and subtle movement is important in a fight." He didn't sound like he was from the North. Or at least not Bolvik, the city her father was from. "You have to find his weaknesses and capitalize on them. Try to anticipate his next move. Be proactive and trust your instincts." He stopped walking and looked over the group of soldiers.

Aris couldn't look directly into his clear blue eyes. She had the sudden, overwhelming conviction that if she did, he would be able to tell she was a fake, that she didn't belong here.

He continued, "The likelihood that you will actually engage in hand-to-hand combat is slim. As a member of a search and rescue unit, you'll generally be arriving after the enemy has left the area. But things happen. Hand-to-hand combat should be your absolute last resort. Our goal, as a unit, is to retrieve our targets with minimal engagement of the enemy. Understood?"

"Yes, sir!" came the unified response.

Major Vidar clapped his hands once, and Aris turned toward her sectormate, stomach tight. With a single well-timed punch, Dysis sent her to the ground again.

Chapter Twenty-One

"A month and a half after this year's disastrous World Council, Ward Vadim is still in quarantine. The other members of the Council have been tested for the highly contagious bacterium found in Vadim's blood; so far, no else has contracted the illness. Ward Vadim's husband, Josef, suspects she may have been exposed during a recent visit to—"

"Off," Pyralis barked. The monitor blinked white and then black, the reporter's voice silenced mid-sentence.

He walked to the window. Beyond the glass, tall, thin trees shook their sharp leaves at him, and blue sky winked between their branches. Panthea would be hot today, thick with sun. Here in the hills, it was cooler.

"Is she getting *any* better?" Bett asked from behind him.

"I don't know." He sighed. "Her menders have been cagey. I suspect it's to avoid overpromising on the speed and extent of her recovery, but it's annoying as hell. I'd like a straight answer for once."

She rubbed her hands over his shoulders. "Maybe you should just go to the clinic. Are they really going to turn you away?"

The speaker on the desk buzzed. "Ward Nekos, you have a visitor." Kellan's voice was strained.

The door to the office slid open to admit a tangle of raised voices.

"Please, just give me a moment—"

"No, *now*. I won't wait any longer."

Pyralis turned, instinctively stepping between Bett and whoever was yelling through his open door. "Kellan—"

"I have to see her." The words fell like bricks into sudden silence.

Pyralis knew that voice. "Josef."

The man didn't move beyond the threshold. The light from the hallway behind him was brighter than the soft glow in the office; it threw his shadow, monstrously distorted, across the floor. "You have no right to keep me from my wife."

In one graceful movement, Bett stepped toward Josef, hands outstretched. "Please, do come in. Let us offer you a drink."

He ignored her; his gaze never left Pyralis's face. "You know it's wrong, what they're saying. You know Galena doesn't have some exotic bacterium. *Contagious*. No one else has fallen ill, so how can it be contagious? It's all a lie!"

Josef's jacket was rumpled, his chin dark with the scattered beginnings of a beard. The skin under his bloodshot hazel eyes sagged.

"Josef," Pyralis said. His heart pounded in his temples and he suddenly felt like a Castalian gladfighter, thrown into the pen with a bull for the first time. "Galena *is* ill. It's difficult, knowing she's in pain . . ." the tiny wobble in his voice was nearly imperceptible, "but you must believe she is getting the best possible care."

"And you don't think it's odd, that she fell ill at the World Council? Just before the vote?" Josef stalked forward until they were nose to nose. He was the shorter of the two men, but his anger lent him height.

Pyralis met his glare. "The vote would not have gone in her favor, either way," he replied, weariness seeping into the words.

Josef's shoulders slumped. "So . . . Ruslana was the only one who would stand against Safara?"

"They didn't need the World Council to impose sanctions. And no one has changed their policies since."

At that moment, Bett came toward them, holding out two cut-crystal glasses full of amber liquid.

"Here," she said softly, handing a glass to Josef first and then to Pyralis.

Josef took the glass and nodded absently in thanks, his eyes still wary. "So there wasn't a plot to poison her? To keep her from turning the vote?"

Pyralis shook his head. "I know the timing seems suspect, but I've heard no whisper of such a plot, and Ward Vadim's menders keep me informed of her progress, just as they do you."

"They won't let me see her." Josef stared miserably at the glass. "Not once. We haven't spoken in . . ." His eyes flew again to Pyralis. "You have to make them let me see her. I don't care if I catch what she has. I *must* speak with her."

Pyralis swallowed a mouthful of the amber liquid, buying time to think. Galena was still on Atalantan soil; if he refused her husband access it could cause tension with Ruslana, and that he couldn't afford. But the entire clinic was quarantined. Even he didn't have access to her. Not yet.

Best to stall. "It won't be long," he said, finally. "They've told you, surely, that she's recovering a little more every day? That the blood tests are encouraging?"

"Not good enough," Josef growled.

Pyralis shrugged, hoping Josef understood that he wished he could do more. "I'm sorry. Even I am not allowed to visit her."

For a long moment, Josef said nothing, just stared at him as if his gaze could pierce Pyralis's soul. Then, with an inarticulate noise, he flung the remains of his drink down his throat and slammed the glass on the edge of the desk. "And you think she'd see you, even if you were?"

With that he spun and left the room.

Chapter Twenty-Two

Target practice was the last place Aris expected to think of Echo.

Once, about a year ago, Echo had invited Aris to her house before a night out at The Toad. When Aris walked into her bedroom, two canvases were set up—one a newly finished painting and the other a large square of unblemished white.

Her dark curls bouncing, Echo gestured to the blank canvas. "I need to relax for a minute before we go out. Do you mind?" When Aris shook her head, Echo grinned and handed her a brush. "You can help."

Echo took her own brush and swept a glistening vermilion trail across the stark white canvas.

"Are you sure?" Aris asked, holding the brush gingerly between two fingers. "I'll ruin it. I'm a terrible painter."

Echo added another slash of color, cobalt this time. "You can't ruin it. This is just for fun. Come on, Aris, throw a little paint up there. Get dirty. I promise, you can't make a mistake."

But holding that brush had felt like a mistake. Aris was certain that if she tried to put paint to canvas, she would ruin everything. She couldn't relax. An irrational fear of failure held her back, kept her from painting her first colorful line.

Eventually she did, of course, and she enjoyed swirling the

emeralds and silvers and crimsons into a great big mess, but in that first moment she was consumed by insecurity.

Now, with a solagun shaking in her hands, the fear that coursed through her wasn't irrational. It wasn't insecurity. The brilliant green shots of energy with which she was supposed to paint the sim monitor wouldn't make a pretty picture. They'd paint pain, danger. Death.

Beside her, a steady series of hisses punctuated Dysis's shooting. She'd already gone through two sim targets, and Aris hadn't taken a single shot.

Noticing the silence to her right, Dysis glanced up. "Everything okay?"

Aris nodded, swallowing. The sim room was loud with the sibilant whine of solagun fire. On her other side, another soldier, Specialist Pallas, was having trouble with his aim. His blank, human-shaped target only had two hits—one at the edge of the shoulder and the other just grazing the line of the head. Pallas was skinny with a pointed chin and short, white-blond hair that fuzzed up around his head like a halo. He kept lifting his weapon to aim, eyes wide, and then letting his hands fall as if unsure of himself.

"Is there a problem?" A voice rumbled over Aris's shoulder. With a start, she twisted and came face to face with Major Vidar. He regarded her steadily.

"Um, no," she replied, flustered. *Keep it together.*

"You haven't fired your weapon."

"I—I . . . I'm just getting used to it. This is my first time," she said, then wanted to smack herself. He was going to see right through her. What man didn't want to practice firing weapons?

The thin pink scar pulled at the edge of his mouth as he gave her an odd look. "Didn't you do weapons training at Pono?"

Oh Gods. Why hadn't Dianthe done weapons training with her? All they did was run and spar! Aris scrambled for something to say, some excuse. "They mostly had me in the air, sir," she said at last, staring at the solagun in her hands to avoid his eyes.

"This isn't my *first* first time," she cleared her throat, "just, you know . . . first time *here*."

He gave a little groan. She glanced over in time to see him run a large hand across the back of his neck. His equally large arm muscles bulged. "Blighting hell."

Aris's throat closed. Had he figured it out? "I'm sorry, sir. I—"

Major Vidar sighed and said, "Not your fault, Specialist," in a long-suffering way. "Not the first time green ears have come to us with subpar training." He reached for her solagun and held it up, aiming for the sim target. "Keep your elbows relaxed, wrists firm, hands steady. Like this. See?"

She nodded, so relieved she wasn't exposed that she almost didn't cringe when he handed the sleek, chrome weapon back to her. He waited while she drew the solagun into position. Her hands still shook, and her breath, trapped between her raised arms, sounded loud in her ears.

"Do flyers really need to carry solaguns?" She couldn't imagine actually aiming at someone, let alone pulling the trigger.

He grabbed the butt of the weapon, curling his fingers over part of her hand. The physical contact nearly made her drop the solagun. "You have to be able to protect yourself. You won't always be in the air." He pulled up on her hands to adjust her aim, then let go. "Good, sight down the line, there. Okay, now fire."

She squinted at the target, took a deep breath, held it, and did as he ordered. The hiss of the solagun was swallowed by the sounds of other guns firing around them. She lowered the weapon and stared at the target; a green hit showed against the lower center of the human shape's stomach.

"Not too bad," Major Vidar said, nodding.

Aris let out a shaky breath.

"Next time, don't close your eyes when you pull the trigger."

He moved down the line. "Pallas, it works better if you aim at your *own* target."

CHAPTER TWENTY-THREE

ARIS AND DYSIS SLIPPED OUT OF BREAKFAST EARLY TO COMM up before morning formation. When a comm from Calix flashed on her digitablet screen, Aris let out a silent breath.

I'm glad the job is going well, Aris. I wish I could say the same. I haven't slept in so long, I feel that if I closed my eyes they might never open again. There was a fight in a village near our station-point a few days ago, and we've been picking up the pieces ever since. For every person I save, it seems another one dies. Can't the whole world close its eyes, just for a moment? Can't it all just rest?

Sometimes at night, I pretend the rumble of distant explosions is the crash of waves, and we're in our cave on the beach, just you and me. I know you're in Panthea now, but I always imagine you in Lux, standing at the edge of the water with the sun setting behind you, all red and gold. I think about you all the time: your smile, the wind blowing your wild hair around, the way you laugh when you fly. You keep me going. Knowing that you're safe, that you're waiting for me . . . right now it's one of the only comforts I have. I love you. ~ Calix

Aris quickly looked up the news on her digitablet. What village was Calix talking about?

Finally, after several different searches, she found a two-line mention in a war report from several days ago. A small village in Atalanta's Mittaka region had been the site of a skirmish between Atalantan and Safaran forces. Wounded fighters were being sent to the two mender points close by: Revening and Mekia. She filed the names away. *Revening. Mekia.* She'd know soon enough where Calix was. He wasn't allowed to tell anyone exactly where he was, but Dianthe had said Aris's S and R unit would take their victims to a single mender stationpoint. Calix's. Her first mission, and she'd know. *Revening or Mekia.* Soon, she'd see him in the flesh.

"Anything good?" Dysis asked, glancing over Aris's shoulder.

"Well, I heard from—"

Lieutenant Daakon's voice cut her off. "Latza, Haan, the Commander would like to see you in his office. Now, please."

Aris started. Lieutenant Daakon stood just behind them.

Aris and Dysis jumped up, exchanging nervous glances. As they hurried down the hall, Dysis whispered, "Do you think it could be about Jax? Everyone knows I'm looking for him. Do you think . . . maybe there's some news?"

Aris wanted to say yes. But—"Why'd they call me, then? Wouldn't Commander Nyx just want to see you?"

"Then what?"

Aris's stomach dropped. "Do you think . . ." She tensed and clamped her jaw shut. They'd reached the office, and the Commander's door was open.

"Latza, Haan, come in," Commander Nyx ordered.

Aris stepped into the small, windowless room first and stood stiffly before the Commander's desk.

He indicated that Dysis should close the door. "Sit."

They sank into the chairs set before the desk. All the furniture was old-fashioned, beat up. The white finish was chipped in some places, and a leg of the desk had a chunk taken out of it, exposing the grain of the wood.

Commander Nyx tapped his monitor. Aris tried not to stare at the ropes of red scar that circled his neck, but she couldn't stop herself from wondering what had happened, if it was a wound sustained in battle, or something older. She couldn't imagine what might have caused the marks, short of someone trying to strangle him. With fire.

"Specialist Haan, you've done poorly in hand-to-hand training. Worst of any soldier at this stationpoint," Commander Nyx said.

Aris swallowed. She wanted to defend herself, to demand that they hold off judgment until they saw her fly, but she was afraid if she spoke up she'd get lambasted for insubordination, so she simply nodded. She squeezed the chair's armrests so tightly her knuckles went white. She couldn't go home. Not now.

"You passed your physical assessment, and your run times have been improving," he continued. "So that's something." Commander Nyx then turned to Dysis. "Specialist Latza, you've shown prowess in target training and your physical assessment was sufficient. In addition, you're quite skilled at hand-to-hand." The stout man sank back in his chair. "And Lieutenant Jax Latza is your brother."

Dysis stiffened at the name but nodded, though it hadn't been a question.

"He was well-known in Military even before his disappearance." Commander Nyx paused.

Dysis's square jaw was clenched, eyes burning. "If he's so well-known, why hasn't anyone found him yet? That's why I'm here, sir. To find him. Whatever it takes." she said, a dangerous edge to her voice.

Commander Nyx placed his hand on the desk, fingers spread, and stood. His movements were slow, deliberate; it was like watching a snake coil to strike. "No. You're here to do your *job*, Specialist," he said.

For a second the silence built, tight and dirty in the small room. But as Nyx's scars pulsed red and his eyes bored into Dysis, she finally murmured, "Yes, sir."

Aris let out the breath she'd been holding.

The Commander straightened, his hands falling to his sides.

"As you are women, I am already taking a risk with you. I need to be able to trust that you're committed to the mission of this unit, above all else. And capable of doing your jobs without exposing yourselves."

Aris's jaw slackened. "You *know?* But . . . but how—"

"And how would the deception work if I didn't, Specialist?" he interrupted. "You have paperwork excusing you from medical evaluations, special dispensations in the event of an injury. Who exactly did you think authorized such measures?"

"I . . ." No words came. Of course she should have known, but the shock kept Aris rooted to her chair.

"Specialist Latza, you've proven yourself to be a useful member of this team. So long as your specialty training remains at a similar level of proficiency, and your brother's circumstances don't distract you, you are welcome to continue with us."

"Thank you, sir," Dysis murmured.

Commander Nyx turned narrowed eyes on Aris. "Specialist Haan. Given your performance to date, I cannot continue to offer you a place at this stationpoint. For you to stay, I would need to see some spectacular flying out of you. And even then, I'm not convinced you have the physical strength and skill necessary for this job."

At first the words didn't register. Then a burning anger caught Aris out of nowhere. Without a second's thought, she stood up and slammed her hand on the desk. "You *will not* tell me I can't do this. I have worked *too blighting hard* to be sent away now."

"Aristos." The warning in Commander's Nyx voice was clear.

Aris lifted her chin. "I'll prove I'm an important part of this team. You'll see."

"I better see you sit down *right now*, or I'll kick you out before you even get the chance." The hardness in his eyes said he was deadly serious.

Aris sat. The shock of her outburst was catching up to her. Did she really just yell at her commander? Another thought sent her reeling. "If . . . if I don't make it, are you going to send me to jail?"

Commander Nyx sighed. "No. That would put the other women embedded here at risk. If you don't make it, we will deal with your dismissal internally."

Aris swallowed hard.

Nyx sat back in his chair. "Specialist Haan, I will give you my decision on your future here within the week. In the meantime, I expect you both to be vigilant in keeping your real identities to yourselves. For any issues arising from your unique situation, you will come to me and me only. You will not discuss this meeting or your 'special circumstances' with anyone outside this room. Is that clear?"

"Yes, sir." Aris and Dysis said together.

Within the week. At least Aris wasn't getting kicked out now. At least she had one more chance to earn her place.

Commander Nyx turned to Dysis. "Specialist Latza?"

"Sir?" Dysis stood and met the Commander's glare straight on. The air thickened between them, and Aris wanted to slink away before something—or someone—exploded.

"Your priority, while you're here, is your team. *Not* Lieutenant Latza. There are people far more important than you looking for him. Understood?"

Dysis gave a slow nod, but the mutiny in her eyes remained.

"Dismissed."

Aris hurried down the hallway, ignoring Dysis's angry muttering. She could barely breathe. *Please let my flying be enough. Please, Gods, make them let me stay.*

CHAPTER TWENTY-FOUR

"Total bloodbath," Dysis mumbled at dinner that night, her mouth full of pea-and-piggin pie.

Galec nudged Aris's arm. She winced. "Hand-to-hand wasn't that bad, was it?" he asked. "Better than yesterday, anyway. Looks like you got one good shot in." He gestured toward Dysis and the puffy, purple bruise along her chin.

Aris grunted, for once sounding like a man without even trying. "I was aiming for his shoulder, but his face got in the way."

Galec laughed. Aris's stomach twisted. She'd tried even harder in combat training today, pushing herself until she thought she'd pass out, and she still got whipped. She could just imagine Commander Nyx's cold eyes when he sent her home.

"Still counts," Otto said, then he belched. The skin around his mouth was shiny with piggin fat.

Jealousy flared within her. Aris had no doubt that Galec and Otto were really, truly male, with nothing to prove and no one threatening to send them home. She'd been watching the other soldiers, wondering who among them was hiding, like her. Sometimes she caught a glimpse—a too-graceful movement, a snatch of conversation between sectormates that sounded *too* familiar, too female—and she'd file the moment away. Specialist Pallas,

114

perhaps, was a woman. Or maybe even Lieutenant Talon. But Galec and Otto? Definitely not.

As Otto shoveled another hunk of pie in his mouth, Dysis grinned, an extra hint of sympathy in her eyes. "You'll get me next time. You just need more practice. Little hummingbird."

Galec and Otto guffawed. Aris scowled. She'd made the mistake of telling Dysis about Calix calling her a hummingbird, and now she couldn't get away from it.

She shook her head and tried to ignore its pounding. "On the ground I'm donkey rot and always will be. Just put me in a wing-jet. By all that is holy, let me fly. Then we'll—"

"Tomorrow. Then *we'll* see."

She spun in her seat. Lieutenant Wolfe, the unit's flying expert, kept walking without looking at her, but the faint smirk on his thin face betrayed his skepticism. Not that his derision was a surprise. Hadn't Commander Nyx made it clear she wasn't impressing anyone? She'd barely passed her physical evaluation, and even now she spent most of her combat training trying to ignore the disgusted look on Major Vidar's face.

Target practice was getting better. She had the sharp eyes of a flyer, but she still flinched every time the solagun went off, which always impaired her aim. At least she usually managed to keep her eyes open now. Still, it wasn't enough.

Aris turned to glare at Otto, who was chuckling openly.

"Have you heard from Helena?" She asked Galec about his wife in an attempt to change the subject.

His eyes glowed with pride. "Got a comm from her yesterday. Calla has started walking. She's taller than all the other girls her age, and Helena says she looks more like me every day."

"Poor child," Otto said under his breath. Dysis punched him in the arm. "Ow!"

"You should be so lucky," Galec replied with a good-natured smile.

Just then, someone on the other side of the room hushed them, turning up the volume on the monitor mounted to the wall.

In the news vid, a pretty reporter in a slim yellow dress was speaking in front of a steep-roofed stone house. ". . . With a heavy heart I announce the passing of Josef Vadim, husband of Ruslana's Ward Galena Vadim, who remains in quarantine," she said solemnly.

Everyone turned to watch, the last murmurs of conversation fading to silence. The woman continued, "Vadim was found early this morning, alone in the home he shared with his wife, dead of catastrophic heart failure. He was taken to the nearest clinic but menders were unable to revive him. Those close to the Ward believe the stress of her illness contributed to his collapse. We've been told Ward Vadim will issue a statement. Her son has still not spoken to or been seen by the press; it is unclear if he was with his father at the time of his death or, indeed, if he's even aware of today's sad events."

Otto sat back in his chair and whistled. "That's a bad business."

"I'm surprised they haven't appointed an acting Ward," Galec said. A vertical line had formed between his brows. "But I suppose they wouldn't, if she'll soon be well enough to issue statements."

The reporter was still speaking, but she'd moved on to interviews with friends and colleagues of Josef Vadim, and the room erupted again into conversation and the clinking of silverware.

Aris took a bite of her pie, staring intently at her plate. That man in Dianthe's apartment had talked about Ward Vadim's husband, how he'd been telling anyone who'd listen that his wife wasn't really sick. It was so odd that now *he* should fall ill. That he should die.

"I wonder why they can't locate her son," Dysis said. "How can no one know where he is? Surely he'll attend his father's burning."

"Will Ruslana continue with the sanctions, do you think?" Aris asked.

From Commander Nyx's briefings, it appeared Ruslana's pressure on Safara was having some small effect. Without the water and other resources Ruslana normally traded for Safaran energy, the dominion was struggling. A little. But Atalanta was still in danger. And no one here seemed to believe that giving Safara access to the Fex River would actually solve anything.

"They better," Galec said, running a hand over the ginger stubble on his head. "Otherwise, there's not much hope for us, is there?"

Aris glanced at Dysis, taking in her worried look, as Dianthe's words echoed ominously in her mind. *We are losing this war.*

CHAPTER TWENTY-FIVE

TODAY WOULD BE DIFFERENT. GALENA KNEW THIS BECAUSE Elom's routine changed. He did not immediately connect her to electrodes. And he didn't unchain her either. He entered the room silently, his dark skin glowing under the bright lights. A digitablet and medigun held in his large, oddly delicate hands, he stood beside her bed and stared at her for a long time.

She was certain this would be the day he killed her.

She'd racked her brain for reasons why someone would want to kidnap her, and then do nothing but hold her captive. There were no ransom demands, no death threats, no torturing her for information. Whatever they'd needed her for, it seemed obvious her purpose had expired.

"Prepare yourself," Elom said. The first words he'd spoken in days.

In that moment, Pyralis's face flashed in her mind. No, she would not let him have her last thought. Instead, Galena held her son, her beautiful son, close to her in the darkness as she closed her eyes.

There was no sting from a medigun needle. No pillow pressed against her face, or merciless fingers snaking around her throat. After a moment, she opened her eyes. Elom didn't touch her, didn't speak. He just placed the digitablet on her lap and turned it on.

Confused, Galena wanted to ask, *prepare myself for what?*

She didn't have time.

"It is with a heavy heart," the reporter announced, standing before a house Galena instantly recognized as her own, "that I announce the passing of Josef Vadim . . ."

Galena opened her mouth, gasping like a dying fish, as the reporter's voice babbled on.

With the last hiss of air remaining in her lungs, she whispered, "It's a lie."

This should have been it. The moment when he explained what was going on, explained his terms. But Elom didn't respond.

"You doctored the vid. You want something from me, and you're using him as collateral," she guessed. Prayed. Josef couldn't be . . .

Still Elom said nothing, just stared at her patiently. Waiting for it to sink in.

Her husband was really dead.

The panic she hadn't shown when she thought Elom was about to kill her surfaced now.

"Let me go!" she screamed and fought against her restraints, cutting her arms on the cool metal. She strained desperately against the sheets that kept her legs immobile. "Stop this! Whatever you're doing! *I know you killed my husband! Let me go.*" The words spewed out of her with all the abhorrence she'd built for him, the flames of anger blazing forth.

She and her husband had had little to do with each other in recent years. But he was not some *pawn* in whatever psychotic game she was being forced to play. And he'd never had a problem with his heart in his life.

"Who do you work for? Ward Balias? *What did you do?*" She kept up her rage-filled tirade until all that came out was a breathless scream.

Elom didn't try to stop her; he waited until the blood from her wounded arms had stained the brilliant white sheets crimson and she'd flopped back against the hard mattress, exhausted.

"Tell me," he said, his voice level, pleasant even, as if he were remarking on the weather, "Where is your son?"

"He is beyond your reach. You will never find him," she hissed, rage burning through her exhaustion.

"You don't think he'll visit you, knowing that you are soon to be released from quarantine? You don't think he will come to pay his respects at his father's burning?" Elom's mild tone didn't change.

"No. He won't come." Let Elom think her son hated his father. Let him think what he wanted; she would *not* give him this.

Elom smiled without showing his teeth. "I see."

The simple response sent a shiver of fear along her spine. Struggling to keep her voice steady, she said, "Is that why I'm alive? So you can destroy my family? Why am I here, Elom?" When he didn't respond, she screamed, "Why don't you just kill me, too?"

"Oh, I have no intention of killing you. For now." He patted her head as if she were a small child. "There is too much of value in here."

He was too close, looming over the bed, and she couldn't breathe; he was sucking the air from her lungs just standing there. "I need to use the washroom," she said.

He removed the digitablet from her lap and released her restraints. She thought about launching herself at him, but by the time she found the energy to sit up, he'd backed away. He leaned against the wall, watching her, ready if she tried something.

For once, he didn't give her a time limit. Galena stood against the sink and stared at herself in the mirror. The light was as bright in here as it was in her cell, and every wrinkle, every rice-paper patch of skin was visible. She stared into her own haunted eyes and saw, for the first time, how much she'd aged in the time she'd been a captive. Her hair, which was normally pulled into a flattering knot, was tangled and greasy. The blonde had dulled, leeching the little color she had left in her cheeks. She looked like a wraith.

She leaned over the old-fashioned chrome sink. Tears broke through the iron wall she'd built in her heart. She hadn't let herself cry, not once, since she'd woken and seen Elom standing over her. She hadn't let herself think much about her circumstances, her future.

But now. Now. Her husband was dead. The father of her child. They hadn't spoken with more than awkward civility, if that, in years, but she had loved him once. After Pyralis left, Josef had saved her—from a nowhere job and a broken heart. He'd found her a better placement, in his own Technology company. He'd set her on her journey to success. She was Ward in large part because of him, whether she'd been willing to admit it in recent years or not.

And now he was dead.

Murdered.

She was sure he had been silenced so her life could be stolen.

Dropping her head to her hands, she closed her eyes, desperately searching for a happy memory, some moment that would abate her helplessness. At first, all that rose in her mind was panic.

Happy memories, she thought. Happy.

The memory that came wasn't so much happy as . . . complicated.

The Ruslanan Council Building, at her welcome gala. A year ago, the day after she'd been elected Ward.

The high-ceilinged room had rung with voices, the clink of glasses. Dignitaries in endless colors flowed through the marble-floored hall, glittering like rainbow prisms within fractured glass. It was the beginning of the evening, before the meal and official speeches. She'd barely had time for a sip of her drink, no time for its heat to run along her veins and soothe her nerves.

"Ward Vadim," Pyralis had said, moving smoothly to her side.

Kissing her hand. She'd been braced for this moment; she thought she'd been prepared.

But that first sight of him, handsome in his flowing emerald green tunic and gold pants, that first touch in twenty-five years . . . There, in front of everyone, she'd almost crumbled.

"Pyralis," she'd whispered, realizing too late that she hadn't addressed him properly.

His face had been pleasantly blank, his grip on her hand distant, appropriate for one Ward greeting another for the first time. But when she said his name . . . in that instant, something in his eyes broke, and his lips paused against her skin. The moment lengthened. Too long. Do *something*, she thought, caught in his gaze. He wasn't moving. She couldn't. *Oh holy, my hand's on fire. . . .*

"Love?" The woman's voice was a shade louder than necessary, even in the crowd. Pyralis dropped Galena's hand as if scorched.

The woman slid her arm through his, staring at Galena. She wore a long carmine dress streaked with orange and blue, like a sunset. Ropes of gold hung from her neck, gleaming against the caramel warmth of her skin. Pyralis cleared his throat. "Ward Vadim, I'd like to present my wife, Bett Nekos."

Bett tilted her head gracefully, her feather-accented black hair twisted into a tall updo.

Galena nodded in response. "Ward Nekos, Bett. It is a pleasure. I thank you for being here this evening." She couldn't help staring. This was the woman. She, the Promised he'd returned to so long ago.

Galena fought back the instinctive hatred. She was a grown woman. She was better than the bitterness of that time, those dark months after Pyralis abandoned her. And the flicker of longing? There was no place for that here. Or ever again.

Bett's brownish-golden eyes flashed at Galena, and the red of her perfectly sculpted lips drew into a thoughtful frown.

"Ward Vadim, forgive my impertinence, but I sense you've met my husband before?"

This was the moment Galena had most wanted to avoid. She didn't want anyone to know of their history, least of all this woman. She opened her mouth to respond, eyes drawn to Pyralis's. What could she say? What had he told Bett about the time he'd spent in Ruslana?

"It was the Tech benefit last year, wasn't it?" Josef's words slid into the awkwardness of the moment, jovial and relaxed. Galena leaned into him as he moved to her side, her knees suddenly weak.

"Yes," Pyralis replied quickly, glancing from his wife to Josef. "Hello, Josef. Nice to see you again." He held out a hand.

"I don't remember—" Bett began, her knowing look fading into confusion.

"For the Meridian refugees," Pyralis continued. "You were ill that day, my love." He nodded to Galena, his eyes blankly polite once more. "On behalf of Atalanta, I welcome you to your new role as Ward and look forward to working with you."

He drew Bett away. Galena smiled back stiffly, long after the crowd swallowed them.

"You alright?" Josef asked. He stood, stocky and comfortable in his dark pants and fitted jacket, his eyes filled with concern. He knew the truth, and still he asked if she was okay. Still he looked at her with sympathy.

It was enough to make her squirm with shame. "Yes. Thank you," she'd said, looking away.

Her feelings for Pyralis . . . they were buried but not forgotten. But *Josef* had been the one who'd stood by her. The one who'd died because of her.

Now, under the harsh lights of her cell, she braced her hands on either side of the sink and sobbed. She wept for Josef, yes, but she also wept for herself. And her son. They would seek him out, try to do him harm. Whatever Elom's agenda, it was not to keep her family safe.

At last, with a deep breath and a stern glare at herself in the mirror, Galena straightened. She dried her face on the one rough towel Elom had provided her.

No matter what Elom did to her, she would keep her secrets. For her husband. And for her son.

CHAPTER TWENTY-SIX

"This morning we'll assess your skill within your specialty," Major Vidar announced at formation. "Gunners, you'll be training with Lieutenant Daakon, retrievers with Lieutenant Talon. Flyers, you'll be with Lieutenant Wolfe."

Aris bounced on the balls of her feet, the nervous energy coursing through her like a live wire. So much rode on how she flew today, and yet all she could think about was how good it would feel to be up there, arcing through the wide, blue sky.

"Dismissed!"

She stepped forward, her knees creaking. Even with Dysis going easy on her, she was bone-sore, bruised and so tired the air felt like mud when she moved. But it didn't matter. Not today.

"The hummingbird gets his wings," Dysis threw over her shoulder as she passed.

"And Guns gets to blow things up," Aris replied. "Much luck to you."

"And you." Dysis jogged to catch up with the other gunners. Aris could hear their laughter, see the loose, confident way her sectormate moved across the plain. She was the only one who knew how nervous Dysis really was, how much she'd built up this day in her head. The more she excelled, the more missions she'd go on. The more chances she'd have to find her brother.

Aris couldn't let herself think about what would happen if *she* didn't excel. The fear of being sent home had dogged her for days.

She and the five other flyers followed Lieutenant Wolfe to the massive landing pad at the front of the stationpoint. Two rows of wingjets lined the open space.

The Military sector flew two different styles of wingjet for S and R missions. Recons—used for reconnaissance and laying down suppressing fire—were small, with space for up to three people. Transports were much larger; they held a flyer, a gunner, and a retriever, with space in the cabin for four or five additional people. This jet was responsible for carrying out the actual rescue.

"Who has flown transports before?" Lieutenant Wolfe's tall frame might have been gangly, if he didn't hold himself with such rigid control. A couple of men stepped forward.

Wolfe scowled at them down his long, narrow nose. "I'll fly with each of you to assess your skill and experience. Or lack thereof. The rest of you pay attention until it's your turn."

Aris swallowed a sigh of impatience.

Lieutenant Wolfe climbed onto the wing of one of the transports and gestured to the nearest flyer, a man covered in colorful tattoos who moved slower than the slugs that plagued Lux's groves. Evander, she thought his name was. Aris watched him with envy; she'd love to fly one of the bigger wingjets, to be a fanax instead of a hummingbird for once.

The other flyers leaned against one of the recons, some sitting on a wing, others on the ground beneath. She lowered herself to the dirt in the shade next to Specialist Pallas, watching out of the corner of her eye to see how the men moved. She tried to sit the way they did, with her legs stretched out, leaning back on her hands. Specialist Mann, a thick-necked, seasoned flyer Aris had never spoken to, scratched his groin, and she fought to keep her expression neutral. She'd walk the way a man does, sit like one, but she would *not* scratch down there.

Beside her, Specialist Pallas leaned back on his hands and

stared up at the sky, where Wolfe was taking Evander through his paces. Pallas's eyes matched the blue above them, and his skin was tan from the endless outdoor training. Nothing in his features or the way he held himself suggested he was in disguise, but Aris had seen the horrified look on his face after their first solagun training session and wondered if he might be a woman. Then again, Dysis was perfectly comfortable handling weapons. Still, there was something about Pallas that Aris couldn't quite put her finger on.

"Too bad about the Ward of Ruslana's husband," Pallas said. The Ward was all anyone had talked about since the news the night before.

Specialist Mann nodded. "Can't be good for Ruslana, what with everything else going on."

Pallas kept his gaze on the sky. "At least the sanctions are still intact."

One of the other flyers, a wiry boy who looked about Aris's age, dropped from the wing and moved to sit next to Aris. "Fat lot of good they're doing. We're still at war, yeah?"

"Commander thinks they're making a difference," Mann said.

"You gotta figure it's better than nothing, right?" Pallas said. "I just wish the other dominions would throw us a branch. Doesn't seem right that they're allowing us to get attacked."

Aris nodded with the others. It *wasn't* right, but the only person who'd tried to help was Ward Vadim, and she couldn't do much from a clinic bed.

"How long you all been flying?" Pallas asked, when no one offered new insights on the topic.

Mann shrugged. "Forever, feels like. What about you, Nyal?"

The boy, Nyal, said, "Since I was fourteen, so four years, yeah?"

Aris glanced up at the large wingjet in the sky, made small now by distance. "I've been flying since I was twelve. My father taught me, when—" she paused. Probably better not to explain. Instead she asked, "What about you, Pallas?"

"Three years. Grew up in Panthea, so no flying there. But

when I was selected for Military they sent me to Cress. That was just before the war. I was meant to be trained as an emergency flyer. Part of the town's protective detail."

"And now you're search and rescue."

"Not much difference, really, except for being away from my family." He dropped his gaze to his feet. Little puffs of dust sprang up under his boots as he scuffed them along the ground.

"Are you Promised?" Aris watched Evander do a lazy loop and head back toward the landing strip.

Specialist Pallas shook his head. "You?"

"No."

"Me neither," Nyal said.

Mann grinned. "Guess I'm the only one. Not Promised, though. Those two years went by in a flash. The wife and I've been married four years."

Evander's landing was a little rocky; Aris could do better.

"Might as well get this over with." Mann heaved himself to his feet and moved toward the transport.

"Much luck," Aris called.

"Flyers!"

She jumped.

Major Vidar was striding toward them. Aris and the others stood quickly, dusted off their uniforms, and straightened their spines.

"Who flies the recon jets?" Vidar asked.

Aris, Pallas, and Nyal stepped forward.

Vidar jerked a finger at Aris, who was standing closest. "Come on."

She moved toward him, stumbling a little in her excitement. For once, Vidar's snort of derision at her awkwardness failed to bother her.

When they were strapped into the recon, Major Vidar consulted the roster on a small digitablet. Without looking at her, he said, "Aristos Haan. From Lux."

"Yes, sir." Her pulse pounded in her temples as her hands slid around the controls.

"When you're ready, take it up nice and easy and do a few laps to acclimate yourself. Watch out for the transport." He sounded bored, and his eyes said he wasn't expecting much from her. Maybe he'd even talked to Commander Nyx and assumed, like Nyx, that she'd be gone within the week.

The navigation panel was the same as her wingjet at home. Aris tightened her grip on the controls, felt the pedals give as she shifted her feet.

And then she grinned.

This was the moment she'd been waiting for. This was the moment she'd prove she deserved to be here.

This was her ticket to Calix.

Aris pressed down on the pedals and the wingjet slowly rose, hovering perfectly balanced just off the ground. It was one of the hardest moves to learn, taking off and landing without the added propulsion of forward movement. But it was also necessary in Lux, where the landing pads and cliffs were small targets.

From the corner of her eye, she saw Major Vidar raise his head.

For a second she let the wingjet hang there, reveling in the feeling of the controls in her hands, the delicate balance of the pedals under her feet.

And then she began to dance.

First a nearly vertical dash into the wide blue sky, followed by a little spin to give her a sense of the way the wingjet handled. Then she nosed upward, steeper and steeper until they looped into a graceful backward flip. She spun and dipped, varied her speed, paused to hover far from the ground below.

Major Vidar said nothing, so Aris kept on, twisting and flipping and soaring, feeling the air stream against her wings, the sun touch her face like the hands of a long-lost friend. The dusty flat training fields and low buildings looked nothing like Lux, but she skimmed along the roof of the barracks as if it were the edge of her cliffs; she rose high and then dove, spinning toward the ground, imagining she could see the sparkling flash of waves far below. She even tried a new move she'd been working on before she left—a double backflip freeze that she completed perfectly.

The pain and confusion of trying to live within a skin that wasn't hers, in a world she didn't understand, fell away. Commander Nyx's warning lost its power. Even her awareness of Major Vidar faded, until it was only Aris and her wings and the welcoming ocean of sky all around her.

"That's enough, Aristos." Major Vidar's rough voice was a splash of reality she wasn't quite ready for.

She suppressed a disappointed sigh, then pointed the nose of the wingjet toward the training ground.

"So you're from Lux . . ." he said, sounding thoughtful.

"Yes, sir." She slowed to hover above the landing pad, determined to show him how precise she could be.

As soon as she landed, the other flyers surrounded the wingjet. She noticed, belatedly, that the transport had returned, but Wolfe hadn't taken anyone else up yet. They were all standing around, watching as she emerged from the jet.

Specialist Evander clapped a tattooed hand on Aris's shoulder and grinned. "So *that's* why they let you volunteer for Military, Hummingbird. We were starting to wonder."

She laughed a little as the rest of the flyers gathered around her.

"How'd ya learn to do that?" Nyal asked, his eyes wide.

"What angle did you use on that backflip move? Sixty-five or eighty? I couldn't tell," Mann said.

As the questions continued, Aris answered what she could, her smile stretching so wide she probably looked half-crazy. She'd never been around so many people who shared her passion before. At home, flying was a way to get from one place to another. No one wanted to talk about pedal angles or jet power levels.

"Specialist Pallas, you're up," Major Vidar said eventually, breaking up the group.

Aris moved back to a spot in the shade, and the rest of the

flyers followed, still chattering about her flight. As she sank to the dusty ground, her smile faded. She'd done well. She just hoped it was enough.

Chapter Twenty-Seven

Pyralis didn't realize he was drumming his fingers on his knee until Bett reached for his hand.

"Nearly there, Ward," Kellan said from the front seat.

The driver guided the long, silver terran up the winding, steep street on the outskirts of Panthea's mountainside. Pyralis's thoughts were just as twisty. *Josef, dead.* How long was it after Josef stormed into his office that he had died? A few days? A week? Galena's husband had been overwrought, wound so tightly with desperation that heart failure wasn't a difficult truth to accept.

But *was* it the truth?

Pyralis stared blindly at the vid embedded in the terran's glass partition. The daily war update played, showing footage of burned wingjets and flattened dwellings. Every day a new village was evacuated, more soldiers killed. He had his war strategies, his secret military maneuverings. And still Safara pushed farther into Atalanta, leaving destruction behind.

Meanwhile, rumors swirled. A Ward in quarantine, her husband dead. Conspiracies . . . conjecture. . . .

What if Josef was right? What if someone had tried to hurt Galena?

The terran glided to a stop outside the back entrance to the small, private clinic. A black-robed man stood guard at the door. Ward Vadim's quarantine was scheduled to be lifted tomorrow. But Pyralis had waited long enough.

"Meet us out front, Kellan, if you would," he said as he emerged from the terran. He didn't wait for his assistant to open the door. "I'll give a statement to the reporters as we leave."

Kellan nodded. He reached in to help Bett; she teetered on her high red heels as her matching fingernails dug into his hand. Taking her other arm, Pyralis steadied her. Today she'd high-lighted her Tech brand with swirling gold make-up to match her shimmering dress. Every time she moved, the multicolored bangles piled to her elbows jangled.

"Thank you, Kellan," Pyralis said, as he walked Bett to the entrance of the clinic. The guard bowed and stepped aside as they approached. With a hiss, the frosted glass door slid open.

"This way, Ward." A tall man in mender's white led them down a long, empty corridor. "This wing has been closed since they brought Ward Vadim here. She's had her privacy."

"Has anyone been given access to her, beyond her menders? Anyone tried to speak with her?" He couldn't keep the edge from his voice.

The mender lifted his chin. "Absolutely not. The quarantine would not allow it, even if she had been strong enough for visitors."

"And how is she now?" He glanced along the blank hall, silent except for the click-clack of Bett's heels and the thud of his boots. The mender's shoes shushed against the floor with a whisper.

"The Ward is still quite weak, often drifts off when you're talking. Her memories are a little hazy." The mender paused by a closed door at the end of the hall. "Don't be alarmed. It's quite natural for someone with her condition."

"I've been told she'll be moved to Ruslana by the end of the week?"

"That's correct, Ward Nekos. She would like to return home as soon as possible."

"Thank you," he said, and the man stepped away, to stand a respectful distance down the corridor. Close enough to be within earshot if he was needed but not so close that he could appear to be listening to their conversation.

Bett reached out to open the door.

"Stay here, love," Pyralis said, catching her arm. The movement set her bracelets jingling. "I need to speak to the Ward alone."

Bett turned, eyes wide. "But I thought—"

"Dominion business. It'll just be a moment. Then you can wish her a speedy recovery, if you wish." He was sure she'd come for appearances, not from any real concern. He had the impression Bett and Galena disliked one another, though that assumption could have arisen from his own awkwardness at Galena's reappearance in his life.

Bett stepped out of his way, tossing her black curls over her shoulder. She was excessively proud of her hair and the fact that it didn't yet show any hint of gray. He looked old beside her now, though they were born only a few years apart. Watching her slink to one of the chairs that lined the hallway, he felt stooped, creaking, ancient. She raised her brows, her eyes asking why he was still standing there. And why was he?

He took a deep breath as he moved into the room and tapped the panel to close the door.

"Ward Nekos." Galena's voice sounded just the same, high, with that girlish whisper that had once driven him mad with wanting. Now, it filled him with relief.

He studied her. She looked almost the same as he remembered. She'd been ill for a long time, and it showed in the lavender shadows beneath her eyes, the paleness of her lips. Her face was thinner, her body more angular. But she was Galena, the Galena who still, even now, haunted him.

As much as he wanted to run to her side, he held himself rigidly by the closed door, hands clasped behind his back so they could not betray him. "Ward Vadim. I am happy to see you are recovering."

Galena smiled pleasantly. "I am grateful for the superb care your dominion has provided."

Pyralis dared to take a step closer. "And you'll be returning to Ruslana soon?"

She inclined her head. "That's what I've been told. I am eager to be home again. It has been a long time."

"I'm sorry about Josef." Moving closer, he let the tips of his fingers drift along the very edge of the bed.

She dropped her gaze to her hands, which were clasped demurely in her lap. "Such a tragedy. I can't help thinking if I hadn't fallen ill, he might still be here."

"You mustn't think that."

A tear made its slow passage along the curve of Galena's cheek. Instinctively, he reached for her hand. As their fingers touched, she glanced up, her shock apparent. He paused, but he took her lead, backing away before making his official speech. "Ward Vadim, I know you are still very tired. On behalf of Atalanta, I am overjoyed at your return to health and am grateful, as always, for your support. May Atalanta and Ruslana ever be allies."

Galena nodded gracefully. "I thank you, Ward Nekos, for your hospitality in my time of need. May our dominions ever prosper."

The words were appropriate, everything as it should be, except for that blank politeness in her eyes. No anger, no chill, no warmth. Just . . . nothing.

With a slight bow, Pyralis left her, eager now to get away.

"How is she?" Bett asked anxiously, when he emerged from the room. She was already standing, hovering just outside the door.

"Recovering," Pyralis replied, striding down the hall.

He berated himself silently for being so foolish. For touching her. Of course she'd recoiled. How else did he expect her to act? Her husband had just died. And their past was just that. The past.

Chapter Twenty-Eight

"Heard you put on quite a show yesterday," Otto said around a half-chewed chunk of roasted goat. He was like a camel: skinny everywhere but that giant belly.

Aris grinned but said nothing as she forked up her own—more reasonably sized—bite of meat.

"And now he's modest." Otto rolled his eyes. "This is the time to tell your tales, son. You don't want anyone to remember your combat skills. Believe me."

"Oh, leave Hann alone," Galec interjected. "We've got enough ego at this table with you sittin' here. A little humility never hurt anyone."

"I figure I've still got a ways to go in the 'impressing people' sector," Aris said. "I mean, after the third time tripping over my own feet in hand-to-hand this morning . . ."

"It was only twice. The third time *I* tripped you," Dysis said.

"Well, you should have seen *me* yesterday. Nobody might be talking about it . . ." Otto paused to swallow, "but I retrieved our sim victims faster than anyone." He patted his belly, which strained against the slim fit of his military jacket. "Well, faster than any of the other porkpies."

Galec snorted. "You *are* a porkpie. You better watch it or they'll make you run extra laps at phys training."

"At least I know I'd catch Aristos, here," Otto said, punching Aris in the arm. "He might be able to fly, but he can't run worth shit."

Dysis smirked. "Oh, I bet he'd run pretty fast if *you* were chasing him."

"Specialist Haan." The voice rang through the room and silence followed, abrupt as if someone had flipped a switch.

Commander Nyx stood in the wide doorway, hands clasped behind his back. His blood-red scars stood out in the bright light of the mess hall.

Aris stood quickly and rushed to the hallway.

Nyx gave her a curt nod. "Major Vidar told me about your training session yesterday."

Her stomach tightened. "Yes, sir. And?"

"And?" Nyx's eyes glittered. "I hope you're ready for your first mission. Suit up and report to the landing pad."

<hr>

FOR A SECOND, Aris just closed her eyes and breathed. She'd made it. Her first mission, her first chance to find Calix.

Major Vidar's deep voice spoke directly into the headset embedded in her helmet. "Haan, Pallas, as the search team, you'll go first. Radio back when you have visual confirmation of the targets. We'll be right behind you in the transport." There was a hiss of static after Major Vidar finished speaking. Aris gripped the controls tighter and double-checked the coordinates on the navigation panel.

"You ready?" In the tight quarters of the wingjet, Dysis's voice was too loud.

Aris nodded. Her helmet tipped forward a little. With a gloved hand, she pushed it back. She took a deep breath. She could do this. It was just her and the wingjet, just a little dance. No problem.

"Now," Major Vidar ordered.

She lifted off beside Pallas, who was flying the other recon.

Green dots on her nav panel showed the position of the two transports behind them. Soon they were all speeding through the clear afternoon sky. They were headed toward a tiny, nameless hamlet near the border, in a part of Atalanta that had been evacuated weeks ago. Soldiers had been fighting to keep control of the region, but daily skirmishes meant frequent rescue missions.

Dysis pressed a button on the side of her helmet, so they could talk without broadcasting to the whole team. "Let's go over our orders again." She stared intently at the nav panel, her hands already gripping the gunner controls.

Aris could feel the same tension in her own arms and willed the muscles to loosen. *Relax.*

"We're fine. We know what to do," she replied. But in her head she went through their instructions one more time.

Fly over the east and north portions of the village, while Pallas takes south and west.

Use the heat-seeking tech to assess the threat and locate the injured soldiers.

If we're targeted by the enemy, Dysis will take them out.

Aris checked the nav panel; not much farther. She couldn't forget the last step of the mission: radioing back to the transports the exact coordinates of the soldiers and status of the enemy, so they could perform the retrieval.

Aris didn't let herself consider what would happen afterward. Once they'd made the rescue, after the danger had passed . . . *then* she could think about seeing Calix. Right now she had to concentrate.

"Can you believe we're doing this?" Dysis glanced at her.

Aris shook her head. "Never in a million lives."

For a few minutes they were silent, watching a bank of clouds grow along the far horizon. Then, softly, Dysis said, "When Jax and I were kids, we'd hide out in the forest behind our house and make believe we were soldiers or spies. We'd pretend sticks were our solaguns and sneak up on each other." She laughed a little, shaking her head. "He always found me, no matter where I went. I'd start crying because I'd get so deep in the woods, so turned around, I didn't know how to get home . . . and he still found me. 'Dys' he'd say, all serious, 'you'll never really be lost so long as I'm around.'"

She didn't have to say the rest, that now that he was lost, *she* was lost, too. That she was afraid he'd never be found. Aris could hear the words, feel Dysis's despair, as if she'd spoken them aloud. She leaned into her arm, trying to offer some small comfort, but Dysis drew away.

"Is 'Dys' your real name?" Aris asked, to say something.

Dysis shook her head. "Nah. That's just what Jax calls me. I was named Dysis for my father. He died a few months before I was born. Jax says the midwife tried to persuade Mother it wasn't a fit name for a girl, but she didn't care. Strange little gift, now, not having to change it. Holy knows what Mother would think of all of this if she were still alive." She gave a twisted little smile.

Aris didn't know what to say. To lose both parents so young . . . her parents drove her half-mad, but she couldn't imagine a world without them. Even now, thinking of them made her heart ache. She glanced at Dysis and was relieved to see some of the sadness gone from her eyes. She was staring at the nav panel, checking their progress.

"My real name is—" Aris started.

"Don't tell me," Dysis interrupted. "If I don't know, I can't make a mistake." Before Aris could respond, she added, pointing to the nav panel, "Look. There's the village."

Aris took a deep breath and tightened her hands on the controls.

"Here we go," Dysis muttered, the hard edge back in her voice.

Aris pressed the comm button on her helmet. "Recon One has visual on the village."

"Copy that," Pallas responded. "Recon Two also has visual."

The nav system started to pick up red and purple blotches of heat. It looked like parts of the village were still on fire.

Major Vidar's voice crackled over the line. "Approach with caution. Any sign of—"

An earsplitting whine drowned out his words. The nav panel erupted in panicked beeping. Aris threw them into a dive, her heart beating madly. Dysis shouted something she couldn't make out.

Another whine howled through the small cabin. Dysis fired on the incoming missile. Just beneath and to the east of them, a bright, golden light blossomed. The roar of the explosion reached them a couple seconds later.

Aris wheeled away, skimming and dodging, desperate to figure out where the firing was coming from. Then she saw it. There, in the ruins of a building, a tight circle of big guns pointed toward the sky. A bright flash signaled another shot being fired. She dove, as Dysis took out the second missile. Another explosion swelled orange beneath them. Partially shielded by the smoke, she skimmed closer to the ground, and set Dysis up for a clear shot on the gun emplacement.

Dysis spoke quickly, "Sir, permission to fire on enemy position?"

"Granted."

Just as Aris swept over the half-destroyed building, Dysis fired. The world below them burst into flame.

Minutes passed. No more missiles were fired.

In the scratchy static of their headsets, Pallas cheered.

"Holy hell," Aris choked out, her heart still pounding. She sat back a little but couldn't seem to relax her hands on the controls. Her eyes kept skimming the nav panel and what she could see of the sky and the land below, bracing for more incoming fire.

"Target acquired," Pallas's voice carried over the line a few seconds later. "I've got a hot spot. Looks like three soldiers, possibly four." He gave the coordinates to the transports, and they moved in.

Aris kept sweeping the village, looking for more flashes of weaponry or the reddish-purple blobs on the nav that indicated living bodies. Their request for retrieval hadn't included an exact number of injured soldiers. They didn't want to miss anyone.

Beside her, Dysis took a shuddering breath.

Major Vidar's transport moved in first, followed by the second jet, while the two recons stayed in the sky.

"Is that . . . it?" Dysis said. "That was . . ."

"Easy?" Aris wiped her damp palms one at a time on her knees, eyes still glued to the nav panel, not quite believing it was over.

"Well, quick anyway," Dysis mused. "I don't know . . . I was expecting . . . something else. Something more?"

"Yeah. Me too."

"Four soldiers rescued," Aris mumbled, scarcely believing it. "So we'll be going to the mender point." Adrenaline still surged through her system, accentuating the hum of the diatous veil. She felt like she was about to shiver right out of her skin.

Could it really be only a matter of minutes now, before she saw Calix?

"You think he'll be there?" Dysis asked. "You don't even know where we're taking them yet."

Aris shrugged. "We always go to the same mender point, don't we? He's stationed at whichever that is."

"I don't think that's how it works, Aristos," Dysis said slowly. Almost apologetically.

Aris stared at her. "What do you mean?"

Dysis didn't have time to reply. Major Vidar's voice rang over their headpieces as the transport wingjets joined them in the sky, "Retrieval complete. Recons, set your coordinates for Feln Stationpoint."

Aris's breath caught in her throat. *Feln?* "Dysis, what did you mean?" she asked again, urgently.

Dysis shrugged, brow furrowed in sympathy. "I'm sorry. It says in the manual, you know. Didn't you read it? We go wherever's closest. There are lots of field mender points."

"But—" *Oh holy nightmare. How will I find him now?*

"It's still okay," Dysis said, obviously trying to reassure her. "You know the name of his point, right? I'm sure we'll get there eventually."

In a daze, Aris shook her head. "But I don't," she murmured.

"I was just told it'd be the only mender point we'd go to." *Dianthe promised . . .*

Dysis patted her arm. "Can't you ask him? Don't you have any idea?"

"Because he's in an area of active fighting, he can't share his location with civilians," Aris murmured. If only she could tell him she *wasn't* a civilian.

Revening. Mekia. The words pounded in her head as Aris flew to Feln. How long would it be now, before she found him?

Why did Dianthe lie?

CHAPTER TWENTY-NINE

ARIS SET HER DIGITABLET IN THE PORT AND WAITED FOR IT TO comm up, hoping for a message from Calix. In her last comm, she'd begged him to tell her where he was. She prayed he would, even though he wasn't supposed to.

Once she'd taken a minute to think about it, it seemed fairly obvious why Dianthe had lied. She'd wanted Aris to stay, after all. But that didn't make Aris any less angry about it.

"You playing?" Dysis kicked the back of Aris's chair as she walked past. She joined Galec and Otto, who had already strewn themselves across the more comfortable chairs along the back wall of the rec room. Otto was eating a piece of cocoa his wife had sent him, and Galec was shuffling a deck of cards.

When Otto saw Aris looking, he yelled, "Afraid we'll have a repeat of yesterday?"

"I *beat* you yesterday. Why would I be scared?" she called back, but her heart wasn't in it. *Come on, Calix. Tell me where you are.*

"Because if you beat me today I'm going to punch you in the face." Otto grinned.

Dysis and Galec snickered as Aris rolled her eyes. She turned back to her digitablet. "That's not much incentive."

"Oh come on," Galec said, laughing. "We can't play splots without you."

"Just a minute." She tapped an icon on her digitablet and one new comm popped up. Her heart sank as soon as she saw who it was from. Her father. Not Calix. But then she leaned closer, panic seizing her. It was always her mother who wrote, not her father. Had something happened? She skimmed the comm quickly.

> *. . . Phae looked beautiful at her wedding . . . still don't understand why you couldn't come . . . your mother is distraught . . . she feels it's my fault you won't visit. Please, Aris. Just a day, can't you give us that? It's been nearly two months! I'm sorry I wasn't supportive . . . I can't bear that I drove you away. We miss you so much. Perhaps we can come visit next week?*

Aris's breath hitched in her chest, relief overshadowed by a slow, inexorable sinking in her stomach. *Phae's wedding!* How could she have forgotten? She'd wanted to at least send a comm. She imagined Phae in her wedding dress, dark skin gleaming against the sapphire silk, black hair twisted into the traditional knot. It was all she could do not to cry.

And her father . . . he'd actually *apologized?* She tried to swallow down the guilt, but it wouldn't go; it just sat there, a great lump in her throat, burning and garlic-bitter on the back of her tongue. How worried must her parents be, for her father to suggest he come to Panthea? He *hated* the city.

Her fingers trembled above the digitablet. She had to write Phae. And her father, too; she had to reassure him, convince him to stay away. But what could she say? She couldn't promise him a visit, couldn't promise him anything, not even her own safety. She couldn't tell him the truth.

She pounded a hand on the table. For the first time since Dianthe had shaved her head, Aris hated *Aristos*. She hated the need for a disguise. If women were allowed in Military as themselves, she wouldn't have to lie to her parents or Phae. Or Calix.

She could at least *tell* them what she was doing, if not where exactly she was. They'd understand, then, why she couldn't be there—

"Aristos! We're dying of old age over here!" Dysis yelled. Galec and Otto were staring at Aris, and now several other soldiers glanced up.

"I have to—"

"You have to get over here," Dysis interrupted, a warning in her eyes.

"Fine, fine," Aris replied. "But it's your burning." She turned off the digitablet. She needed quiet anyway, to figure out what to say. This wasn't the time. The room was crowded, all the sagging chairs full, and several other card games in progress. In one corner, a group of soldiers sprawled on the floor watching the news. The noise wasn't deafening, but it was definitely not quiet enough to think in here.

Otto whistled. "Big words from a little man."

"And little words from a big man," Dysis retorted.

Galec groaned.

Aris flopped onto the stained, deep-cushioned chair across from him and tried to keep up with the banter. When Galec leaned closer to deal her a card, he met her eyes. "Are you well, Aristos? Bad news from home?"

Your mother is distraught. . . .

Aris locked the words away, did her best to shut off the part of herself that longed for her father's embrace, longed to have danced at Phae's wedding. She smiled. "I missed a friend's wedding, that's all."

"I'm sorry. Makes the time feel even longer, when you can't be home for important moments," he said. "Was it a close friend?"

She nodded. "Yeah, she—"

"She?" Otto interjected.

For half a second, Aris forgot to breathe. Then she steeled herself to brazen it out. "Yeah, *she*, Otto. Don't tell me you have no female friends." She'd learned she could say just about anything without arousing suspicion as long as she made it sound like a challenge.

"None I tell Dori about," he said, but he grinned, no sign of suspicion in his eyes.

Dysis swatted him with her hand of cards. "You're a lug. Let Aristos talk."

Aris sighed. "My friend, back home, she married another good friend. He was Military, too, got sent away when they were Promised. He was injured, though, so he's back home, probably for good."

Galec stared at his cards. "Was it bad?"

"Firebomb burned away half his face," she said, glancing at the older man. "But he's in pretty good shape, considering."

"It's a tough break," he said, "something like that happening. But at least he's home. And your friend got to have her wedding day."

Aris smiled, the pain in her heart easing. "You're right. That's the important thing."

"Can we play now?" Otto flicked his cards at her. "You have a punch in the face waiting for you."

Suddenly, a disembodied voice echoed from the stationpoint intercom. "All soldiers, report to the briefing room immediately."

Aris stood as the room filled with the sound of squeaking chairs and thudding boots. "We don't have a briefing scheduled for tonight."

Dysis shrugged, her brow furrowing. "Maybe something's happened."

"It has," Pallas said, unfastening his digitablet from its port and moving to join them. "I just saw it on the news. Ward Vadim is out of quarantine. She's about to give a statement."

ARIS SAT with the rest of her unit, eyes locked on the monitor at the front of the briefing room. Commander Nyx, Major Vidar, and the other officers stood at attention along the wall.

"I must thank the people of Ruslana for your patience as I've recovered from my illness," Ward Vadim said on-screen. She was standing before a panel of windows, probably in the lobby of the Ruslana Council Building. Beside her, Amadi Balias, Ward of Safara, stood at a respectful distance. What was he doing there?

"It has been a difficult journey, especially with the loss of my dear husband while I was unwell. I would not have been able to overcome these trials without the expertise of Atalanta's finest menders and the support and well wishes I have received from all across the Five Dominions. I would like to assure you my illness has, finally, run its course, and I am now able to resume my duties as Ward of Ruslana." She paused. Applause filled the room.

When her audience, a small group of reporters just off screen, quieted, she said, "I am as aware as you are that these are confusing, dangerous times with much at stake."

Even bathed in the golden, wholesome lights they'd set up, Aris thought the Ward looked pale and thin. Then she remembered how she'd felt after *her* long illness and was impressed at how well the Ward looked after all, at the fact that she was actually standing.

Ward Vadim continued, "Therefore I felt it necessary to sit down with Ward Balias, as my first order of business, to discuss the reports of abuse to his people and atrocities on the battlefield in Atalanta. As Ward of Ruslana, it is my duty to give each person an opportunity to defend themselves against their detractors."

Aris found Ward Balias's expression unsettling; he was smiling a little, his chin held at an arrogant angle. In news vids, he often looked like he knew something the reporters didn't and was pleased at the knowledge.

She glanced at Dysis. Her sectormate was tense, all of her attention and energy focused on the monitor.

"In our meeting," Ward Vadim said, "Ward Balias laid out proof that the information my sources had gleaned was, in fact, *mis*information. On each point of concern, he presented me with facts instead of conjecture, with truth to counter the lies."

There were murmurs from the soldiers watching, so loud Lieutenant Daakon had to hush them. On Aris's other side, Pallas stared silently at the screen, his face pale.

"As such," Ward Vadim continued, "I have determined that the sanctions I instituted before my illness are not, in fact, in the best interests of the people of Safara. And indeed, they could be dangerous. I cannot in good faith continue a policy that has endangered the health and lives of everyday Safarans."

Explosions of "What?" and "No!" sounded around the room. Aris's own, "I can't believe it!" blended into the uproar.

"Silence!" Lieutenant Daakon shouted.

Ward Vadim turned to look at the Ward of Safara. "But I am deeply concerned by your actions against Atalanta. I must caution you, Ward Balias, in pursuing this ill-advised war. The access to the Fex River you seek will only cause prolonged suffering and strain your dominion's resources. With our newly agreed-upon trade terms, surely ongoing fighting is no longer necessary?"

The briefing room was suddenly eerily silent as the soldiers waited to hear Ward Balias's response. Aris held her breath. Could this be the end of the war? *Right now?*

Ward Balias nodded, smiling wider, and all of Aris's muscles tightened, as if she were caught between his strong, white teeth. As if she were his prey.

"Thank you, Ward, for meeting with me," he said. "I applaud your decision and am grateful, on behalf of my people. It is a difficult time to be Safaran. Clean water has become our most precious commodity. We are still struggling to contain the resultant illnesses and starvation. My desire for access to the Fex River is only out of necessity; I cannot stand to watch my people die when I have the means, however unpleasant, to save them. Our new trade agreement with Ruslana will go a long way in sustaining the lives of Safaran children and their hard-working parents. And I will, of course, take your recommendations concerning our current conflict with Atalanta under advisement."

Reporters began calling out their questions to the two Wards.

"Off," Commander Nyx snapped, and the monitor went black. Lieutenant Wolfe and the other officers stood frozen, silent, as the room erupted in loud-voiced questions and conjecture. Lieutenant Daakon rubbed his chin, shaking his head in disbelief.

Major Vidar's eyes narrowed and his lips twisted in disgust, and Aris knew what he was thinking, because she could feel *her* eyes narrow, *her* lips twist into the same expression.

She'd seen Ward Balias's face. His glee. He'd gotten exactly what he wanted from Ruslana.

And it wasn't going to stop him.

CHAPTER THIRTY

WHEN ELOM CAME TO RELEASE GALENA FROM THE BED, HE brought her a brush so she could tidy her hair. He also gave her a new white robe and five extra minutes in the washroom. She cleaned up, reveling in the feel of clean fabric against her skin, the pleasing pull of the brush through her tangled hair—wishing she didn't feel so suspicious of the new routine.

After she ate a meal of brown, tasteless soup and a hard chunk of bread, Elom invited her to sit on the chair by the bed. "It's time for your statement," he said.

Galena looked toward the door. Was there a camera crew? She heard nothing; the silence hadn't changed in all the time that she'd been here. Glancing back at Elom, she narrowed her eyes. If she was the captive she felt like, why would he let a camera crew in? Why would he give her the opportunity to denounce her kidnapper?

"Will you be filming it?" Perhaps he would coach her on what to say, film it himself, and give the vid to that pretty reporter, as if he really were her mender, carefully managing her illness and stress after the death of her husband. What did he want her to say?

Elom bared his teeth in what she supposed was meant to be a

smile. His bald head gleamed. "You misunderstand me," he said. "One moment." With that, he abruptly left the room.

Galena sat with her hands folded in her lap and awaited his return, because it was the only thing she *could* do. The one thing that kept her going was the very thing that had most assuredly led to her imprisonment—her job. She was Ward of Ruslana. Her absence from her post could only go on so long. They *needed* her. She couldn't just disappear.

The door hissed open. Elom reentered the room. Galena sat up straighter and looked behind him for the news team. But he was alone, a small black digitablet in his hands. Why was he holding that? Did he mean to record her using the device?

Her confusion mounted when he placed it on her knees, as usual.

"Is it another report? I thought you said we were going to record my statement."

Elom tapped the screen. "We are going to watch your statement."

Galena froze. Slowly, the world tilted. What did he mean, *watch*? She hadn't made any statement. How—

And suddenly there she was, her pale blond hair smoothed back in her habitual style, a flattering pink shirt warming the color of her cheeks.

"But, how . . . I don't understand." Galena whispered the words, felt them slip sluggishly though the rapidly closing space in her throat.

Because she wasn't the only Galena speaking.

"I must thank the people of Ruslana for your patience as I've recovered from my illness," the woman on-screen said. "It has been a difficult journey, especially with the loss of my dear husband while I was unwell . . ."

Galena's hands and legs were shaking so hard Elom had picked up the digitablet and was holding it for her. He *wanted* her to hear every word, to watch her own mouth form each one.

"I would like to assure you my illness has, finally, run its course, and I am now able to resume my duties as Ward of Ruslana."

NO!! Galena didn't know if she screamed it aloud or only in her mind. She threw herself out of the chair to the door and scrabbled desperately to open it. It didn't move. From a distance she could hear her voice, *hijacked by that imposter*, faint beneath the words clawing their way from her throat, "You can't have my life! I won't let you *have my life*!"

A sting. The cold fire of Elom's medigun slid through her veins.

This time, she was grateful for the darkness.

CHAPTER THIRTY-ONE

A SHUDDERING CRASH YANKED ARIS FROM HER DREAMS. HEART in her throat, she blinked against the utter black of the room; the wind didn't so much whine as scream as it pummeled the thin outer wall behind her head.

A fist pounded against the door. "Haan, Latza. Up! Now!" As the door slid open, she threw a panicked hand to the back of her neck. She always slept with the diatous veil on, but—

The almost imperceptible smoothness of the device against her fingers addressed her most pressing fear. She was still Aristos.

"Report to the landing pad. Now." Major Vidar's voice rumbled louder than the storm.

"Yes, sir!" she responded, Dysis's voice a softer echo.

Aris leaped from the bed and closed the door behind Vidar as he stalked down the hall.

Dysis touched the pad on the wall, and light flooded the room. "What's going on?" she asked, her deep voice still thick with sleep.

Aris yanked on her pants and threw a shirt over her head. "I don't know, but it can't be good."

A gust of wind buffeted the building.

As soon as they were dressed, they ran along the dimly lit hall toward the door that led to the fleet of wingjets.

Major Vidar was standing with Lieutenants Wolfe and Daakon at the edge of the landing pad, rain pummeling them.

Aris and Dysis skidded to a halt in the open doorway.

Vidar nodded toward the swirling mass of water and lightning that roiled beyond the yellowy lights of the landing pad. "Can you fly in this?" he shouted.

Aris glanced out into the flashing darkness and felt a shock of fear down her spine. Fly? In *this*? But she nodded, because she knew Major Vidar wouldn't ask unless it was absolutely necessary.

"We got an emergency call from Tarik, a village in Southwest Mittaka." Major Vidar briefed them as they ran to the nearest recon and transport. "There was a raid by Safaran troops, and several of our men were injured." He stood by the wing of the transport, his face all hard lines and angles, wet with rain. He stared at Aris. "They can't wait till morning."

She nodded. "Yes, sir."

He turned away to look at Wolfe. The thin man gave a curt nod as another flash of lightning lit his ghost-pale face. They climbed into the transport with Daakon.

Aris and Dysis flung themselves into the smaller recon, snapping the dome closed as quickly as possible, though they were both already soaked.

"Can you really fly in this?" Dysis hissed.

Aris didn't look at her. She flipped on the nav panel and felt the faint hum beneath her feet as the wingjet came to life. She squeezed the controls tightly, to calm her shaking hands. The rain clattered loudly against the glass dome.

She'd been caught in weather like this once in Lux. She'd been flying along the cliffs, just playing around, when a storm blew up out of nowhere, flinging her through the air as if she were a child's kite. At first she'd panicked and fought against the wind, fought to steady herself, to push through the wild currents of air.

And she'd almost crashed.

But a fanax had been caught in the storm as well, and through the gray, whip-fast clouds, she'd seen it, flipping and coasting *with* the wind. The bird had *let* the gusts fling it through the air, only correcting when it got too near the cliffs. And slowly, circuitously, it made its way back to the grove, to its home among the scattering leaves.

She had followed, riding the currents of the storm, until it finally blew her out behind her parents' house, and she'd landed, legs shaking and hands, wet with terror, clinging to the controls.

"I can do this," she told Dysis, as she slammed the helmet on her head.

At first, it was like that day on the beach. They swayed and slid through the darkness, thrown by the wind. In the black, it was harder to tell the direction of the air currents, how close they were to land, but she kept an eye on the nav panel and felt the shudder of the wingjet in her bones, telling her which way to go. Lightning lit the sky with the precision of a sat-photo; rain stood out as individual drops of light against the black, over and over as they tumbled through the dark.

Thunder boomed. The recon shivered as if it were about to rattle apart.

"Oh Gods," Dysis whispered, her deep voice shaking. "We're going to die."

Aris, busy at the controls, didn't answer.

Gradually, as they moved away from Spiro, the lightning and crashing thunder eased, though rain continued to whip against the dome of the wingjet, leaving silvery trails along the glass.

"Aristos, any damage from the storm?" Major Vidar asked over the comms.

"No, sir. We're fine."

Dysis grunted under her breath, disagreeing.

"You?" Aris added.

"All fine," Lieutenant Wolfe reported. He sounded as cool and remote as ever, and she wondered what it would take to break through his impassive shell.

"ETA ten minutes, Specialist. Be on your guard. There could be enemy fire." Major Vidar's voice crackled, gruff but otherwise expressionless, in her ear. Dysis shifted in her seat, hands ready on the gun controls.

But as they flew over Tarik, the land beneath them and the sky around them stayed quiet. No flashes of airfire lit the night, no attack set the nav panel beeping. Even the lightning had subsided; all Aris could see were faint strikes in the distance. The only sounds were the hiss of static over the radio and Dysis's breathing. A faint orange flickered far beneath them. Even with the rain, the village still burned.

"Sir?" Aris asked, after she'd done two loops above the village.

"Turn on your heat sensor," came the reply.

Dysis touched the nav, and a red-purple glow filled the cabin. In the center of the village, a group of strong signals revealed the presence of the injured soldiers. Elsewhere, deep purple blobs showed the buildings that were still aflame.

"Center of the village." Aris gave Major Vidar the coordinates.

As he commenced the retrieval, Aris circled above, scanning for any signs of the enemy. On her third pass, she noticed something on the nav screen. At the end of the far eastern row of houses, a slight hint of pink.

"Do you see that?" She pointed to the spot.

Dysis nodded. "Yeah. Looks like we missed a couple."

"Sir, we've got another heat sig, to the east."

"We're almost done here. Stand by," Major Vidar said.

"The heat signature's weak, sir," she replied.

"Hold your position."

She followed the transport's progress on the nav panel as Lieutenant Wolfe returned to the air, then flew down toward the house with the faint pink glow.

Vidar's voice crackled over the radio, startling her. "Need you on the ground this time, Haan. Debris on the landing pad.

There's a small clearing behind the building, just to the south of a patch of trees. Can you make that work?"

Aris dipped toward the house, studying the topography on the nav panel. "Yes, sir."

"The soldiers we recovered said they have two men unaccounted for. They were sent to confirm that all civilians were evacuated. We need to get them out of there."

"Will do, sir." Aris slid into a hover above the open space.

"Easy now," Dysis whispered. Her hands clutched the gun controls and she kept staring out of the glass toward the ground, as if she could see through the darkness.

With a jolt, the wingjet touched down.

"Report as soon as you find the soldiers," Major Vidar said. "We'll look for another landing spot, where we can transfer them to the transport."

"Understood, sir." Aris touched the nav panel, and the dome hissed open. Taking a deep breath, she flicked a glance at Dysis. "Ready?"

Dysis nodded. They slowly emerged from the recon, solaguns held at the ready.

Cold pricks of rain stung Aris's face. Her helmet protected her head, but the wind still tore through her clothes, leaving an icy chill. The air was thick with the smell of mud and mold.

After listening for any sign of movement, Dysis flipped on her solar-powered torch.

One side of the roof had collapsed, but the entrance was clear. The open door thudded rhythmically against the remains of the wall.

"Do you see anything?" Aris whispered as she followed Dysis into the entryroom.

The torch light flicked across a broken table streaked with rain, a mud-splattered tile floor, and what looked like shattered plates, bits of food still clinging to them.

The shiver of unease under Aris's skin intensified. "Major Vidar, do you know if the soldiers found civilians?"

Dysis stepped further into the house, sweeping the torch before her in slow, steady arcs.

"No, but I'll find out," Vidar said. "Keep moving, Specialist. The signals are fading."

Aris swallowed as she stared at the destruction; every room they walked through was torn apart, water pouring through still-smoking holes in the roof. In one, a dollhouse had fallen on its side, tiny furniture and figurines scattered across the floor.

"There," Dysis said quietly. The light touched on another open door, with the black hole of a stairwell beyond.

A chunk of solar panel tumbled through a hole in the roof, crashing to the tile floor in a rumble of noise and water. Aris sucked in a breath and tried to keep the solagun in her hands steady. Behind her, something popped. She whirled, weapon raised, but it was only a broken lamp in its death throes, flashing and hissing in the whisper of the rain.

"Still no other heat signatures, sir?" She panned her torch back and forth, wishing the light could fill the dark corners. There were too many places where someone could hide.

"Losing the signals we do have."

"Got my back, Hummingbird?" Dysis asked, before descending into the basement.

Aris took another deep breath. "Right behind you."

Dysis stopped so suddenly at the bottom of the stairs Aris bumped into her. "What?" she whispered. She couldn't see past the taller girl's shoulders.

Slowly, Dysis moved out of the way.

In the pale light of the torch, Aris saw an overturned bench. Behind it, a series of humps scattered across the floor.

"Are those . . ." Aris's light revealed more details. Two Atalantan soldiers sprawled on the floor, face down, their legs spread straight. Behind them, a woman, her faded blue eyes wide, mouth open in a soundless scream. A man's red-clothed arm flung out toward her. And between them, so small and pale in the shaking torchlight, a girl. She was lying on her side, as if sleeping, the front of her lovely white dress stained black with blood.

"By all that is holy . . ." Aris whispered. It was a plea, soft as a breath, painful as a scream.

Dysis moved quickly to check for pulses, to assess their wounds, but Aris stood frozen, staring at the little girl. As Dysis bent over the open, unseeing eyes, Aris felt a wave of ice crackle and snap through her, from her head to her heart to her shaking knees. She should be over there, helping . . . she needed to . . .

"We've landed and are heading to your location." Major Vidar's voice filled her head as darkness threatened to overwhelm her. "Report!"

Dysis stood from where she'd crouched by the bodies. Their eyes met.

"They're dead, sir." Dysis's voice was quiet, but it didn't shake. "Two soldiers. And . . ." She swallowed. " . . . and a family. There's a child, sir. No more than five years old. They were all shot in the back of the head. Recently. They're still warm." Light flashed along the mottled bundles of clothing. Dysis's hand, the one that held the torch, was trembling. "They were executed, sir."

Aris couldn't breathe.

She stumbled up the stairs, banging her knee and bruising her hand as she tripped. With a hoarse sob, she fell out of the darkness and into the rain.

Strong arms grabbed her, hauling to her feet. She screamed.

All her training, everything she'd learned, left her. She scratched and writhed, shrieking, as she struggled to escape, tears soaking her cheeks. In that moment, everything about her that was *Aristos* broke, exposing who—and what—she really was.

Without warning, the restraining arms released her and she fell hard against the shattered tile floor. A figure loomed over her.

Major Vidar.

CHAPTER THIRTY-TWO

THE FLIGHT BACK FROM FELN, WHERE THEY'D DELIVERED THE surviving soldiers, was agonizing. Aris and Dysis didn't speak. Major Vidar's voice filled their helmets, giving details to the nearest stationpoint with the manpower to retrieve the bodies of the family and soldiers who hadn't survived. By the time they landed at Spiro, the cloud-choked sky was easing slowly from black to gray.

Aris dropped from the recon to the tarmac on stiff legs.

"Specialist Haan, debrief. Now." Major Vidar swept by her, heading toward the building. She fell in behind him, with a quick, panicked glance over her shoulder at Dysis, who was following slowly, Lieutenant Daakon at her side. Dysis shrugged miserably, face pale.

Aris wiped again at her face. She knew her skin was red and blotchy; not for the first time she wished the diatous veil could hide pigment as well.

Men didn't cry.

But she had, when she'd seen those bodies. When she'd seen the blood spattered on the small face of the little girl.

Even now, the image refused to fade.

Dysis had checked the cellar for other victims. Her face had gone tight and grim, but she'd stayed in control. And Aris, she'd run weeping from the building and straight into Major Vidar's arms.

Now he would reveal Aris's secret, expose her for the weak, whimpering woman she was. Expose her and send her to jail.

It was over.

And the worst part? At that moment, as she followed him into the building and slumped into the chair before his desk, as he closed the door and turned to her, she didn't care. She didn't care about her future, or Calix, or flying. She didn't care about anything.

Except that she'd been too late to save that little girl.

"I'm so sorry, sir," Aris said, her voice close to breaking, as Major Vidar sat on the edge of his desk, facing her. "I didn't expect . . . a family. And . . . and they were dead. And then I thought you were the enemy grabbing me . . . I'm sorry." She swallowed, desperately hoping she wouldn't cry again. How could someone shoot a person like that, so clinically? And a *child?* Two soldiers and a whole family, gone from this world. Her stomach churned and for a moment she thought she might be sick.

Major Vidar cleared his throat. This was it. When he told her he could see through her disguise. When he sent her home.

"What you saw today upset you." It didn't sound like a question, but he paused as if expecting an answer.

"It did, sir." She resisted the urge to wring her hands.

Vidar leaned back slightly against his hands and studied her. "Your reaction is perfectly reasonable."

"What?" Her eyes widened.

"The things we see in this job . . . they can turn the stomachs of the most hardened soldiers." He stood and paced the room.

She wondered what awful things he'd seen.

"But." He paused. "Even among the horrors of war, a soldier must do his job. And, above all, he must protect and support his team. Your sectormate, Specialist Latza. He can't have you falling apart when it might put him in danger."

She nodded, remembering with shame how she'd fled, how

she'd cried while Vidar had barked orders at her. For the first time, she considered what could have happened if the Safaran soldiers hadn't been gone. If they'd been lying in wait, deeper in the cellar. And she'd left Dysis there, alone.

"I know," she murmured. "I'm so sorry, sir."

"You're the best flyer I have," Vidar said, so matter-of-factly Aris hardly noticed the compliment. "I need to be able to trust that you can handle this. Can you prevail, even when faced with the kind of tragedy you saw today? If only for the safety of your team?"

The questions echoed in her mind, with the memory of the executed child. *Can I?*

She grimaced. "I feel like it's my fault, sir. We were so close, if I'd flown just a little bit faster, gotten there sooner, maybe—"

"You must fly as fast as you can, save as many as you can." Major Vidar stopped pacing and turned to look down at her. "But you won't be able to save them all. Can you accept that?"

She met his eyes. Their intense blue reminded her of the ocean at noon on a hot day. He looked tired, younger than he did when he stood before them in formation. As if he'd relaxed his guard, just for a moment.

Without warning, she heard another voice in her head: Dianthe's. *You have a gift. I can't let it go to waste. This isn't about your mender friend, it's about saving lives. Don't you understand that?*

And she did. She finally understood. "Yes, sir," she said, nodding. "But I'm going to try. To save them all, I mean."

"I won't ever tell you not to try." His smile was small, sad. Then he straightened, again the hardened officer. "Now, get out of here."

Aris stood slowly, taking a second to collect herself.

Major Vidar moved behind his desk, to the monitor mounted there.

She paused at the door. "Why was the family there?" she asked. The question had been nagging her. "Wasn't the village evacuated?"

Vidar didn't look up from the screen. "It was. They didn't get out in time."

"Do . . . do you think there were other families there, sir?"

He looked up at her, his eyes softening just a hair. "Commander Nyx will debrief the team shortly. In the meantime, don't talk to anyone about what you saw. This kind of information must be handled carefully. Ward Balias will find it more difficult to deny war crimes now that we have proof."

But Aris wasn't thinking about Ward Balias. She was wondering how those Safaran soldiers had stomached shooting that little girl.

They *weren't* soldiers. They were murderers.

Chapter Thirty-Three

"How did you do it? How did you give that imposter my face?" Galena asked, the next time Elom came to free her from the bed.

He grunted, jerking his finger toward the washroom door.

"The electrodes, that awful hum under my skin? Was that it?" She moved her legs to the edge of the bed but didn't stand. When he didn't say anything, she continued, "It's really quite clever. Why assassinate me and risk someone with similar ideals being elected when you can just transform me into an ally, with no one the wiser?"

Still no response. And what did she expect, that he'd reveal his entire devious plot?

She dropped her feet to the floor with a slap. "Clever, maybe, but stupid, too." She slid toward Elom, as close as she could stand, and growled, "It takes more than a face and a voice to be Ward. To be *me*."

Elom turned, finally, and smiled at her, teeth gleaming. "Of course it does. That's why you're not dead yet. Why we won't kill you as long as *you're* Ward. You're going to tell us all your secrets. You're going to help us make the deception work."

Galena glared at him. "No chance."

The corner of his mouth twitched, as if he were about to laugh. "We'll see."

"Who's 'we'? Balias?"

"*We* do not have to share *our* secrets." With another disturbing smile, he pointed to the washroom again.

When she emerged, he waited until she sat before placing a tray on her lap. This morning, breakfast was dirty yellow custard and a glass of milk that smelled strongly of goat.

It had to be Ward Balias. Galena's shoulders sagged. And now Fake Galena was recovering at home, Josef—who might have seen through the disguise—conveniently dispatched. Now that imposter could support Balias in his effort to destroy Atalanta. Galena had been elected only a year ago; that meant four years of wreaking havoc before the next election.

And there was nothing she could do.

She handed Elom the tray and paced her cage, her body shaking. All would think she, Galena, had betrayed her country. And the trust of Atalanta. Of Pyralis.

The world would fall to ruin at her hands.

She paused in the corner of the room, leaned forward to rest her forehead on the cold, smooth wall. But they hadn't found her son. If they did, Elom would gloat, show the footage on his digitablet, make her watch. So they hadn't found him. Yet. *Don't go home*, she prayed with every fiber of her being, as if just by willing it, he would be able to hear her. *Don't go home. Keep fighting.*

Elom could threaten her all he wanted; she wouldn't tell him anything. Someone would see Galena had changed. *Someone would guess.*

Pyralis would know.

Chapter Thirty-Four

A trail looped around the Spiro stationpoint. It curved through the dusty, open plain and up into the scrubby woods that surrounded the grounds, and every morning the S and R unit ran it together.

In the quiet twilight after dinner, when all the other men went to check comms or play cards in the rec room, Aris found herself pounding along the dirt track. Three months ago, she never could have imagined running willingly, but now it was the only thing she could do to be alone and think. Her feet pounded, her limp finally gone. It had disappeared so gradually she'd hardly noticed.

The evening was cool and smelled of dying leaves and earth. She missed the salty scent of the ocean, the sound of the waves. As she ran, she imagined the ebb and flow of her breath was the lap of water on sand.

Phae had finally written her back. But her words provided no comfort or absolution. Instead they dogged Aris; she couldn't outrun them.

You're right. I don't understand. How can you think so little of our friendship that you couldn't be bothered to come to my wedding?

It was colder in the long shadows of the trees. The air burned against her cheeks as she pushed herself faster, felt sweat slide down her back in the groove between her shoulder blades. Phae's words, her parents' worry . . . it had all worn a spot of pain into her heart that twinged and ached like a sore muscle each time she thought of home. But what bothered her more than the pain was the size of it. It was so small, a pebble in the groundswell of anger she'd felt since she'd seen that murdered girl.

She pumped her arms harder as she flew up a rise in the path. Her life in Lux had become a pleasant dream that lingered with the scent of basilis and wine upon waking. It was nothing like the nightmares that drove her forward now.

Sweaty and trembling with exhaustion, she swept onto the hard landing pad and slowed to a walk, slipping into the building just as night fell.

"Evening," Pallas said as he passed her in the corridor. She nodded, continuing to her room. Dysis would be wondering where she was. She'd been out later than she'd meant.

She touched her key to the wall beside the door. "Sorry Dysis, I'm . . ."

She stopped short. Her sectormate was standing in the middle of the small room, head tipped back slightly, gazing into Lieutenant Daakon's eyes. He was very close to her, the fingers of one brown hand threaded with hers.

At the sound of her voice, they broke apart.

"Uh . . ." Aris stood there, still panting from her run, mind whirling. *What the blighting hell is going on?*

Without a word Daakon pushed past her, eyes down, the lines of his round face tight. For another second, Aris and Dysis stared at each other, mouths open. Then Dysis moved to close the door, yanking Aris into the room.

"Dysis, what were you *doing?*"

"Don't look at me like that." Dysis flopped onto the bed. She propped her head on her bent arms and stared at the ceiling.

Aris sank onto the edge of her cot, still trying to erase the tenderness of Daakon's expression from her mind. It wasn't a look she'd been meant to see.

And then she realized what it meant. "You told him about us, didn't you? How could you!" Her voice shook. They'd lose their positions, be sent to jail. *Gods, not now.*

Dysis glared at her. "Of course I didn't tell him. I'm not stupid."

Aris relaxed slightly, confusion creeping in. "But then . . . you're saying he thinks you're a man?"

"He doesn't seem to mind, does he?" Dysis's broad cheeks were flushed red as boiled crawgigs.

"What exactly was going on? Because it looked . . . well, it looked like—"

Dysis sighed. "It was nothing. We've been doing extra training together, that's all. He's been helping me a lot. He's actually really nice, you know?" She paused, but when Aris didn't say anything she continued, "We just . . . started talking."

"You were *talking?*" Aris bent to pull off her boots. Had she imagined it? No, they'd been holding hands. And Daakon's dark eyes had been locked on Dysis's. It had almost looked like they were about to kiss, or they just had.

"Yeah, talking." The hard edge was back in her sectormate's voice. "About *Jax.* Lieutenant Daakon seemed okay with me asking, so I kept pushing, hoping he'd have information for me." She sat up, drumming her hands on her knees. "And then, I don't know. He seemed interested."

"You can't *let* him be interested!" Aris stood. The panic was building again, tight in her chest. "What happens if he touches you? Or takes your clothes off? He thinks you're a man and you're not! Do you think he'll just smile and say that's okay? Not to mention he's an officer! If he finds out, we're *gone*."

In a flash, Dysis was off the bed and standing nose to nose with Aris. "I know. Don't you think I know? But he'll tell me, now, if he hears news of Jax. He'll—"

"So you're using him? That's your big plan to find Jax? Seduce the Lieutenant?" Aris gave her a little shove, forcing more space between them.

Dysis threw up her hands and turned away. "Yes, that's my plan," she said, but there was bitterness as well as anger in her voice.

"But that's . . ." Aris didn't know what to say.

"What? Terrible? Cold?" Even though Dysis's voice was soft, it hummed with tension. "I don't have a *choice*. Jax isn't safe, like Calix."

Before Aris could protest, Dysis went on. "And so what if I *did* have real feelings for Daakon? It's like you said. Nothing can ever happen between us."

Aris stood in the center of the room and watched Dysis pace. It was like being in a cage with a lion. She had the sense that if she moved, even a little, Dysis would snap. "I'm sorry," she murmured, trying to calm her own pounding heart.

Dysis didn't say anything. She moved to the doorway of the washroom and stared at herself in the mirror. Her face twisted, and then she was scrabbling at the back of her neck. There was a click, and as the veil shimmered and melted away, her face crumpled, and tears ran down her soft female cheeks. She turned away from the mirror, her head down. "Holy hell, I can't do this."

"Dysis . . ." Aris held her hands up, palms forward, in a placating gesture. Without warning, the taller girl threw herself into Aris's arms.

"I can't. I know I shouldn't like Daakon, but I do. And every single time he looks at me, my heart breaks because he doesn't *see* me. He's not looking at *me* that way." Dysis sobbed against Aris's shoulder. "And you know what *I* see everyday? I see Jax. Every time I look in the mirror, I see him staring back at me. We always looked alike, but now, with this. . . ." She threw her diatous veil onto her pillow.

Aris led Dysis to her cot. They sat, Aris's arm still around her sectormate's shoulder.

Dysis sniffed. "I have nightmares," she whispered, "Jax is in a hole in the ground, and there are worms crawling on his face, and I'm there, right beside him, and I can feel them, too, against my skin . . ."

Aris tightened her arms around Dysis, trying to banish the awful image called up by her words. "Shhh . . . shhh . . ."

"I'm here to *find* him, blight it, and then I'll catch myself making moon eyes at Daakon and wishing I really *was* a man!" She choked back a sob. "I don't know who I am anymore."

"Dysis, you're Jax's sister. And you're a gunner. That's who you are." Aris swallowed her own sob. "It's all going to work out, remember? You're going to find Jax, and I'm going to find Calix, and in the meantime, we're going to keep on saving lives. Remember what we said?"

"About winning the war?" The bitterness in Dysis's voice was an ugly thing. "Grow up."

Aris gave her a little shake. "Stop it. What we're doing here *matters*. You know that! We found that family in Tarik, didn't we? Because of us, Ward Nekos has proof that Safara is killing innocent people. We've already made a difference."

Dysis pulled herself slowly from Aris's arms. Her face was red and streaked with tears. She shook her head, as if clearing it. "They would have found that family, that whole village, without us. You're here for Calix, and I'm here for Jax. That's all. We'll stay until we find them, fight with them as long we can, but when they go home, we'll give this up. Go home with them. That's all this is."

"Is it?"

"You know it is."

Aris twisted her hands together. Would she really leave her unit, just walk away, if Calix returned to Lux? "I forget sometimes that we're not real soldiers." She glanced at Dysis. "We're not, are we?"

Dysis heaved a deep breath and wiped at her face. With a final sigh, she straightened her shoulders and carefully replaced her veil. In a moment, she looked like the Dysis Aris knew—square jaw, steady brown eyes. "Well, we are for now."

Chapter Thirty-Five

Pyralis sank onto the edge of his bed with a sigh. The meeting with his advisors had run long—hours and hours too long—and he wanted nothing more than a hot shower and the oblivion of sleep. Not that he'd find oblivion.

He kneaded the perpetual sore spot at the base of his skull. These days, when he finally closed his eyes, all he found were endless parades of numbers. Numbers of soldiers dead. Numbers of villages razed. Refugees. Civilian victims. The months it would take Tech engineers to develop new, more effective weaponry. The number of times he thought about comming Galena, only to change his mind before hitting send.

She was back in Ruslana now, buddying up to Ward Balias. Letting Atalanta burn.

What he couldn't figure out was why. What could possibly have happened to make her change her views so completely? Was it the memory loss her menders spoke of? Some other, more nefarious design? Was she being coerced? Threatened?

He kept playing their last conversation in his head, wondering if he'd missed something. Her blank politeness. Her shock when he'd touched her hand. Was it all some kind of message? Was he meant to know something from what she *didn't* say? How she *didn't* act?

But his spies had found nothing suspicious. And his feelings were just that. Feelings. No proof that she'd done anything but change her mind.

He dragged off his clothes and stepped into the shower, his thoughts as tangled and elusive as a basket of writhing snakes.

He'd thought he could trust her, that their past connected them. When she'd been willing to help Atalanta, he'd hoped she might even have forgiven him. But she'd made it clear her support had nothing to do with him. The sanctions and all the rest were because she believed it was the right thing to do. She wouldn't make his dominion pay the price for his transgressions.

When he'd moved to Ruslana so many years ago, he'd just been selected for Military. He was young, Promised, and bright-eyed at the thought of learning Military strategy from some of the most influential officers of the Ruslanan Military.

He'd met Galena in a park. It had been freezing, snow was falling, the world was white and gray. She was dressed in a yellow coat, like a bolt of sunshine. When he'd said hello, that's all it was meant to be. Just a short conversation among strangers enjoying the chilly afternoon.

It was never supposed to go as far as it did.

Pyralis let the hot water run over his face and rush in his ears. He'd thought he was doing the right thing, leaving her. He had his commitments back in Atalanta. Bett was waiting for him. He'd thought it was the noble, honorable thing . . . ripping out his own heart for his dominion. And the Promise he'd sworn to keep.

But he hadn't thought about what his decision would do to Galena, or what would become of *her* heart. And he never guessed how his choice would haunt him, what it would cost him, even after twenty-five years.

There had been bitterness in her eyes often enough recently. Perhaps despite her noble words, she'd let the ugliness, the pain, win. It was disappointing. But who was he to pass judgment? How could he expect her forgiveness, when he'd never forgiven himself?

Chapter Thirty-Six

Commander Nyx called an early-morning formation to announce the next mission. "We've received reports that a combat wingjet went down last night in a particularly hazardous portion of Mittaka. From radio transmissions, it is believed at least one of the soldiers survived. There were three men aboard. Because of the terrain and number of targets, we'll be sending only one recon and transport jet for this mission. Haan, Lieutenant Wolfe, you're our flyers. Latza, gunner. Galec, retriever. Stay here for briefing with Major Vidar. The rest of you are dismissed."

Aris stood at attention as the rest of the soldiers filed back inside the building.

Please let it be Revening or Mekia this time.

She told herself that's what mattered, finding Calix, but truthfully, she'd settle for any mender stationpoint, Calix or no Calix, if it meant the soldiers they were retrieving were still alive.

"Specialist Latza, you'll be gunner for Lieutenant Wolfe," Major Vidar said. "Aristos, I'll fly with you."

Aris flicked a glance at Dysis, surprised. It was the first time she'd been called for a mission without her sectormate as her gunner.

As Aris climbed into the recon beside him, she tried to

divine the reason he'd chosen to fly with her. Did it have to do with the last mission? Was it some kind of test?

She tightened her damp palms on the controls and fought to keep her face still. She would keep it together this time. It was her job. She would do it right.

"First time out on your own?" Major Vidar asked, after they'd flown in silence for a while.

She covered her start of surprise with a shrug. "What do you mean, sir?"

"This your first time out of Lux?"

"No, sir. I've spent some time in Panthea as well, sir."

"I've never been to Lux. You like it?"

Granite cliffs and the yellowy green of the olive groves filled her mind. She smiled. Her hands relaxed a little on the wingjet controls as she pictured the turquoise of the ocean, the loveliness of the scenery. "I love it there. It's as beautiful as the women, sir." Men always talked about women when they mentioned home.

"Are you Promised?"

"No, sir." She was going to leave it at that, but heard herself saying, "I have a girl, back there. But I didn't think it would be fair to ask her to Promise when I would be gone, not knowing when I'd return."

"Chivalrous, Aristos," Major Vidar said, sounding amused. "Don't you worry she'll decide to Promise to someone else? Or ring around?"

"Of course I—she wouldn't do that," she blurted, the question throwing her off. She snuck a glance at him. He'd raised an eyebrow, which pulled the scarred corner of his mouth up, accentuating his perpetual sneer. Flustered, she kept talking, "My girl . . . she's loved me since she was twelve, sir. She told me before I left that she'd wait, no matter how long it took. She wanted to Promise." It was strange to talk about herself this way, as if *she* were Calix.

"Ah. But you weren't ready." Major Vidar nodded.

"No, I was ready, sir. I just thought . . ." She didn't like the conversation all of a sudden. "Promise is all about growing closer, learning about each other. And we couldn't do that with me here. As soon as I get home, we'll be together." She could hear the defensiveness in her voice as she gave Calix's reasons.

Major Vidar seemed oblivious to her inner turmoil. "And what is she doing, while she waits so patiently for you?"

"She's just a village girl, sir. Works on her father's farm." That life seemed alien now. She could be describing a stranger. She tried to imagine going back to Lux with Calix, spending the rest of her life dusting olive groves. But all she saw was her father, leaning against an olive tree, smiling, hand up to shade his eyes as he stared along the line of softly rustling leaves.

That was *his* place, not hers.

Without warning, tears built behind her eyes. She fought them back, refusing to explore the tangle of feelings clogging her throat. This wasn't the time. Major Vidar wouldn't be so understanding if she got emotional now, with no dead bodies or danger threatening.

"And what about you, sir?" she asked, pushing back just a little. "Are you married?"

Major Vidar laughed, but the sound had a bitter edge. "Not even close." He shifted in the small jet, his shoulder brushing hers. "You know what they say about women and scars, Aristos?"

She had no idea. "Yes, sir."

"Don't believe it. More frightening than appealing, I've found."

She snuck a glance at the pink line that ran along his pale skin. Personally, she thought it was neither frightening nor appealing. More . . . intriguing. She cleared her throat and returned her eyes to the nav panel.

He sat up and pressed the button on his helmet. "Lieutenant Wolfe, I've got a lock on the location. Going in for a closer look. Stand by."

"Standing by, sir," Wolfe's voice scratched over Aris's headset. At Major Vidar's order, she dove and glided closer to the tree line. Vidar switched on the heat-seeking setting on the nav panel.

Below them a carpet of trees rippled along curving ridges, the remains of ancient roads peeking through the green in twists of pale gray. A flash caught Aris's eye. At first she thought it was a missile, but her nav panel didn't go crazy, and Major Vidar didn't react.

"Did you see that, sir?" She dipped lower and turned to make another pass.

"What?" He looked intently out the window.

"A light—there." She pointed right in front of them and slowed further to get a better look.

A rocky hill emerged from the trees, an umber island in an ocean of green. Upon the hill two small figures jumped up and down. One of them held something that flashed.

"They're signaling us, sir!" She halted their forward movement and hovered, slowly losing altitude. "Shall I land?"

Major Vidar stared at the men, eyes narrowed. "No. They're gesturing toward the trees, perhaps toward their downed wing-jet." He pressed the button on his helmet, "Lieutenant, we have visual confirmation of the target." He gave the coordinates. "Commence retrieval. Haan and I are going to try to find their jet; still one soldier unaccounted for."

He turned to her. "Can you see the direction they're pointing? To the West."

"Yes, sir." She tipped her wing at the men, to acknowledge their message, then wheeled away in the direction they'd indicated.

"Do you think their comrade is still alive, sir?" she asked as they flew over the trees, looking for signs of the crash.

"He survived the landing, at least. Those men wouldn't be sending us elsewhere unless they believed he was still alive. But he's injured, or he'd be with them."

"Sir, why wouldn't the Safaran soldiers who shot them down go after them?" Just the thought gave her chills. According to

Commander Nyx, they'd gone house by house in Tarik, executing anyone who wasn't able to evacuate in time.

"It's possible they did but couldn't find them in the rough terrain. Or they assumed there would be no survivors."

"That's lucky, sir."

His voice took on a stern edge. "Luck has nothing to do with it, Aristos. Whatever they did, it was a tactical decision. And we've made our own choices in response."

Another reflection caught her eye. "Sir, I see something." As she pointed, a red splotch bloomed on the nav panel.

He peered down at the wreckage as Aris did a sweep.

The downed wingjet had dug into the side of a hill; the ground was black and bleeding where the jet had ripped through the forest. There was the narrow, churned-up path through the trees, but no larger clearing.

"Do you think you can land there?" he asked.

She tipped her wings and skimmed along the tops of the trees to get a better look. Without answering, she straightened and manipulated the pedals. Soon they were hovering, and she smoothly took them down. At the last minute, she made a slight adjustment to account for a deep groove through the cleared dirt.

When they were on the ground, she released the glass hatch and climbed out onto the wing.

"Weapon," Major Vidar barked.

She pulled her solagun from its holster. It still felt awkward in her hands. They climbed down to the broken earth and made their way to the wreckage.

A great sooty gouge marred the silver side of the jet, and one wing bent unnaturally against the hill. Aris didn't see the third soldier. Her stomach tightened, remembering the sight of the family in Tarik, the little girl's white dress stained with blood. *Please let him be alive.*

Major Vidar waved her closer and went to inspect the cockpit. The glass had spidery cracks along its domed surface, so it was hard to see inside.

Suddenly, with a hiss, it slid open.

"You the cavalry?" a hoarse voice asked.

The words were followed by a cough. Aris let out a relieved breath. Major Vidar leaned into the cockpit to inspect its occupant. "Identify yourself."

"Lieutenant Illias Santos, sir. You are?"

"Major Vidar and Specialist Haan. Search and Rescue. We've come to retrieve you. Do you know the extent of your injuries?"

The man coughed again. "Maybe some internal bleeding, broken rib. Broken leg, and a pretty nasty bump on the head. I can't walk, so my comrades went to find help."

"Aristos, get up on the wing there. We're going to make a chair with our arms and lift him out. Understand?"

She nodded, mouth dry.

She positioned herself on the upper wing, so Vidar would have to support more weight as they were lifting Lieutenant Santos down. All the physical training had strengthened her arms and legs, but she was still weak compared to him.

Santos hissed when Aris slid her arm under his leg. After a moment, Major Vidar grabbed her hand. Her other arm went behind the Lieutenant's back, linking with Vidar's. There was no time to worry about how large or "manly" her hands felt to him. She was desperately afraid that her palms would sweat and her grip would slip, that they'd drop Lieutenant Santos and cause him even more pain. She took a deep breath and tried not to look at the blood. *You can do this*, she coached herself, saying the words over and over in her mind like a prayer.

"On three." Major Vidar said. Santos put his arms across their shoulders; his fingers bit into the flesh at the base of her neck. Vidar nodded at him. "You ready? This will probably hurt."

Lieutenant Santos tensed. Through clenched teeth, he said, "Get me the blighting hell out of here."

"One. Two. Three."

They lifted.

Santos screamed.

Once, when Aris was much younger, a donkey had fallen

from one of Lux's cliffs. It had broken its back but hadn't died. For hours it screamed, until men from the village could get to it and put it out of its misery. The sound had given her nightmares for months.

This was worse.

Her knees wobbled. She almost dropped Santos, but Major Vidar tightened his grip on her hands and kept pulling. Through the noise, he said, "We have to keep going. If we don't, he'll die."

With a final heave, they freed his legs and lifted him from the cockpit. At that moment Santos slumped, his head rolling back and the inhuman scream gurgling to silence.

"Is he dead?" Aris asked, panicked.

Major Vidar waited until she could get her feet on the wing nearest the ground. They stepped down slowly. "No. Just unconscious. It's a mercy."

She couldn't help but agree. Slowly they hauled the limp body to the jet.

"Sir, where will Lieutenant Wolfe land?" She was out of breath and the words came out raspy and quiet.

"He won't. Santos is going in the recon." He heaved himself onto the wing and she had no choice but to follow, Santos lolling against her.

"But sir? The jet's only equipped for two passengers. With the weight of three, I don't know if—"

"I'm not going back with you."

"You're not?"

As gently as they could, they lowered the Lieutenant into the seat.

Aris released Major Vidar's hands and slid her arms free. Immediately they ached as blood rushed back into them. She rubbed her wrists and stared at him in alarm.

Vidar reached behind his seat and grabbed a pack she hadn't noticed before. He clapped her on the shoulder then hopped down from the wing. "Reconnaissance mission. Solo. Commander knows." He glanced back at her. "Good work today,

Aristos. Now, get Lieutenant Santos to Revening. Call it in to Lieutenant Wolfe. Until I get back, he's in command."

Aris watched him walk into the woods, her mouth open. He was going to hike off into the forest, just like that?

A groan from her injured passenger got her moving. She ran to the other side of the wingjet and slipped into her seat, closing the glass shield. She swept her hand over the display to start the jet, then pressed the button on her helmet. "Lieutenant Wolfe, this is Specialist Haan. Major Vidar and I retrieved the third soldier. I have him ready to transport to Revening. Major Vidar said he had a solo mission to complete?" She ended the sentence as a question.

With a crackle, Wolfe replied, "Message received. We've retrieved the other soldiers. Taking off now. You can follow us to Revening."

She pulled slowly on the controls, and the wingjet rose. When she was clear of the trees, she glanced at Lieutenant Santos. His helmet had fallen off, and the bump on his forehead was oozing blood. Accelerating in a wide arc, she headed in the direction she'd come from. Ahead, she could see the transport. She tapped the nav panel and adjusted her flight path to match the other wingjet's. Soon, they were speeding through the air.

Revening. Would Calix be there?

Oh Gods, what if he was?

"So what is it, really?" Lieutenant Santos's cracked voice made Aris jump.

"What, sir?"

"What's your real name?"

She glanced at him in surprise. His eyes were open, and he was clutching his side. "What do you mean, sir?"

Santos shook his head. The movement made him cough. "Aristos is a man's name," he said gruffly. "And you're no man."

CHAPTER THIRTY-SEVEN

For a long moment, Aris couldn't breathe. The wingjet's wing tipped. With an effort she got it under control.

Finally, she whispered, "Don't tell."

Lieutenant Santos laughed. Aris looked at him, and he bent his head, revealing his Military brand. In the bright sunlight streaming into the cockpit it glittered faintly.

Aris gasped. "Wait. Are *you* . . . ?"

"Illiana Santos. At your service." The soldier coughed.

"How did you know?" It was the first coherent thought that came to mind.

"When I put my arm around your neck I could feel your veil. You should be more careful."

Aris blushed and reached back to touch the device self-consciously. "I was a little busy trying to save your life, sir. Uh, ma'am?"

"Sir is fine," Illiana said, amused. "I only told you because you have to help me get to a specific mender at Revening."

"Of course." Aris was struck with a sudden thought. "Is his name—I mean, what's his name?"

"Zaro. Why?"

Oh well. She'd have been more surprised if Illiana *had* said

Calix. "It's nothing. A . . . friend . . . from my village is a field mender. I was hoping we would meet sometime."

"At Revening?"

"Maybe. I'm not sure."

"His name?"

"Calix Pavlos." Aris held her breath.

Illiana cocked her head. "I've never heard of him. But that doesn't mean he isn't there. Revening is a big stationpoint. Where else have you tried? Mekia's close."

Aris's heart knocked wildly against her rib cage, creating a seasick feeling in the pit of her stomach. She took a couple slow breaths through her mouth, willing her heart rate to slow.

"Haven't been to Mekia. I haven't actually been to many mender points yet." Oh Gods, she could see Calix today. What would she do—say—when they met? Would he recognize her? Suddenly, she really did feel sick.

Illiana reached out to pat her arm and winced. "Don't worry. You'll find him." She leaned back and took a couple deep breaths.

"I can't believe . . . you're really a woman?" Aris asked. Her hands were starting to shake. *Focus on the mission. Don't think about Calix.*

Illiana's laugh came out as a hiss. "Silly question. I think you meant to ask why. 'Why are you in Military, Illiana? Why are you here in this blighting hellhole with your bone sticking out of your leg?'"

Aris swallowed. She hadn't seen the bone. She forced herself not to look. "So, why?"

"Because I got selected Commerce. *Me.* The tallest, ugliest girl in my year. I'd have been stuck running numbers for a store, or stocking shelves. All the good Commerce placements go to the pretty ones. The only thing I'm good at besides calculations is flying. And flying is a *lot* more fun."

"So you just joined because you wanted to be a flyer?"

"There are more of us than you think. The dominion will

never openly admit it, but women make the best flyers. They recruited me. My unit has two other female flyers as well." Illiana's breathing was ragged, the words dragging more and more slowly from her chest.

"How long have you been doing this?" Aris asked lightly, trying to mask her alarm. *Keep her talking. Keep her awake.*

"Two and a half years, since just after the war began."

"That long?" Aris's mind reeled. "What did you tell your family? Don't they wonder why you never visit?"

"I'm not close to my family." Illiana winced and shifted, her face going deathly pale.

"Does it bother you?" Aris asked, thinking of all the lies she'd told. "That you have to be in disguise? That you don't get to be yourself?"

"It's not a disguise for me. This is who—" Illiana coughed, sounding for a moment as if she was choking, "—I am."

"Is there anything I can do?" Aris asked, glancing worriedly at her passenger. "You don't sound—"

"Just get me to Zaro," Illiana said on a groan. "Fast. I think I'm going to pass out again."

Aris flew the rest of the way in silence, her heart pounding.

ARIS LANDED the wingjet as smoothly as she could. Illiana was still unconscious, and her breathing had become a strange gurgling. Each time it hitched in her throat, Aris's stomach clenched.

After opening the dome, she stepped out onto the wing and jumped to the ground. Lieutenant Wolfe had just landed. Soldiers were filing from his transport: Dysis and Galec, and the two rescued men. They rushed to her recon.

"How is he?" one of them asked. He was slight, not much taller than Aris, but his head was large and boorish, with heavy dark brows and a bulbous nose. He had two broken teeth; the stumps were still there, jagged and yellow.

She glanced up at Illiana, slumped against the side of the wingjet. "I don't know. He needs a mender as soon as possible. He asked to see someone called Zaro. Can you find him?"

Just then a flood of white-robed menders and assistants spilled from the long, windowless building that lined the landing pad. Revening was much larger than Spiro, and the buildings were older, just a single story, their flat roofs covered with massive solar panels.

The first mender to arrive at the wingjet was tall with a narrow face and golden eyebrows. "What have we got?" he asked, jumping on the wing to inspect Illiana.

"Are you Zaro, sir?" Aris asked.

"No." The blond mender didn't look at her; he was too busy inspecting Illiana's injuries.

"He asked for Zaro specifically, sir," she said, taking a step closer to the recon. What would she do if they didn't respect Illiana's wishes? How could she protect her?

"Move aside," came a voice from behind her. Through the crowd, which, in its controlled chaos, was efficiently arranging a stretcher and various machines in preparation for moving Illiana, a man wove until he was standing at her side. "He asked for Zaro?" the man asked, voice pitched low.

She nodded, staring at him. As he lifted himself up on the winget, Aris couldn't help but notice his arched brows and smooth skin, the graceful way his body flowed into place.

The blond mender helped Zaro shift Illiana onto the med-bed. She didn't wake, didn't make that horrible noise she had when Aris and Major Vidar had moved her. Aris took this as a bad sign.

She pushed around the broken-toothed soldier, who still stood beside her, and hurried to Zaro's side. The throng was breaking up now that Illiana was on the stretcher and hooked into a small collection of beeping, wheeled machines.

"Let me come with you." She hated the paleness of Illiana's skin, beneath the blood. "I have information on h—his injuries."

Zaro glanced at her, still steadily pushing the stretcher

toward the hissing glass door of the stationpoint. Whatever he saw in her expression made him nod. He moved Illiana into a small room with pale yellow walls at the end of the first long hallway.

When Zaro had shut the door behind them, he moved to Illiana's side and got to work.

"Are you a woman, too?" Aris asked quietly.

Zaro didn't look up from the patient. There was a quiet hiss as the medigun he held released its contents into Illiana's arm.

"So you know that much about the Lieutenant," he said.

"I won't tell."

"Of course you won't," he said. "You have your own secret."

"Is it so obvious?"

"If you know." Zaro glanced up and met her eyes. "If you're looking." Then he reached behind Illiana's head with gentle, precise fingers and released her veil. The flyer's face melted, reformed. In the end, she didn't look that different. Her features were harsh, her jaw blunt. She wasn't, as she said, beautiful.

Zaro moved to the wall by the door and pressed a button. "Caldi, Dex. Room Fourteen. Now." He turned to Aris. "Time for you to go."

Aris looked one last time at the still figure on the bed. "Will she be okay?"

"There's a lot of damage, and she's lost a lot of blood. Give me an hour to know for certain, but I believe she'll live."

The door opened, and two assistants filed into the room.

Aris was almost in the hall before she remembered. *Gods, how could I have forgotten?*

"Zaro?" she asked. The three were already flitting around the bed, white cloths turning red with blood, machines beeping and sucking and shooshing.

"Yes?" he said, without looking up.

"Is there a mender named Calix Pavlos here?"

"No," came the answer, before she had time to hold her breath.

She nodded, then closed the door behind her. Dazed, she followed the green glowing signs to the lobby.

No Calix. But Illiana would probably live, all because Aris had gotten her here in time.

CHAPTER THIRTY-EIGHT

ELOM WALKED INTO THE ROOM CARRYING THE FAMILIAR digitablet and an object Galena couldn't identify. It looked a little bit like a solagun, but it was thinner and made from a shinier material. The way he held it—so lovingly—made her heart quiver.

He didn't release her from the bed. He just raised the back so she was sitting up, her legs stretched before her.

"Come to torture me with another news report?" Galena asked, trying to brazen it out. She kept her chin up and met his glittering dark eyes.

"You're only half-right," he replied, with one of his little disturbing smiles. He dragged a metal stool into the room, screeching it against the floor like a dying animal, and set it by the bed. Sitting perched on its edge, he studied her face in silence.

"I'm going to ask you some questions," Elom said. "I would like you to think very hard before you answer. But you will answer." His eyes met hers and she could find no emotion, no empathy in their depths.

She nodded that she understood. "We've played this game before."

He smiled. "Not like this."

Galena glanced again at the object in his hand. "Why now? Why are you asking now and not before you gave that woman my face?"

"We had to make sure the procedure worked before . . ." he paused, ominously, ". . . taking the next step."

"I told you. I will tell you nothing."

"I respectfully disagree. You will tell me everything." Elom's unconcern sent a chill through her. "Now, where to begin. How about an easy question. What is your name?"

Galena tilted her chin up, just slightly. "Galena Vadim, Ward of Ruslana."

"Sadly, you are Ward no more. But we shall proceed. Who of your family still lives?"

She wanted to crush his face with her fist. "You know the answer to that question."

Before she'd even realized he'd moved, a line of pain erupted along the side of her face, from her forehead through the key brand at her temple to her chin. She screamed.

He sat back, the pointed tip of the mysterious device glowing with blue flame. The tears that streamed from her eyes made the pain worse; her whole face was in agony.

"Now, please answer the question."

She tensed against her bonds, wishing again for a way out, for the rescue she knew wouldn't come. Panic rose from her stomach to her throat. She opened her mouth, but the only thing she could manage to voice was a whimper.

He held up the object again, adjusting the intensity of the flame. She pulled against her bonds, trying to get as far away as she could. Scrunching her eyes closed, she whispered, "I have a son still living, that is all."

"Thank you for your honesty, Galena." Elom sat back slightly, as if satisfied.

He asked her about the members of Ruslana's Council, personal details about their families, what she knew of their non-work activities.

"I . . . I don't know," she whispered at one point. "I haven't seen these people in so long, I don't know if they still—"

He cut her off with another line of flame, this time across her other cheek and the edge of her mouth. Another scream ripped from her throat.

He painted her face with the fire until she told him exactly what he wanted to know. She told him as tears slid down her cheeks and her skin burned. Her arms ached from straining to protect her face. She talked until she had nothing left. Until she *wanted* him to kill her, so she wouldn't have to live with the knowledge of her own betrayal.

"It hurts, doesn't it?" He brushed a lock of hair from her face, not in a kind way, but to clear his canvas. "I've taken you from your family, your job. No one even knows you're gone. No one suspects that you're here, with me, giving up all your secrets. *Their* secrets. And the most delicious part?" He paused to draw a flourish on her skin. "I'm taking your face as well. Your friends would turn away from you in disgust if they saw you now. No one would believe you were Galena Vadim." He smiled. "You are nothing now."

It wasn't until his final question that Galena dared defy him.

"Where is your son?" he asked, passing the device from hand to hand. Everything about him spoke of a man relaxed, comfortable with his place in the world. His role as interrogator.

Torturer.

She relaxed her fists, turned her hands palm up in their restraints. An entreaty. To whom, she didn't know.

Closing her eyes, she shook her head.

The flame bit into the skin along her nose, between her eyes. She clamped her lips shut, terrified that if she opened her mouth to scream, she'd swallow fire. Inside, she begged for release, for it all to end.

The searing agony didn't stop, and Elom asked his question again.

Finally, when she felt sure she would die and welcomed the

darkness, she forced her blackened lips to smile. "I don't know where he is, but I know *you'll* never find him."

She couldn't tell anymore if he was touching flame to skin or not. Her face burned, would forever burn.

In the darkness, in the pain, she heard him say, "Hold on to that secret then, if you must. I have taken everything else."

And she knew, in the empty tatters of her soul, in the lines of fire in her disfigured face, that he was right.

CHAPTER THIRTY-NINE

FOR WEEKS, ARIS FLEW WITH MAJOR VIDAR AS HER GUNNER. Almost every mission, he'd order her to land, sometimes far from where the rescue operation took place, and he'd haul his pack onto his shoulders and disappear.

He never told her where he was going, and a day or three later he would appear at morning formation, as if he'd been there the whole time.

"You *really* don't know?" Dysis asked one morning, as they left the training ground. Major Vidar had just returned after another of these mysterious missions.

Aris shrugged, hiding her own questions behind bland nonchalance. "He never says."

"And you don't ask?" The wide door hissed open, admitting them to the building.

Aris gave Dysis a hard look. "If I was authorized to know, he'd tell me." Had she wanted to ask? Yes, a million times. She'd even tried once, but he'd ignored her. The truth was, she had so many questions. Where he went, how he'd gotten his scar. How he could be so cool and level-headed all the time, even when the world was exploding.

"Your ability to follow the rules is truly admirable." Otto made it sound like an insult.

"Who *cares* where he goes?" Aris grumbled. "It obviously doesn't concern us."

"I've never heard of officers going on solo missions like that," Pallas said, looking thoughtful. "It does make you wonder."

"Could it be something to do with Tarik?" Galec suggested. "Maybe he's looking for more evidence against Safara?"

Dysis pounded the flat of her hand against her leg as she walked. "If he is, I hope he hasn't found it. Tarik was enough."

"I don't know," Galec mused. "Helena says there are many who believe Ward Balias's explanation, that it was all a terrible mistake."

Otto harrumphed. "Only because Ruslana is backing him. The bacterium must have eaten Ward Vadim's brain. It's the only explanation for her nonsensical support of such a snake."

Pallas's shoulders tensed. "It's all such a mess."

As they rounded the corner, Dysis stopped abruptly. The Commander and Lieutenant Daakon were standing in the middle of the corridor talking.

"—getting closer. It's imperative we follow this lead quickly and discreetly," Commander Nyx was saying.

"Commander, is there news of my brother?" Dysis burst out.

Commander Nyx went still. Slowly, he turned to stare at Dysis, and Aris fought the overwhelming urge to flee. "Excuse me, Specialist," he said coldly and, turning to Daakon, "My office." Daakon nodded, shooting a wary glance at Dysis.

Aris reached to take Dysis's arm, to drag her the other direction before she said something stupid, but she didn't get a chance.

"Why is there no news of Jax? It's been months, and nothing! You could let me go and look for him. I could be doing something." Dysis sputtered, the words tumbling over themselves.

The red scars around the Commander's neck pulsed. "Specialist Latza. We've discussed this before. I thought I made myself clear."

Lieutenant Daakon took half a step away from Commander Nyx. It appeared to be out of deference, but Aris caught a hint of worry in his eyes. She rather thought Daakon was stepping *toward* Dysis, as if his instinct was to protect her. Well, *him*. Daakon still didn't know Dysis was a woman.

Otto elbowed Aris in the ribs; she turned to glare at him. He was backing away. Galec and Pallas were already halfway down the hall. They were smart to retreat, but she couldn't leave her sectormate. *Blight her.*

Commander Nyx continued, his voice icy, "There can be no possibility that you do not understand the rules you are to adhere to, so I can only assume you meant to be insubordinate."

Dysis's chin went up, but she blanched. "No, sir," she said gruffly. "I meant only to offer my services."

The air was so thick with tension, Aris could hardly breathe.

Commander Nyx raised his brows. "Well, then." He nodded to Lieutenant Daakon. "Please ensure Specialist Latza runs an extra three miles today."

Daakon gave a smart nod. "Yes, sir."

Dysis swallowed, but she didn't say anything more, for which Aris was grateful. Commander Nyx suddenly seemed to notice Aris lurking in the hallway and turned his scowl on her. She fought to keep her knees from shaking. With a final nod, the Commander barked, "Dismissed," and they hurried back the way they came.

"Why did you *do* that?" Aris hissed, punching her in the arm.

Dysis clamped her jaws tight, raised her chin, and kept walking toward their room.

Aris slowed. "Okay, well. I think I'll go check my comms, so . . ."

When Dysis didn't answer, Aris turned the other direction and headed for the rec room. She was desperate for a shower, but her sectormate obviously needed some cooldown time. She'd just send a quick comm to her parents with a new, hopefully more effective, excuse for not visiting. They were threatening to come see her in Panthea again; it was a blessing her father couldn't stand the city. Otherwise, she'd never have been able to put them off this long. But they wouldn't wait forever.

Truthfully, she wasn't sure what to do. Maybe if she hinted that—

Whomp. Someone flew around the corner and slammed into her, knocking her to the ground.

Somehow Major Vidar kept his feet, but it took him a second to regain his balance. "My apologies, Specialist. I wasn't paying attention." He reached out to help her up.

Aris stared at his outstretched hand for a beat too long. Would he see the ripple of the veil when they touched?

"Specialist?"

"Sorry." She gripped his fingers to pull herself up, then let go so quickly she almost stumbled again.

He made no derisive noise at her clumsiness, which was unlike him. As he pushed past her, she noticed the harried, faraway look in his eyes. He hadn't lost his hard edge, exactly, but he definitely seemed distracted. Had something happened?

She continued on her way, mulling over this question. Ignoring the heat that clung to her fingers from his touch.

In the darkness of her room, Major Vidar whispered her name.

Aris pulled on her uniform, still groggy, and followed him through the dim building to the wingjet landing pad.

"Sir?" she asked, her voice small in the moon-soaked night.

"Just us tonight, Specialist. Very dangerous mission. You ready?"

She nodded and stepped onto the wing and into the wingjet cabin. He settled into the seat beside her, his arm brushing hers. The moonlight glowed against his pale skin, highlighting his cheekbones and the straight line of his nose.

Before she could ask their destination, he tapped the coordinates into the nav panel.

She closed the shield, and they rocketed off into the night.

"Tell me about the girl," Major Vidar said.

Aris blinked. She was too tired to concentrate on flying and interpreting his inexplicable questions at the same time. "Sir?"

"The girl you left in Lux. Tell me about her."

She tensed, uncomfortable with the question. But she had to answer or risk giving herself away. So she thought of Calix, and how he saw her. "She has the most ridiculous hair, sir," she said, remembering the feel of Calix's hands threaded through her hair, the way he laughed when it flew wild in the wind. "It's long and dark, like the shadows of sunset on the sand."

"Most men begin with a woman's lips or breasts, Aristos. And you talk about her hair."

A tiny sigh escaped her lips, as she remembered the warmth of Calix's hands against her breasts, the pressure of his lips on hers. "Her figure is fine, sir. And her lips are soft, softer than anything I've ever touched." She wanted to tell him how smooth Calix's skin was, how his lips felt on her throat, on the hollow of her collarbone.

"Did you say goodbye to her properly at least?" he asked, his voice soft in the close darkness of the cabin.

For just a moment, she closed her eyes, imagined, as she had countless times since that night on the beach before Calix left, what it would have been like if he had let them make love, if they'd stayed there in their cave, let their legs entwine, really been together. "I wanted to. More than anything in the world."

The nav panel beeped, and she began her descent. The landing spot was at the edge of a cliff, a waterfall deep in the heart of Mittaka. In the moonlight the water flashed and winked at her as it threw itself over the edge.

The wingjet hummed onto the ground but Major Vidar made no move to leave. Suddenly, Aris was very aware of his arm against hers, the sound of his breathing. The wingjet had no center console; there was nothing between them but the darkness.

"Do you miss her?"

She tried to imagine herself before the selection ceremony,

when her future with Calix had stretched happily, painlessly before her.

"I . . ." Her voice faded into the rumble of the waterfall. She turned toward Vidar's shadow, saw the thin gleam of his scar. He was staring at her. For an infinite moment, they looked into each other's eyes.

Before Aris could take a full breath, his lips crushed against hers. His hands clasped her face, and somehow, suddenly, she found herself pulling him closer, he was filling the cockpit, pressing her against the curved side of the shield.

She felt the warmth of his body against her, gasped as he teased her lips open with his tongue. Somehow she'd slid sideways on the seat and her leg was wrapping itself around his back, drawing him down to her.

Her loss of control was complete. Liberating. One simple truth filled her mind: She wanted him.

He ran a hand down her neck, gripped her waist, his mouth hot on hers.

Everywhere he touched her, she burned.

"Aris . . . ." He whispered her name and somehow it was the right one, her true name. She didn't know how he knew, didn't care, didn't dare respond except by arching her hips against his. She let her hands slide along his face, felt the slight bump of his scar, traced it from his eye to his lip.

He turned his head slightly and took her finger in his mouth.

She moaned.

"Aristos?"

The voice wasn't Major Vidar's.

With a gasp, she yanked herself out of the dream.

The room was still dark, and her legs were tangled in the sheets, her tunic hitched to her waist. She was panting.

"Are you well? You were . . . making noises." Dysis sounded like she couldn't tell whether to be embarrassed or concerned. "Were you having a nightmare?"

"Blighting *hell*." The words exploded from her chest. Aris

tried to relax, tried to settle her racing heart. *What the hell was that?*

"Yeah, it was a nightmare," she said, finally. As soon as the lights flipped on she was out of bed and heading to the washroom. She didn't look at Dysis.

When she was disguise- and clothing-free, Aris turned on the shower and let the cool water pound against her hot cheeks.

She was just missing Calix. Spending a lot of time with Major Vidar on all these special missions. It was just her subconscious confusing what she really wanted with what she had to deal with everyday.

I want Calix and no one else.

Later, as she lay in bed, she drafted a comm to Calix, saying the words over and over in her mind, so she'd remember them until she could get to the rec room the next day.

> *Calix, I miss you so much. There are so many things I wish I could talk to you about, so many questions I want to ask you but know I can't. Sometimes I wonder . . . I get this feeling like everything I've thought about the world, everything I've thought about myself is all upside down and inside out. I start to think maybe I don't know anything at all. But I know if you were here, you'd help me figure it out. Be careful. Aris*

CHAPTER FORTY

THE TREES OUTSIDE PYRALIS'S OFFICE WHIPPED BACK AND forth in the wind. Heavy storm clouds darkened the sky, but it hadn't started raining yet.

Standing by the wall of glass, Pyralis watched Kellan's reflection pace back and forth. His anxious energy and wild hair made him look like he'd been struck by lightning.

"The heads of the other sectors want you to call a meeting," Kellan said. "They need reassurance we're doing everything we can. And the Tech sector has several new weapons at the final stages of development. We could—"

"Set up the meeting with the sector leaders." Pyralis didn't turn around. "And another one with the head of Tech. We need to get those new products to our soldiers as soon as possible."

Kellan's reflection nodded as he made notes on his digitablet. "Also, troop strength is weakening in the Mittaka region. Do you want to redistribute several units from along the Fex?"

Pyralis sighed. "I suppose we'll have to. But send word to the riverside villages that their protective details—fire fighters, law enforcers, all of them—should report for combat training. We need them to be ready if Safaran forces break through our defenses. And send an extra squadron of wingjets to patrol the river."

"Got it," Kellan replied, tapping furiously on his tablet.

"Contact my most senior commanders. Move up our next scheduled vid call to tomorrow. That's all, Kellan. Thank you."

Silence met Pyralis's words. He turned; his assistant still hovered in the center of the room, running his hand through his already-disheveled hair. "What is it?"

"We've had reports that Ward Vadim is doing more than funneling resources into Safara," Kellan said, his furrowed brow betraying his reluctance to impart yet more bad news. "It's still unconfirmed, but it appears she's also provided them with a small supply of weaponry."

Pyralis fought the urge to bang his forehead against the wall of glass. "A small supply? What does that mean?"

After Kellan explained and exited the room, Pyralis sank into his chair. The reality of the situation—that Galena had completely turned against him—was more than he could bear. He thought back to when she'd wanted to start a life with him. Their secret, stolen romance so sweet and unexpected.

But, inevitably, he always returned to the same memory. The moment he regretted more than any other in his life.

They'd taken a holiday to the mountains just before he was scheduled to return to Atalanta. On their last evening, he'd walked up to the overlook outside the retreat to think. He'd known what he had to do, but the thought of leaving her, never seeing her again, had been eating at him for months. Now, with the moment at hand, he wasn't sure he could go through with it.

He'd stood at the edge of the overlook, studying the craggy points of the mountains dip in and out of a wispy line of cloud. Wondering what he could possibly say to Galena. How he could possibly say goodbye.

The sun sank along the edge of the furthest peak, gilding the snow that blanketed the valley below. Behind him, Galena called his name.

He had turned as she walked toward him. She was bundled in a white coat, the fur-lined hood framing her beautiful face.

When she smiled at him, her ice-blue eyes glowed as if filled
with the soft warmth of prayer candles.

He couldn't remember the words he'd chosen to break her
heart. But he'd never forget how that light in her eyes had died.

CHAPTER FORTY-ONE

Sorry it's taken me so long to write, Aris. There was another raid and we've been busy picking up the pieces. I wish I had good news, I wish I could say I enjoy patching people up, that the number of injured soldiers is dwindling, but it would be a lie. The truth is I'm exhausted. I've seen so many faces over the past months, so much blood. Every time I let myself think we'll have a reprieve, there won't be any violence for a while, another explosion lights up the horizon. And the bodies follow.

I miss you. Before I fall asleep, I always think of you, pretend you're resting in my arms with your hair spread across my chest. As soon as I get home, you're going to get us one of your father's mangoes, and we're going to sit on the beach and watch the sunset and eat mango until our faces and hands are sticky. I haven't had fresh fruit in weeks.

I love you, Hummingbird. Must go now. It never ends.

ARIS STARED AT THE WORDS ON HER DIGITABLET. HER FINGERS were poised to type a reply, but she didn't know where to begin. She didn't know how to quiet the guilt that welled up in her heart each time she read his words.

She had dreamt of Major Vidar again, just last night. And each day she had to stand in formation, fly missions with him, sitting there in the cabin of her wingjet, the fabric of his uniform brushing hers.

"Specialists, report to the gym. Now." Major Vidar's voice made her leap halfway out of her chair. She glanced up at him and immediately looked away, her cheeks burning.

"Yes, sir," she murmured with the others. She tapped the screen of her digitablet; she'd have to write Calix later.

The unit convened in the old sock-scented room Aris had entered her first night at the stationpoint. As usual, she was stuck at the front of formation with the other short men. Major Vidar stood before her, along with Lieutenants Daakon and Talon.

She snuck a glance at Vidar. Why *him*, of all the soldiers she could have dreamed about? She still didn't understand it. Looking at him, at his pale skin, icy blue eyes, and the scar that ran along his cheek, at the sharp edges of his nose and jaw, the pale gold of his eyebrows, she didn't find him handsome. He was well-muscled, a fierce fighter in hand-to-hand, as she'd seen often enough in training. But not handsome. Still, she thought, there *was* something . . . arresting about his features. If he was in the room, it was hard to look at anyone else.

"Tech sector's come up with a new weapon," Vidar began. "It's unlikely it will be of particular use to us, given its nature, but we'll be training with it and supplying each of you with one on all future missions."

He held up a thin round item, about the diameter of a stylus but longer, with pointed ends. It gleamed silver in the dim light. "This is a sythin. It works like a tranq, incapacitating rather than killing. But it works only in close quarters. You have to press this button—" He twisted it so everyone could see the small round knob on the side of the smooth metal, "—and hold the weapon against your enemy's body to activate it."

A few murmurs rumbled through the men. "How the blighting hell do we get close enough to use that without getting our damn heads blown off?" someone said, loud enough for Aris to hear. The tone of the whispers suggested this was the general consensus.

"Enough!" Major Vidar said, restoring silence to the room. "As I said, because of the mechanics and purpose of the weapon, it may not be useful to us in the field. But there's some indication it could sedate injured victims for transport without causing harm."

Lieutenant Talon flipped the lid off of a chrome box in the corner of the room. "Divide into pairs. We'll demonstrate how much pressure you'll need in order to make a contact with your target and which locations provide the easiest access, but you will *not* activate the weapons. I don't want any unconscious soldiers on my floor."

Daakon and Talon passed out the sythins. Aris and Dysis took their familiar positions across from one another, weighing the unfamiliar devices in their hands.

"Seems kind of pointless, no?" Dysis murmured, brandishing her sythin.

Aris twirled hers from hand to hand, thinking of the agonized sounds Lieutenant Santos made when they'd lifted her from the wingjet. If they'd been able to safely knock her out first . . . "As a weapon, maybe," she said. "But Major Vidar is right. For injured victims, I could see a use."

"Specialist Haan, please put your sythin down." Major Vidar's sudden presence at her elbow caused a sudden shock to run through her.

Aris dropped the sythin as if scalded.

Major Vidar gazed skyward in obvious exasperation. "I said *put*. As in place carefully on the floor. Not fling down as if it's going to bite you."

Aris stared at her boots. "Sorry, sir."

Without warning, he grabbed her arms, raising them until they shot straight out from her sides. The heat of his fingers seeped through her uniform. When he let go, she stood frozen. He turned to Dysis. "Specialist Latza. As I run through the best contact points, I'd like you to demonstrate on Haan." He glanced around the room. "Watch carefully, everyone."

First, he tapped Aris's neck with the side of his hand. Blood rushed to her face. He was so close, touching her, and all she saw was his faint scar, the soft fullness of his lips, while those *damn* dreams played over in her mind.

"The juncture of neck and shoulder is your best option," he said. "The sythin works through clothing, but it's most effective if you can make direct contact with skin."

He had Dysis jab the sythin at Aris's neck, cheek, armpit, belly, tapping each place himself first. Aris stood, arms wide, in an agony of anxiety. What if, this close, he noticed the subtle shimmer of the diatous veil? Worse, what if he noticed the way her pulse raced under her skin every time he touched her?

<hr>

WHEN ARIS KNOCKED over her boots, dropped her digitablet, and misplaced her jacket in quick succession while getting ready for bed, Dysis's voice broke the silence. "What's with you?"

"Nothing. Sorry. I'm just clumsy tonight." Aris flopped onto her cot, half-dressed.

"You've been on edge for days. Your hand-to-hand has regressed so much Wolfe is ready to throttle you." Dysis sat on her own cot, facing Aris. "Are you sure you're alright?"

Aris dropped her eyes to her hands and slowly finished slipping her sleep tunic over her head. What could she say? That every time Major Vidar barked an order, her dreams invaded her mind? That she was haunted by the memory—the fantasy—of his warm hands against her skin, even now? She rocketed to her feet. "I need to go for a run."

Dysis widened her eyes. "It's lights out in ten minutes. You can't run now."

Aris paced to the door and back, stopping before the cubby that housed her few belongings. Staring down at the pocked wood, she willed her heart rate to slow.

"Do you and Daakon still 'talk'?" Aris blurted out.

Dysis didn't answer right away. "Not the way you mean. He hasn't spoken a word to me beyond orders since you walked in on us."

"I'm sorry." Aris leaned against the wall. "What I said that night . . . I didn't mean . . ."

Dysis shrugged, eyes down. "It's for the best. You were right. There isn't any future for us, and it was dangerous, getting close to him." Her deep voice wobbled a little. "It's better this way."

"And Jax?"

"Daakon doesn't know anything. Maybe if he hears something he'll still tell me." She sounded so sad Aris wanted to give her a hug, but she sensed Dysis wouldn't welcome it.

"Still. I'm sorry about what I said that night. It wasn't my place."

"There's nothing to be sorry for."

Aris moved back to the bed and sat on its edge. She lowered her voice to just above a whisper. "I've had a few dreams about Major Vidar." She couldn't look Dysis in the eye.

"Okay."

"We were . . . kissing."

When Dysis gasped, Aris looked up. And almost laughed at her sectormate's hungry, knowing look. It was a distinctly *Echo* expression. With a gruff squeal, Dysis moved to sit next to her on the bed. "Tell me everything."

"You know I'm talking about a *dream*, right?"

"Of course. Sorry. I just haven't felt like a girl in a really long time." Dysis smiled wistfully.

"Me either," Aris replied, some of the tension in her shoulders easing.

"So, what happened?"

"Well, in one, we were on a mission. It was just us, and he was asking all these strange questions . . ."

"About?"

Aris cleared her throat. "Well, about Calix. And me. I mean, he was asking about my 'girl back home.' But I was thinking about Calix."

"And?" Dysis tucked her legs up and leaned close, practically bouncing on the cot.

"And . . . um . . . then we were kissing. That's all." A blush rose in Aris's cheeks.

Dysis leaned back on her hands and sighed.

"What do *you* think it means?" Her stomach still twisted at the memory. "I've been walking around feeling so blighting guilty."

Dysis giggled, which, with her low male voice, came out sounding disconcertingly like the grinding of gears. "Well, I don't blame your subconscious one bit. Major Vidar is luscious."

Aris grunted. "You're not helping."

Her eyes turned serious. "It doesn't mean anything, except that you're a human being with feelings. Calix has been gone a long time. And you're a woman stuck with nothing but men all day."

Aris snorted. That was no excuse.

"Just because we look like them doesn't mean we're not still women underneath." Dysis pursed her lips, and the skin around her eyes tightened. "I've dreamt about Daakon many times."

"Then why didn't I dream about Calix?" Aris asked, voice rising. "I should be dreaming about *him*, not . . ." She couldn't bring herself to say his name.

"You dreamt of Major Vidar because he shouted at us at the end of training those days and he was on your mind. Or because you flew with him?" Dysis waved a hand. "Believe me, you haven't been unfaithful to Calix."

Aris relaxed slightly at her words. "I've never thought about Major like that before."

Still, she was troubled. It wasn't just the dreams, really, if she was honest with herself. Over the past few weeks, she'd been so consumed by their missions, so busy flying for Major Vidar, she'd hardly thought of Calix at all.

"What if I've changed too much?" she whispered, more to

herself than Dysis. She ran a hand along her shaved head. "When Calix finally sees me, when I explain . . ." Gods, it could go so badly. "How much of what he loves about me is left?"

Dysis caught her eye. "You *have* changed. It could always be you who doesn't want him anymore."

Just then the lights went out.

"Go to sleep, Aris," Dysis said.

But she couldn't. Not for a long time.

CHAPTER FORTY-TWO

GRADUALLY, THE DEMONS EASED, THE FLAMES COOLED. THE torture stopped. Slowly, slowly, Galena began to remember what merely moderate pain felt like. Then mild. Then the absence of pain all together.

But still she kept her eyes closed and screamed.

Because when she screamed, when she writhed in the fiery aftermath of what he'd done to her, Elom left her unrestrained. When she was incapacitated with pain, she was free.

And while hell laughed in her face with the gleam of Elom's smile in the endless black night, she formed a fever-foolish plan.

AT LAST, when she felt ready, Galena stopped screaming. Eyes closed, she let her breath drift, whisper-thin, in and out of her lungs, and she kept her body still as death, her unshackled hands turned up at her sides.

It was hours before Elom entered the room, to find her quiet as the grave.

He had the nerve to whistle a cheerful tune under his breath as he bent to examine her. When he was so close his breath nearly choked her, she silently sucked in more air. *Now.* She shoved the base of her palm into his face with all the force adrenaline, terror, and rage could muster.

His head snapped back.

Galena surged up and hit him again. He fell back against the bed, and she clamped one of the arm restraints onto his wrist. He grunted and scrambled for her, hatred in his eyes, but his nose was pouring blood, his arm was chained to the bed and, for a few seconds at least, she was free.

She ran to the door, pulling her white robe closer around her, and slipped out of her room. Elom yelled and rattled the bed but she didn't turn around. She waved a hand over the blank white wall outside her cell, and the door hissed closed.

Her breathing was shallow, her heart pounding in her throat. Already she felt weak; though the near-coma state had been an act, she'd had little food and no exercise for a long time. But it didn't matter. She would keep going until she fought her way to freedom. Or they killed her.

She found herself in a long white hallway lined with doors. They were all closed. And there was no helpful red blinking light indicating the exit, as most buildings in Ruslana had. She listened for a moment, heard nothing but the faint rumble of Elom's voice within the room.

Only two choices: right or left. She chose right.

Her bare feet slapped on the cool carbonate floor as she fled down the empty hall. As she passed the endless blank doors she wondered if they held other prisoners, felt regret that if they did, she could do nothing to help. She tried sweeping her hand across the scan pads along the wall, but none of the doors opened.

Just as she reached the end of the hallway, a crash exploded behind her. She skidded around the corner, snuck a glance back, and found to her horror that Elom had already escaped and was barreling after her, blood streaming from his nose.

She ran faster.

Air heaved and rattled in her lungs and her throat burned. Her face burned. The muscles of her legs burned. Galena was a woman on fire.

She burst through a doorway into a large open room and slid into a table, slamming her shins against the bench bolted to the floor. The whole room was filled with tables where people sat eating something that resembled the brown soup Elom often fed her. The murmurs of conversation died and dozens of faces, most gaunt, some battered, stared up at her. Along one wall, pallets were set up. Along the other, a line of grim-faced guards.

Panicked, she looked around, desperately seeking a door, a way out. No one moved. She started to weave through the tables when she heard Elom's voice yelling, "Stop her!"

A rush of movement. All around her, people were standing up. Some started shouting. The guards sprang to action, raising their weapons. One slammed the butt of his solagun into a gray-haired man's head, knocking him out of the way.

She weaved through the rush of prisoners, trying to duck out of view of the guards. But they kept tracking her movements, pushing bodies aside to get closer.

A scream built inside her chest. She would not let them take her.

Dodging around a bench, she tripped over a young woman who cowered on the ground, arms up to protect her face. The noise increased, screams of pain now punctuating the chaos. Galena twisted and pushed in the opposite direction, narrowly avoiding a guard. In a break in the crowd, she caught a glimpse of Elom's bloody face. He'd made it to the doorway.

He kept a hand on his nose, and somehow, even through the movement and madness, his piercing, merciless eyes immediately found hers. She turned away, looked instead at a man sitting at the table beside her, an island of stillness. His short hair suggested that he was a soldier; the fresh and fading bruises that covered his face spoke of prolonged torture.

"Please help me," she begged him. Carefully, he stood, hands splayed across the table. His eyes shifted to the left once, twice. A signal. She glanced in the direction he indicated. There, through the crowd . . . she wasn't far from a wall. A door. In all the upheaval, the door had been left unguarded.

Out of the corner of her eye, she saw a guard raise his sola-gun. She turned away from him and ran toward the door.

But it was too far. She wouldn't make it.

Still, she didn't stop, didn't slow. She wanted her last moment to be her own. She would die knowing she didn't cower or beg.

She, at least, would know that she'd fought to save herself. To save her dominion.

A shot rang out, and an incredible pressure exploded in her back. She slammed into the floor face first. As the smooth, hard surface caressed the destruction that was her face, she gave the scream that had been building its release.

Too soon, the sound died.

With a final prayer that her son would be safe, Galena closed her eyes.

CHAPTER FORTY-THREE

"Two for two this week, Hummingbird," Dysis said as she leapt from the wingjet. "Not bad."

Aris grinned as she released the clasps on her body armor. A cool, early-evening breeze blew across the landing pad, raising goosebumps along her neck. "You and Lieutenant Daakon were amazing. That Safaran jet just screamed out of nowhere, and the way you two got the guns around in time. . . ." She whistled in admiration.

"And don't forget my superior retrieval skills." Otto pushed his way through the crowd of returning soldiers. His shiny, round face broke into a sly grin. "The cable wasn't even *close* to snapping this time."

Dysis rolled her eyes. "Only because you retrieved a five-year-old girl. A girl so small she was practically smothered by that belly of yours, I might add."

"Many women would consider that a glorious way to die."

Aris and Dysis erupted in laughter. Eyes flashing mischievously, Dysis had just opened her mouth to reply when Lieutenant Daakon bumped into her, throwing her off balance. In the second it took her to rock back on her heels, a blush bloomed along her cheeks. But all she said was, "Watch where you're going," under her breath.

Daakon didn't look back at their small group. Aris sighed and followed the straggling line of soldiers entering the building.

Galec caught up to them as they reached the door. His breath was coming fast and his eyes shone. "Did you hear?"

Aris raised a brow. "Hear what?"

He looked at Dysis and opened his mouth. "Your—"

"Haan, Galec. Commander's office. Now." Major Vidar's roar filled the narrow hallway.

Galec shrugged and hurried after Major Vidar, Aris trotting to keep up.

"Close the door," Commander Nyx ordered when they arrived. His bald head was shiny with sweat and his uniform the slightest bit rumpled, as if he'd been working all night. The rest of the officers stood along the wall. Aris glanced at Galec; he kept brushing a hand over his fuzz of ginger hair.

"We have a situation that must be handled delicately." The Commander's eyes flashed from his monitor to the row of men standing before him. "And quickly. Two wingjets: one recon, one transport. Specialist Haan, you'll fly Major Vidar. Galec, you'll be Lieutenant Wolfe's retriever. Lieutenant Talon will be gunner."

Major Vidar as her gunner, again. Lovely.

"I've received intel that a soldier has escaped from a Safaran prison camp," he continued. "He's probably injured and most certainly being pursued." The Commander ran a finger along one of the many scars that crisscrossed his neck. Aris glanced from his face to Major Vidar's; they both wore matching unreadable expressions.

With a sigh, he continued. "We believe the soldier in question may be Dysis's brother, Lieutenant Latza."

Aris's face lit up. She wanted to cheer. "That's wonderful news! Sir," she said, restraining herself with an effort. "Have you told Dysis yet? He'll be so—"

The Commander held up a hand. "Specialist Latza will not be part of this mission."

Aris looked at him in confusion. "But that's why he came here, to find his brother . . ."

"We don't have confirmation yet that Lieutenant Latza is the escaped soldier, and we know nothing of his condition. But if it *is* him, we must proceed with utmost caution. The Lieutenant is an important asset and, contrary to his brother's beliefs, his recovery is a top priority of this sector. I can't have Dysis on a mission this crucial and risk the possibility that his personal feelings could jeopardize our efforts. Do you understand?" He turned to Galec, who looked just as shell-shocked as Aris felt. "Specialists?"

Together they murmured, "Yes, sir." Aris tried to keep her face blank, but already she was torn between excitement for Dysis and terror that something would go wrong. Without meaning to, she glanced at Lieutenant Daakon. His jaw was clenched, and a vein throbbed at his temple.

"You have one hour to eat and then I need you all on the landing pad. Aristos, wait until after dinner and then tell Dysis to come see me," Commander Nyx said.

Before she could nod, Daakon stepped forward. "Commander, I've spoken with Specialist Latza about his brother before. With your permission, I'd like to be the one to tell him."

Commander glanced from his monitor to Daakon. "Very well, Lieutenant. I'm certain I don't need to remind you that it is paramount that Dysis understand he is *not* authorized for this mission. He *will* stay on point. You will impress on him the severity of punishment should he choose to disregard my order."

Lieutenant Daakon nodded. "Yes, sir."

"Galec, Haan. You're dismissed."

As they left, Aris could hear the murmurs of Commander Nyx speaking with Major Vidar and the other officers. She glanced at Galec. "Not letting Dysis go on the mission . . . I don't know. If it were my brother—"

"I wouldn't want to go," Galec said.

Her eyes widened. "But what if things went wrong? Wouldn't you blame the others, wonder if the outcome would have been different if you'd been there?"

Galec shrugged. "I'd be devastated regardless. And you heard what the Commander said. This mission is bigger than Dysis. As much as I hate to say it, I do think his feelings would get in the way."

"Still. Blighting hell." Aris rubbed a hand over the back of her neck, across the nearly imperceptible hardness of her veil. "I suppose we shouldn't say anything to him at dinner, but I don't know if I can hide it."

He smiled grimly. "You won't have to. There are rumors already. That's what I was trying to tell you earlier."

"Wonderful."

"Just get Otto talking. That heathen could distract anybody."

BUT DYSIS DIDN'T APPEAR for dinner. In fact, Aris didn't see her until she went back to their room to collect her body armor. Her sectormate was sitting on her bed, alone, when Aris walked in.

Dysis didn't look up.

"Did Lieutenant Daakon speak with you?" Aris asked, when it became clear Dysis wasn't going to say anything.

Slowly, Dysis nodded. Voice hoarse, she murmured, "He said he wanted to be the one to tell me."

"Are you okay?"

"I'm not allowed on the mission. I've been *ordered* not to save my brother." Her face twisted, teetering on the edge of emotion, but her voice remained flat, expressionless.

"I know. I'm so sorry."

Aris took a step closer and pressed a hand on her sector-mate's shoulder.

Dysis raised her face, her brown eyes glassy. "You bring him back," she said, the agony finally emerging, lining the edges of her words. "Whatever you have to do, you bring him back to me, you understand?"

Aris didn't remind her that they weren't even sure it *was* Jax. She didn't explain how dangerous the mission was, how it wasn't just up to her but to the entire team. She didn't do anything but nod and squeeze Dysis's shoulder once, hard, before leaving the room.

CHAPTER FORTY-FOUR

"THE VILLAGER SAW THE MAN, ON FOOT, TRAVELING EAST toward Bieza," Major Vidar said into his comm, transmitting to Lieutenant Wolfe's transport.

Aris listened as she steered the recon toward Hevensak, a small town near Atalanta's border with Safara.

"Hasn't Hevensak been evacuated?" she asked. "It's so close to the border. Bieza is farther east, and it's held by Safaran forces."

"The man's an old salt. He refused to comply with the evacuation order. Didn't want to leave his farm. It's not the first time he's called in something suspicious, apparently." Major Vidar glanced at her. In such close quarters, holding his gaze without blushing was a trial.

Quickly, she asked, "But—why didn't the villager offer to help the soldier, sir?"

To her relief he turned forward again, and she did the same. "He didn't know he *was* a soldier. He just saw an injured man in tattered clothing hiking under cover of darkness to the north of the village. The villager had the impression the man did not want to be seen. About two hours before the sighting, we got a hit on an old, unused emergency transmitter in the area. We think Lieutenant Latza—or whoever it is—activated that transmitter intentionally."

Aris concentrated on the topographical map on the nav panel. She was constantly making small adjustments to their course; the night was blustery and damp, the wind buffeting them as they flew.

"Enemy threat?" Lieutenant Wolfe asked over the headset.

"We believe the missing person is being pursued. Enemy engagement probable," Major Vidar replied.

Aris swallowed.

"Turning on thermal imaging," she said as they passed over a village to the east of their destination. Between here and Hevensak ran some of the roughest country in Mittaka. The rolling land was pocked with crumbling ruins, deep ravines, and hills that had been carved into vertical drops millennia before. It was beautiful, but deadly all the same.

"Sir." Aris gestured to the nav panel. Deep within a narrow ravine, the faint pink blob of a heat signature glowed. "Could that be Lieutenant Latza?"

Major Vidar nodded. Over the headset, he said, "Possible target located. At the bottom of the ravine. Proceed carefully." He glanced closer at the monitor. "Wolfe, you see the wider stretch at the southern point?"

"Yes, sir," Wolfe's voice scratched over the line.

"Land there. We'll head farther in, toward the target."

Aris skimmed along the edge of the crevice. She spared a moment's regret that it wasn't a daytime mission—flying in close quarters was easier when she could see where she was going instead of relying on the nav. She descended farther, until the black around her changed, felt more solid.

Aris fought back a sudden wave of claustrophobia. She glanced at Major Vidar. "It feels a little close in here. Are you sure—"

The nav panel exploded into panicked beeping, just as the night swelled with yellow light.

"Evade!" Major Vidar yelled, hands busy returning fire.

Aris pulled sharply on the controls, and the wingjet shot up out of the ravine. She flipped them sideways so they were hugging the edge of the cliff, giving Vidar a clear shot at the emplacement at the edge of the promontory. Another flash. She spun, narrowly avoiding the missile. How had the enemy's heat sig not shown up on the nav? The pink blob they'd seen had been small, human-sized. Not large enough to indicate a wingjet.

"Wolfe, come in. We're under fire. Status!" Major Vidar yelled into the crackle of the headset.

Aris sent them down into the ravine again, spiraling and swerving to avoid two more flashes.

Lieutenant Wolfe didn't respond.

"Wolfe, Talon! Status!" Major Vidar's voice was harsh. "Aristos, take us up, I want to give the sons of asses something to worry about."

She pulled out of the dive and blasted into open sky, taking her cues from the insistent beeping of the nav panel. Her palms damp, she kept her elbows pinned to her sides so her arms wouldn't shake.

The ominous silence on the headset lingered. "Sir, the transport . . ."

"Wolfe! Specialist Galec—one of you report immediately!" he yelled again.

Aris skimmed along the cliff a second time. Fire bloomed beneath them as Major Vidar's missiles found their targets. But still the flashes continued.

"Lower now, Aristos. Beneath them." His voice was tight, and instinctively she knew what he wanted to do. According to the map, the lip of the canyon protruded slightly, curving back into the hill. If they could destroy enough of the ledge, the whole thing would go.

Then a blast rocketed them sideways. They tumbled toward the canyon floor like a burst balloon.

"Aristos!" Major Vidar's voice thundered over the whistling of air through a gash in the wingjet's side.

Desperately she manipulated the pedals and levers. A

screeching crash erupted around them. They'd grazed the side of the cliff. Her fingers slipped on the controls.

In a last-ditch effort to save them, she increased their speed, engaging the jets to propel them forward, while yanking as hard as she could on the controls.

"What the hell?" Vidar roared.

"The thrusters are out!" she shouted. "But if I can get her nose up—" Slowly, too slowly, the wingjet's trajectory shifted. It wasn't going to happen.

She slammed her feet on the pedals, arresting their forward movement as much as she could. Without the thrusters she couldn't hover.

They were going to crash.

Aris did her best to slow them down and get the nose up, but in the end, they still went careening along the stream bed, plowing a gash through the mud-dark water. When one wing hit the cliff wall and they went spinning, a sudden jerk and *crunch* threw her back against her seat and into darkness.

CHAPTER FORTY-FIVE

ARIS AWOKE TO A RAGING HEADACHE. HER FINGERS SHOOK AS she touched them to the tender spot at the base of her skull, just above her veil, from which the pain radiated. When she returned her hand to her lap, it was sticky with blood.

She tipped up her helmet, which had jammed itself over her forehead, blinked a couple of times, and made the hazy observation that she could still see. Night was just beginning to ease into dawn.

What happened? Some instinct cautioned her not to say the words aloud, not to draw attention to herself.

A small noise sounded to her right. She turned her head. The pounding at the base of her skull increased, and she shifted her shoulders in an attempt to lessen the pain.

Beside her, Major Vidar breathed shallowly, his eyes closed. A gash on his forehead, just below the rim of his helmet, sheeted blood.

Sickness roiled through her belly. "Sir?"

He didn't respond.

She shifted again, carefully, to look out the hole of twisted metal and shattered glass that had once been the wingjet's dome. The memory flashed again before her. The concussion of explosions as the night lit with fire. The screech of metal as they tore into the ravine wall. The coppery smell of blood. The wingjet was facing into the cliff wall; she couldn't get a clear view of their location. She tapped on the nav screen, but it didn't power on. No way to tell if or where their enemy lurked. Or call for reinforcements.

After taking a couple deep breaths, she wiped her shaking hands against her knees. A glance at Major Vidar told her he hadn't moved but was still breathing.

"We've got to get someplace safe," she whispered. She nudged Vidar's arm. Nothing.

She reached out and yanked on the manual release for the dome. Praying that there were no Safaran soldiers waiting, weapons ready, she listened to the hiss as the remains of the shield slid back.

Cautiously, she twisted to look around. The wingjet had landed more or less on its belly. It listed slightly toward the shallow stream at the bottom of the canyon. Several yards away, its missing wing had pierced the muddy ground, stabbing into the air. A monument to destruction.

When she turned to look the other way, toward the north end of the ravine, she gasped.

Wolfe's wingjet.

She glanced around once more, ears strained for footsteps or the skitter of rocks down the ravine wall. The steep red-clay cliffs would be difficult to navigate, but it was only a matter of time before those Safaran soldiers came looking for them.

Ignoring the pounding of her head, she scrambled out of her seat and stumbled onto land. Solagun at the ready, she made her way toward the transport.

"Lieutenant Wolfe? Galec?" she called as she approached the wingjet. The jet was on its side, wedged into the wall of the cliff. It was still smoking trails of wispy gray that twisted up into the lightening sky and burned her nose.

"Lieutenant Talon?" She slowed, her steps dragging. A bird cried far above, and the sudden noise made her jump. She stared up at the rim of the canyon, where the missiles had come from, but saw no movement.

With a deep breath, she wiped an edge of the cracked glass of the shield and looked inside the cabin.

Galec stared up at her with one perfect, lifeless eye. The rest of his face was gone.

Wolfe and Talon, slumped beside him, were just two blackened husks.

Aris turned away, stumbling, and fell to her knees. Hands down, she retched into the shallow, sun-warmed water that wended its way through the canyon.

She closed her eyes, heaving, sobbing, wishing she hadn't looked, wishing she could go back, erase the last months of her life.

Erase everything.

"It's not worth it, it was never worth it," she mumbled, the vision of Galec's demolished face static and endless in her mind.

The skitter of kicked pebbles caught her attention. She froze. Without taking a breath, she moved into a crouch and worked her way along the shadow of the wingjet. A moment later, two black-uniformed soldiers rounded its nose.

Before she had time to think, she was shooting, the solagun clenched in both hands.

The two soldiers went down without a word, their faces drawn into grimaces of surprise and pain.

Still she kept shooting, blind with horror and sick with rage.

Eventually the solagun ran out of power. She didn't look at the soldiers, didn't wait to see if more were coming.

Instead, she ran.

CHAPTER FORTY-SIX

WHEN ARIS REACHED THE RECON, MAJOR VIDAR WAS STILL unconscious. She watched his chest rise and fall for a long moment as she panted and tried not to pass out.

They were the only two still alive.

But just because she saw no sign of other Safaran soldiers didn't mean they weren't there. She needed someplace safer, away from the jet, but she wouldn't be able to carry Major Vidar very far. She looked around, squinting in the glare of sunlight that had found its way to the base of the ravine. A few hundred yards away, she spotted a darker shadow along the canyon wall. A cave, maybe?

Aris scrambled onto the wing next to Vidar and shook his shoulder, more roughly this time. "Major!" she yelled, voice hoarse and throat burning.

A soft, pained moan left his lips, but he didn't open his eyes.

She yanked her pack and the aid kit from behind his seat and carried them to the darkness along the wall of the cliff. It was indeed a cave. It wasn't tall—she had to duck to avoid hitting her head—but the narrow opening went deep into the hill. It wasn't much of a hiding place, but it would have to do.

Aris stumbled back to the jet and shook Major Vidar again.

Blood still flowed from the wound on his head; she couldn't tell if he had any other injuries.

She stood back and looked at him, at his long arms and legs. He was so tall. How the blighting hell was she going to get him into the cave?

Taking a deep breath, she grabbed his arm and pulled until she could wedge her neck under his armpit. With a grunt she hauled him over her shoulder. When she stepped back along the wing to pull his legs free, his weight overbalanced her. She tried to keep her footing, tried to keep from falling, but he was too heavy, as inert as an enormous sack of donkey feed. His legs slid out of the jet and they both tumbled off the wing onto the muddy ground.

For a long time, Aris lay on her back, gasping. Major Vidar had fallen on her and knocked all the breath from her lungs.

With a groan, she sat up, head throbbing. Major Vidar lay on his side, half in the muddy water and half draped across her legs. His breathing was shallow. She worked her legs free and stood, knees shaking, to look down at him.

Now what?

It took longer than she could have imagined, but eventually, through a combination of dragging, rolling, and heaving, she got him to the mouth of the cave. They were both filthy, covered in sweat, blood, and the slime of the stream bed. She got him into the shade of the cave, where the air was cooler. He still hadn't woken; she wouldn't let herself entertain the thought that he might never wake.

Flopping beside his body, she drew off her helmet and let it fall to the ground. She knew she had to clean Vidar's wound, inspect him for other injuries. But for a moment, she just breathed.

When her hands stopped trembling, Aris rose and peered from the mouth of the cave, again searching the ravine floor and cliff edges for signs of Safaran soldiers. Aside from a pair of birds skimming the breeze above and a small brown lizard skittering along the edge of the stream, there was no movement. No sound, save for the tittering of the birds and the distant burble of running water. Cautiously she emerged, gripping her empty canteen like a talisman.

To the south, she could hear a distant rushing. When she'd flown over the canyon, the glowing green nav map had indicated a waterfall, with a large pool of water at its base. She headed that direction, keeping to the shadows along the canyon wall. Her eyes flickered constantly across the open space, but she didn't look behind her, didn't let her eyes fall on the transport.

The sound of the waterfall grew louder until it filled her head. When she came to the pool, she kept walking until the cold water had reached her chest. The icy liquid revealed cuts and scrapes she didn't know she had; they burned as the water flowed against them. She dipped her head beneath the surface, washing the bile and sweat from her face and the blood from the back of her neck. When she emerged, her teeth were chattering but she felt clean once more.

Aris filled the canteen and walked slowly back to the cave, her cold, wet uniform dragging against her. The sun beat down on her aching skull; the warmth seeped into her skin but couldn't entirely kill the chill.

Major Vidar was lying where she'd left him. She removed his helmet carefully then used her wet jacket to wipe the blood from his face and neck and the gash on his forehead. They'd had basic aid training, so she knew what to do to disinfect and dress the wound. When she was finished, she propped him up on her arm and got him to swallow some water from the canteen, though he didn't fully wake.

All the while she listened, waiting for the sounds of enemy soldiers. Once, she heard a scream and shot to her feet, banging her head on the curved roof of the cave, but the sound warbled into a howl as it faded. And then, quite close, a rustle as the animal scurried after its prey.

When she noticed her hands shaking, she dragged herself to the pack and removed a pouch of nutrigel. It tasted vaguely like cherries and slid down her throat like oil, but her hands steadied once the nutrients reached her stomach.

All through the day, Aris watched the rise and fall of Major Vidar's chest, stared at the pale scar that ran from his eye to his lip, studied the wide white bandage circling his head. As the sun slid toward the horizon, she replaced the wrapping, now dotted with blood, and poured more water into his mouth.

She wondered when they would be rescued. If they would be rescued. Would Commander Nyx tell Dysis that the mission had been unsuccessful? Her stomach clenched. And she remembered, for the first time, that faint pink blob at the northern end of the ravine. Had that really been Jax? Was he still there?

The questions ran like dogs in her head, chasing their tails and finding no resolution.

Aris was sipping from the canteen and staring intently out at the shadows lengthening along the ravine floor, watching for movement, when a hoarse cough broke the silence.

Aris spun around and smiled with relief to see Major Vidar's eyes open, his piercing gaze locked on her face. "Who the hell are you?" he demanded.

Aris paused. "Sir! Don't you remember me?" Had he lost his memory? "It's Specialist Aristos Haan, sir."

He squinted at her in the gloom. Maybe he couldn't see her in the dark? She grabbed the lantern from her bag and brought it to his side. The light bloomed, golden and comforting. He still looked pale. Tilting his head, he studied her face more closely.

"You aren't Aristos." His voice was quiet, but in no way uncertain.

She sat back on her heels, confusion making her frown. If he knew who *Aristos* was he couldn't be having trouble with his memory. "But, sir—"

And then she knew. Her voice . . . it was *her* voice.

Her hand flew to the back of her neck. The large bump at the base of her skull, right where her military brand was. The veil.

It had shattered.

Chapter Forty-Seven

"Major Vidar," she whispered. She held her hands out, an entreaty.

"Who are you?" he repeated.

"Sir, I *am* Aristos. Really I am. Only . . ."

"Only you're a woman." His eyes ranged slowly from her face to her chest; the tight, still-damp fabric of her Military-issue shirt left little in question, even with the band binding her breasts. She couldn't meet his eyes.

"Yes, sir," she whispered.

"How." It was more command than question.

She opened her mouth to answer but saw his face go pale. Blood was seeping through the bandage. "Let me help you." She scrambled to her bag and returned with a pouch of nutrigel and some clean dressings. In silence, he let her tend him. By the time she'd changed the bandage and he'd eaten the gel, his color was a little better.

He raised one eyebrow, and the scar pulled his lip into a more pronounced sneer.

With a sigh, Aris felt along the back of her neck and released the device. She handed him the transparent—now cracked— rectangle. "It masks my features. And changes my voice." A hole had started widening in her stomach. She would be kicked out of

Military and sent to jail. She forced back the tears that built behind her eyes.

He held the disc up to the light so he could inspect it more closely. She waited for him to yell at her, to tell her the game was up and she was going home.

"How does it work?" he asked instead. His eyes found hers again, glowing a darker blue in the dim light.

"You have to get your body mapped and an implant put in your voice box." Her hand went to her throat, where she could feel the tiny bump. He reached out and touched the spot, lightly, moving her fingers out of the way. His touch sent a shiver through her; she told herself it was because his hand was cold.

"Where did you get it?" He was staring at her like she was a puzzle he was determined to solve.

"Please, sir," she said, leaning back. "Don't make me say. I don't want anyone else to get in trouble."

Major Vidar let his hand fall. "Ar—wait, what is your real name?"

"Aris," she whispered.

"Aris, I need to know." He looked away, his eyes thoughtful. "Do other dominions have this technology?"

She shook her head. "Atalanta is the only one. They didn't sell it to other dominions."

For a long time, Major Vidar didn't say anything. Finally, as he looked carefully at the device in his hands: "I think perhaps someone did."

"Sir?"

He shook his head, as if clearing his mind, and looked up at her. "We've got to find Lieutenant Latza and return to point as quickly as possible. Have you been in communication with Lieutenant Wolfe?"

This time she couldn't contain the tears. "They're dead." The image exploded in too-vivid detail in her mind. She thought of Galec's family. Helena, little Calla, who would grow up with his face. What would they do when they found out? She swallowed back a sob.

"You're sure?" Vidar's voice was hard.

Aris nodded and turned away.

"Signs of pursuit?"

"Two soldiers, over by the other jet. I . . . took care of them." She busied herself with her pack, pulling out more nutrigels and a couple hard loaves of bread, wishing she could erase the image of the soldiers' crumpled bodies from her mind.

"And no contact with Lieutenant Latza, or anyone else?"

She shook her head.

"We have to find him. It's even more important now, you understand?"

"Yes, sir," Aris said, but she didn't, really.

Major Vidar held up her nearly empty canteen. "Where did you find the water?"

"There's a pool at the end of the ravine, sir. I'll go get us some more." She stood quickly, nearly bumping her head again. He handed her the canteen, but as she turned to go, he grabbed her arm with his other hand, his cool fingers sliding down her Enviro brand to rest on her wrist. Goosebumps skated along her skin, and her pulse picked up.

"Aris." He waited until she looked at him. "Well done, Specialist."

WHEN SHE RETURNED to the cave, Major Vidar had moved farther away from its mouth and was leaning against the rocky wall. He'd removed his jacket and his pale, defined arms were crossed, which made the muscles stand out.

She reached for her still-damp jacket and put it on, uncomfortably aware of her own body now that it was no longer hidden by the veil. Vidar gestured to a spot beside him, but as she handed him the canteen and sank to the ground, she scooted back a little, to put distance between them.

He tossed her a loaf of bread, and she chewed until it turned to dust in her mouth.

"We need more light to conduct a proper search for Lieutenant Latza. We'll wait until just before dawn," he said.

"Wouldn't he have come to find us, sir? After all the noise last night?"

"He may be injured. Or not realize that we were the ones shot down."

Aris tried to get comfortable against the craggy side of the cave, but it was difficult. Her racing mind, and sweating palms didn't help. She felt like a hog, waiting for the blade. She didn't know whether to ask Major Vidar outright what he planned to do with her when they got back, or if she should just keep silent and hope, somehow, that it would all work out.

He turned off the lantern, plunging them into darkness. "Why are you here, Aris? Why did you join Military?"

The questions caught her off guard.

"There were a lot of reasons," she replied, after a moment. "It started because of someone I knew, back in Lux." She slid down the wall until she was lying on her back. Her head throbbed, radiating pain down her spine. "He was selected Military and sent away."

"And he left you, alone and Unpromised." Major Vidar broke in. He must have remembered their conversation about her "girl back home."

She shifted, uncomfortable with his tone. "He was trying to protect me."

Major Vidar let out a bitter laugh. "Apparently, Specialist, you are very hard to protect."

"I love to fly," she said softly. "Back home, no one really understood that. And it wasn't important, not like it is here. What I'm doing here, the people I've saved . . . Calix came first, but now this is who I am." She paused, steeling herself. "Please don't report me. I'll find another disguise. I can't do any good from prison."

His clothes rustled as he slid down to stretch out on the hard ground. The cave was narrow, and when he shifted, his leg brushed hers.

"I'm not going to report you. Not now, anyway," he said. "I can't. You're the best blighting flyer I've ever seen." He cleared his throat. "And the only one I've got at the moment."

"And when we get out of this?" She ran her hands over her skull, the prickling beginnings of stubble catching against the tips of her fingers.

"We'll worry about that when we have to."

Her stomach sank. It was such a diplomatic, noncommittal answer. With a deep breath, she closed her eyes against the darkness and whispered, "Does it bother you?"

"Does what bother me?"

"That I'm not Aristos. That I'm a woman." She was strangely comforted, in spite of everything, by the sound of her real voice.

"Not for the reasons you think." He sighed. "Now go to sleep. Only a few hours until dawn."

"Yes, sir," she said, wondering what he meant.

A few moments later, his voice floated a last thought into the darkness. "The simple village girl from Lux. You didn't do her justice."

As she drifted off, she saw the lone figure of her former self, standing still as stone on the edge of a beach, the edge of the world, the sunset tangled in her long, wild hair. And Dianthe's words, from so long ago, echoed in her head.

There are no women in Military, Aris. We're all just ghosts.

Chapter Forty-Eight

Aris woke at the touch of a hand on her arm. Major Vidar's face loomed over her in the glow of the lantern. She sat up too quickly and hissed when her head cracked against the wall of the cave.

She'd dreamt of Lux, and Calix. It took a moment for the sound of crashing waves to fade from her mind.

"Sorry," Major Vidar said, rocking back on his heels. "No more beauty sleep for you. Time to go."

In an effort to avoid his eyes, her gaze swept up and caught on the bandage binding his forehead. A little blood had seeped through. "Let me check your wound first, sir."

"We have to hurry."

"It'll just take a minute. The dressing needs to be changed." She pushed on his shoulder to get him to sit and grabbed the small canister of disinfectant and a fresh length of gauze. He held up the lantern so she could see better.

"You don't strike me as the mender type," he said as she reached up gingerly to remove the bandage.

"You're right." She smiled. "Usually I'm the one getting mended."

He laughed a little. She accidentally met his eyes, and her hands froze against his forehead.

He didn't look away. An unfamiliar expression flitted across his face: surprise, with a bemused sort of recognition. Like he was seeing her for the first time.

She held his gaze and felt herself sway just the slightest bit toward him, as if drawn by a string. Under her hands, his head tilted back. Her lips parted.

Then he blinked, and the spell was broken. She rocked back on her knees and dropped her hands, as if scalded. "I . . . I think —" she stuttered, turning away. What was she *doing*?

Major Vidar's hand snaked out and circled her wrist. His touch made her skin tingle, hum like the diatous veil had done, only these vibrations echoed deep beneath the surface. "You're injured, too," he said, sounding concerned.

"I am?" She looked down as if she expected to find fresh blood on her shirt.

His fingers gently touched the back of her skull, and pain flared. She winced.

"Sorry," he said, his other hand still warm on her wrist.

She pulled free, not looking at him. "It's fine, sir. We should go."

"Are you sure? It looks like a nasty bump."

"It's fine," she said again.

"Alright, then. I trust you." There was something in his voice she couldn't quite identify.

She started to move away, but he cleared his throat. "Aris?"

"Yes, sir?" She glanced back at him, and caught his amused smile.

"Could you finish my dressing? I'm a bit undone here." He lifted the edge of gauze that dangled along the side of his face.

Heat rushed from her scalp to her toes. "Of course. I'm so sorry." She finished disinfecting and bandaging the wound as quickly as she could, relieved that he kept his eyes trained on the cave's entrance. By the time she was done, the amusement was gone from his face, and his eyes were narrowed in thought.

He stood, hunching to avoid hitting his head. "We'll refill the canteen at the waterfall, then head north. By now a search team should have been assembled. We'll check the wingjet for comms, but our priority is finding Lieutenant Latza."

"Very good, sir," she said, and moved to the entrance of the cave, looking around before venturing into open ground.

They kept to the wall of the ravine, solaguns drawn. Major Vidar stopped at the recon to see if the sunlight had recharged any of the instruments. Nothing worked.

"So where's this Calix? Does he know what you've been up to?" he asked as they made their cautious way toward the transport.

Glancing at Vidar, she found his eyes on her. "No, he doesn't know. I haven't seen him. But I think he's at Mekia."

"A mender?"

She nodded. Vidar turned his attention back to their progress through the canyon. The walls of the ravine were steep, with patches of red clay in some places and gravity-defying trees clinging in others. It would a difficult climb to freedom. As their shoulders brushed the wall, leaves and little stones were dislodged, tumbling to the ground. Aris jumped at every noise, worried it would *expose* them.

The closer they got to the wreckage of the transport, the harder it was for her to breathe.

When they reached it, she shrank back. The bodies of the two Safaran soldiers still lay on the muddy ground beside the stream.

Major Vidar moved away from the wall, toward the jet.

"Sir, I think I need to stay here," she whispered. The charred skin, the rusty stains . . . Galec's ravaged face. She turned away, afraid she might be sick.

"Keep going. Stay along the wall, in the shadows if you can. Keep your eyes open. I'll be just a moment."

"Are you sure you have to go over there?" she asked. "It's . . . not a pleasant sight."

Major Vidar moved closer to the transport, his eyes scanning the lip of the canyon. Without looking back, he said, "I have to see for myself. Lieutenant Wolfe and I . . ." He paused. "We worked together for a long time."

Wolfe and Talon . . . they were men she'd come to trust, rely on during missions. Galec had been more than that. He'd been her friend. Now they were dead, gone from this life.

They'd given their lives for the mission. For Lieutenant Latza. Aris couldn't fail them now. *I will find your brother, Dysis. I promise.*

She crept along the wall, her hands steady as they held her solagun. No more fear. Not with Dysis in her head.

The canyon curved, effectively cutting off her view of the northern portion. Safaran soldiers could be waiting just out of sight. She paused, listened. All she heard was Major Vidar's footsteps behind her, the ripple of the stream, and the faint call of a bird far above. She tilted her head back and watched for a moment as it dipped and soared. Trapped down here, the wing of her jet behind her like a giant gravestone . . . she felt like a bird with clipped wings, broken and alone.

She moved forward slowly, her eyes scanning the curve of water and the muddy stream bed, the rocky edge of the canyon.

And then she saw it.

A great hulking shadow, there in the middle of the ravine.

Another wingjet, black and shining, the red flame of the Safaran flag curled along its tail.

She raised the solagun. She waited, watched, but saw no movement.

"Sir!" She didn't dare yell, but she hoped Vidar could hear her loud whisper.

After a moment, he rounded the curve of rock and stood behind her.

He, too, stared at the wingjet.

"What should we do?" she asked, torn between fear that it was a trap and hope that it could be their means of escape.

Without answering, Major Vidar approached it. She followed, covering him. As they moved into the open, she expected to hear the whine of a missile or see the flash of solagun fire. But the morning remained serene.

He stared through the dome to the cabin. "It's empty. Must belong to the men you shot." He turned to glance back at her with a grim smile.

Aris knew that one day she was going to wake up with the horror of what she'd done washing over her. But in this moment, she felt nothing but joy. Joy that she was still alive. Joy that they'd found their escape.

"Don't move." The voice came from behind them.

She whirled and tried to get the solagun up, but her reflexes were too slow this time.

A man in a Safaran uniform had his weapon pointed directly at her head.

CHAPTER FORTY-NINE

"IDENTIFY YOURSELVES," THE MAN BARKED.

Aris shot a panicked glance at Major Vidar and saw him putting his hands up, his solagun dangling from his finger. His face was blank. How could he be so calm?

She tried to keep her shoulders straight as she faced the enemy. Her mouth was desert-dry.

"Lieutenant Latza?" Major Vidar asked mildly.

Her eyes flew to his face and back to the stranger. *This* was Jax? He was dirty from head to toe, as if he'd been rolling in mud. His jacket was Safaran Military, but he wore pale flowing pants, now stained dark with dirt and blood. He held his left foot off the ground, leaning heavily on a branch dotted with brilliant green leaves.

The man's voice stayed hard, and his hand on the solagun didn't falter. "Identify."

Before Major Vidar could say anything, Aris burst out, "Are you really Jax? Dysis's brother?"

The solagun in his hand wobbled. "You know Dysis?"

Aris took a step forward, excitement drowning her fear. "Oh, *Jax*. Dysis will be thrilled. She's been looking for you."

"Wait, Dysis is a woman too?" Major Vidar's exclamation broke the tableau.

Jax lowered his weapon, and suddenly they were all talking at once, questions bumping and interrupting, with no opportunity for answers.

Finally, Aris raised her hands. The two men stopped talking. She walked over to Jax, put a hand on his arm. "Your sister has been searching for you ever since you were captured. She joined the Military sector to find you."

His eyes widened. "She did *what?*"

Aris gave him a wry smile. "It's more common than you might expect. I'm Aris, by the way. And this is Major Vidar."

Jax shook her hand, though he still looked confused. When his fingers closed around hers, they were cool and clammy.

And suddenly he swayed.

Major Vidar was at his side in a moment, and together they held him up.

"You're injured," Vidar said.

Jax shook his head slightly, as if shaking off a dream. "I was traveling at night, didn't see the ravine until it was too late. Broke my leg in the fall. And I haven't eaten anything in a couple days."

"We'll get you to safety," Vidar said. He and Aris helped Jax to the Safaran wingjet. "Can you fly her?"

She looked at the panel on the side of the jet. "Probably. But I don't know the passcode."

"Zero-nine-zero-nine," Jax said. When she stared at him, he shrugged. "Military Intelligence. All the Safaran wingjet passcodes are the same."

"You're a spy?" she asked, awed.

He smiled down at her; she thought he was probably good looking, under all the mud.

"Just open it," Major Vidar said.

As soon as they were secure and the jet was powered up, stinking and loud with Safaran fuel instead of solar power, Major Vidar adjusted the communications to Atalantan frequency.

Soon he was in contact with the Commander.

"Search and rescue is on its way, Major," Commander Nyx's voice rang over the in-helmet speakers. He sounded relieved.

"Sir, we've recovered Lieutenant Latza. He's injured. Please advise S and R to meet us at Mekia." He turned and met Aris's widened eyes.

Her stomach flipped. Vidar was sending them to *Mekia*?

"Noted. Will pass the intel along. Status on Wolfe, Talon, and Galec."

After a pause, Vidar said, "Deceased, sir. We'll need a recovery crew."

Silence. Finally, Commander Nyx said heavily, "Noted. And Haan?"

Major Vidar glanced at her again. "Specialist Haan is fine. He's acclimating himself to the new wingjet."

Aris let out a breath. If she spoke, Commander Nyx would know her disguise had been blown. And if Major Vidar wasn't sharing that information, she wasn't going to.

The takeoff wasn't quite as smooth as usual; the controls were slightly different, and the machine didn't have the same hover capabilities as Atalantan jets, but they were soon on their way to Mekia. No one fired at them, and as they flew along the edge of the ravine, she saw why; the rest of the Safaran ambush had been destroyed in the firefight. She kept her gaze from the bodies baking in the sun.

"Mekia?" she asked softly.

"It's the closest mender stationpoint," Major Vidar replied, clipping the words.

"Of course. Sir."

Her palms began to sweat. What would Calix do when he saw her? Her heart beat faster, whether in fear or anticipation she couldn't tell.

THE MEKIA STATIONPOINT WAS SMALL, much smaller than Revening. She landed on a dusty pad behind a low row of buildings. The town rose behind the stationpoint; the white-roofed houses, which reminded her of Lux, climbed into the hills, disappearing within the shadowy green of an immense forest.

Two men rushed to meet the wingjet. She looked at them closely as they approached, but neither was Calix. Her stomach was doing a series of what felt like double spindrops, and maybe a blackflip freeze or two.

As a group of soldiers and menders gathered, Aris noticed stares and confused looks, but no one spoke to her. They were too intent on helping Jax out of the jet.

Major Vidar grabbed her arm and drew her away from the throng. "You need to stay out of sight until we figure out what to do with you," he said. "For now, we'll say you're a villager who helped us locate Lieutenant Latza. You're injured, so you'll stay to be treated here. Specialist Haan is sleeping off his own injuries if anyone asks. Understood?"

She nodded.

"Good. Let's see if we can find you more appropriate clothes."

She started walking with him and then stopped abruptly, impervious to the pressure on her arm as Vidar kept moving. There, on the edge of the pad, striding toward them . . .

Oh holy. Calix.

His face was thinner than she remembered, stark without the frame of his thick brown hair. But the way he walked . . . from miles away she would recognize him.

Major Vidar said something but she couldn't focus on the words. She couldn't move, couldn't breathe. *Calix*.

If she'd been Aristos, if her veil was still working . . . maybe she could have given herself time to work up to her revelation. She could have eased Calix into the idea. But now . . . He was right here, walking toward her. Mere yards away. *Mere yards away*.

Oh Gods, he's really here. It was sinking in. Excitement momentarily overtook the other emotions coursing through her.

She pulled away from Major Vidar and ran to Calix, skidding to a stop before him.

He glanced over her head toward the jet, his green eyes narrowing in confusion. "Are you one of the crew? Are you injured?"

She ran a nervous hand along her bald head. "Calix," she said, heart pounding, "It's me. Aris."

His eyes widened, and he looked more closely at her, taking in the shaved head and the Military uniform.

"Aris?" His voice was full of disbelief. And then worry overshadowed his features. "Are you okay? What happened? Who did this to you?" He stared at her shaved head.

"No one. I'm fine." And she was, mostly, except for her trembling hands and a chill in her bones that wouldn't leave her.

He grabbed her arm, as if to support her, and then stared as if surprised at her hard muscle. "But . . . but what are you doing here?" he asked, still looking dazed. "And why are you dressed like that? Are you sure you're okay?"

"I really am, I promise, but I need to talk to you." There were so many things to say, so much to explain. But not here. Not with the flood of menders pushing med-beds and a dizzying array of equipment toward the wingjet. Any moment, someone was going to notice her and ask her who she was. They'd want to take her away to assess her injuries . . .

"This is a closed stationpoint, no civilians allowed," Calix said. "Did you, um . . ." He stared again at her head. "Did you come in disguise or something? Did someone let you in?"

"I'm not a civilian. I can explain, just—"

"We need to get you out of here." He glanced toward the buzz of activity just a few yards away. "You're going to get in trouble."

He started pulling her toward the gated entrance, as if he meant to escort her off point. She planted her feet, resisting the pressure of his hand. "You don't have to do that, Calix. I'm allowed to be here." Well, *Aristos* was.

"You're not, Aris. I'm sorry. Women aren't—"

"Stop. Listen to me." She grabbed his wrist. "I'm a member of the Atalantan Military, just like you." He opened his mouth to argue, but she shook her head. "It's true. I have a veil . . . this device . . . it makes me look male. But we crashed, and now it doesn't work." Her hand went to the tender spot behind her head. "I know it sounds crazy, but—"

"You crashed? Your veil? What are you talking about?" He squinted down at her, an unfamiliar expression on his face. *Suspicion?* Dismay filled her.

"I'm a flyer," she tried again. She turned and pointed to the Safaran wingjet, where several menders were securing Jax on a med-bed to transport him inside. "That's Lieutenant Latza. He escaped from a Safaran prison, and we rescued him." Her voice caught. Major Vidar was walking toward them.

Calix saw him and stood straighter, reacting to the officer's emblem on Vidar's uniform.

"Sir . . ." she started when he reached them.

He grabbed her arm and pulled her along. "I've just been informed that Dysis and crew are on their way. We need to get you changed."

She stumbled along next to him. "*Dysis* is on the rescue mission?" Commander Nyx must have changed his mind. "Did someone tell her we found Jax?"

"Not yet. He—she came after you. Well, us. Presumably she's aware of your . . ." his eyes grazed her body and he raised a brow ". . . condition, but I doubt the others know?" Aris shook her head. "So it's even more important to find you female clothes and stick to our villager story, until we figure things out. I'll inform anyone who asks that Aristos isn't fit for visitors."

Vidar glanced at Calix, who was hurrying along next to them, his face blank with confusion. "You must be Calix."

Calix's eyes widened, obviously surprised Major Vidar knew who he was. "Yes, sir." He looked again at Aris, but she shrugged. Further explanations would have to wait.

Taking her other arm, so she was pinned between them, Calix said, "I know where there are some extra clothes, sir. I can help."

The two of them shuttled her across the landing pad, as if she were a criminal.

With a grunt, she pulled away. Stopped. They both turned to her, brows raised, and she noticed Calix was shorter than Major Vidar. He'd always seemed so tall.

"I can walk perfectly fine on my own, thank you. Sir," she added, nodding at Major Vidar.

"Fine. Walk, Specialist."

She kept her head up and her eyes straight ahead. She'd known it would be a lot for Calix to accept, her arriving at his point as a soldier. She'd known he'd be confused. Shocked. But suspicious? Wasn't he even a *little* bit happy to see her?

And why did it bother her so much to see him side by side with Major Vidar?

Calix led them to a glass door around the corner of the building, away from Jax and his entourage of menders. With a hiss, the door slid open.

"All we have is extra mender uniforms, sir," he said as he walked.

"That'll do for now," Vidar replied. "Aris, remember. You're a village girl who saw an injured soldier and helped lead Aristos and myself to him. You hurt your head when you were showing us the way, so we brought you along to get treated. Got it?"

"Stupid village girl who hit her head. Got it." Aris fought back sudden, inexplicable tears. She'd rather have just been Aristos, veil or no veil.

"Let's look for something we can use to cover your shaved head," Major Vidar added.

When they reached a closed door at the end of a long hallway, Calix swiped his hand across the monitor, and the door slid open. It was a storage room: cleaning supplies, shelves stacked high with linens, and a rack of white mender tunics like the one he wore. Only, unlike his, they didn't have a name or Military emblem stitched into them.

Aris yanked one off the rack and started to remove her jacket. She glanced over her shoulder. Major Vidar and Calix were squeezed awkwardly into the small space by the closed door, looking anywhere but at her.

"A little privacy?"

With some throat clearing and mumbling, the two men left the room.

Alone, she sagged against the wall, hugging the mender tunic to her chest. *Foolish. Stupid. Silly.* All the names that Dianthe and Dysis had called her, she was every single one of them, and worse. It wasn't supposed to be like this.

Why couldn't I have found him sooner? Or later . . . but not now. Not when her veil was broken, when Major Vidar knew who she really was. When her fellow soldiers were dead.

Aris bent forward, unable to hold back the tears any longer.

CHAPTER FIFTY

A COUPLE HOURS LATER, MAJOR VIDAR ESCORTED ARIS TO Jax's room. "I have to take care of something," he said. "I'll be back in a moment."

Aris adjusted the scarf covering her head, took a deep breath, and entered.

Inside, several menders stood before a monitor along the back wall, discussing an X-ray of Jax's leg. Dysis was sitting beside Jax's bed, holding his hand so tightly his fingers were going white.

Dysis stood when she noticed Aris at the door. "But—"

Aris cut her off. "I'm Aris." She held out her hand and gave Dysis a look.

Dysis's eyes flicked to one of the menders and widened in understanding. She ushered Aris to a seat and whispered, "What happened?"

"Veil broke," Aris whispered back. She smiled shyly, as a local village girl would.

Jax grinned, as if enjoying the joke.

"How are you feeling?" she asked. Without all the mud and blood, he was indeed good-looking. Dysis was right; with her disguise, they could have been twins. The resemblance was eerie.

Jax's eyes sparkled. "You should ask them to give you some of the purple stuff." He gestured to a tube of liquid attached to his arm. "Pretty sure I could fly without a wingjet right now."

She couldn't help but laugh. "That good, then?"

Major Vidar strode into the room. The bandage on his forehead had been replaced with a smaller, neater dressing. Without preamble, he said, "Lieutenant, I need to ask you a few questions. Do you feel strong enough? Or shall I give you more time?"

Jax's face was suddenly serious. "I'm ready, sir," he said. "What can I do for you?"

Major Vidar glanced at Aris and Dysis in turn. It was clear they were being dismissed.

Dysis started to lean over, as if to kiss her brother's forehead, and then remembered herself. Instead, she squeezed his shoulder and grinned. "See you in a little while, brother."

As soon as they were in the long, sterile hallway, Dysis bumped Aris in the arm. "So Major Vidar knows about you? And he wasn't mad?"

But Aris didn't answer. "Dysis, he's here," she whispered instead.

It took Dysis a second to understand, and then she let out a low whistle. "Calix?"

Aris nodded and resisted the urge to wring her hands.

"What did he say? Was he happy to see you?" Dysis asked eagerly.

When they came to the end of the hall, Aris ducked into an empty room along the next corridor, pulling Dysis after her and closing the door. A frosted panel separated two white-sheeted med-beds, and a vid strip ran along the walls, projecting a rotating array of calming landscapes.

"I don't think so." Aris sank onto the nearest bed. "He didn't recognize me, and when I tried to explain, he couldn't stop staring at my head." She pulled the scarf loose and ran her fingers along her now-prickly skull. "And when I was finished changing, he was gone. He just left, without saying anything."

"Maybe he got called away," Dysis said, plopping down next to her. "What did he say when you told him?"

"Nothing, really. It all happened so fast. We arrived, and he was right there. I didn't have time to *think*. I didn't know what to say." She still didn't. Why did everything have to be so complicated?

"You should find him. Talk to him," Dysis said. "It's a lot to process. Even though you'd already told Jax, he was still shocked when he saw me. Calix had no warning. Not to mention he's figured out by now that everything you told him for the past few months is a lie."

"Are you trying to make me feel better? Because—"

"I'm just saying you have to give him time."

"I'm not sure how much time I have to give." Aris plucked at her white tunic. Major Vidar could say what he wanted about her being a good flyer, but they wouldn't be able to keep up the deception that "Aristos" was resting and wanted to be alone for long.

"What did Major Vidar say? Was he mad?" Dysis asked.

Aris shook her head. "He didn't seem angry. Just . . . not sure what to do with me." *And he almost kissed me. Maybe.* Gods, had he? Had *she*? She'd just imagined it, right? Nothing had happened. Nothing was *going* to happen. *Why am I even thinking about this?*

Dysis bumped her arm. "You okay?"

"I don't know what to do," Aris said miserably.

"Well, what do you *want* to do?" Dysis gestured to Aris's clothes. "You're a girl again. You can stay that way. Find a little place in Mekia, maybe, and be with Calix? That's why we did this, wasn't it? To find them?"

Aris shrugged, twisting her hands together, clenching and unclenching until her fingers were red. "I don't think it matters what I want. Calix can't stand the sight of me, and Aristos is gone. What choice does that leave?" *Aristos is gone.* A tightness built in her chest.

Dysis squeezed Aris's shoulder. "You can't give up so easily,

Aris! You're the romantic, remember? Your little fantasy came true. We found Jax and Calix. That makes this a happy day." She smiled but there was sadness in her eyes. Not entirely happy, with Talon and Wolfe and Galec dead. "Talk to him. It can't make things any worse, right?"

"I *am* happy, Dysis," Aris said softly. "I'm so happy you found Jax and that he's okay."

"Me too, Hummingbird, me too." She stood. "I think I'll check on him, see if Major Vidar's done."

"Dysis, wait."

Dysis paused at the door, eyebrows raised.

"Major Vidar knows about you too. In the confusion, with finding Jax . . . I'm sorry."

She didn't respond right away. And when she did it was with a shrug. "It's okay. It doesn't matter. Not anymore."

"What do you mean?"

"I came here—I did this—for Jax. Wherever he goes, that's where I'll be." Dysis opened the door. "I don't think Major Vidar will turn us in. I'll just disappear, leave when Jax leaves."

But Dysis was so *good* at being a soldier. How could she walk away?

"What about Lieutenant Daakon?"

"What about him?" Her voice betrayed nothing.

"So, you're really giving it up? You'll go home with Jax and teach mechanics again? And never look back?"

Dysis glanced over her shoulder, her expression unreadable. "I'll be looking back for as long as I live. But it doesn't change who I am."

Aris fought sudden tears. Dysis turned to go. They were sectormates. *Friends.* They were supposed to stay together, protect each other. But now . . . "Wait," she whispered again, but couldn't go on. "I . . . Dysis . . ."

She didn't know how to say goodbye.

Dysis didn't turn around. Just froze for a moment in the doorway, shoulders tense. And then, without another word, she slipped away.

CHAPTER FIFTY-ONE

IT WASN'T HARD TO FIND CALIX. ARIS JUST TOLD THE FIRST soldier she passed that she had an urgent message for him from Major Vidar, and the man led her to his room.

She knocked softly on the wall beside the open doorway. Inside, it looked just like her bedroom back at Spiro: two beds, two chrome trunks, the closed door to the washroom. Calix was sitting on one of the beds, leaned up against the wall, his forehead resting on his bent knees. He was thinner than she remembered, more muscled. Harder, like she was.

"Calix?"

He didn't move. She was about to say his name again, when he murmured, "You really joined Military? You've been pretending to be a man all this time?"

"Yes." She stepped around the edge of the bed, until she was standing beside him. "Won't you even look at me?" She let a hand run along his shaved head. "You were the only thing in my life. You were everything. And then you went away." Her voice broke.

He finally looked up. "What made you even think of it, Aris?"

She let her hand drop from his skin, felt the memory of the touch as if it were seared into her palm. "I was recruited to be a flyer." She couldn't bring herself to admit she'd done it for *him*. Not when he was looking at her like that.

"There aren't any women in Military. It's not allowed."

Was that really all he cared about? *The rules?*

"You told me to keep flying! This was my chance. And it *is* allowed. Sort of. If you know the right people."

"I knew you liked to fly, but I just can't believe you did *this*." He looked at her more closely. "How *did* you do it? You're not strong enough for the physical training. Did they—"

She cut him off. "I *was* strong enough." Holy, he sounded just like her father. "I went through everything you did . . . the running, the weights, the combat training. I passed all the tests."

He shook his head in disbelief. Which annoyed her, but she couldn't blame him for it either. Why shouldn't he have doubts? She'd been just as convinced that she'd fail.

Still. She sank to the bed beside him. "I thought you'd be proud. I thought you'd be happy to see me."

Calix sagged forward, staring at his hands resting on his knees. "Happy? Oh Gods, I don't even know what to think. You should have told me."

"I couldn't, Calix. I gave my word. The risk of exposure was too great."

"So no one knows where you are? Your parents think you're working some silco-pushing job in Panthea and that you're—what—just too busy to visit? What do you say when they write you and offer to come see you?"

She sighed. "I tell them that I want to see them, but it's a bad time, or that I'll try to visit next week."

Anger sparked in his eyes. "And what if something had happened to you? How would they have ever known? How would I?"

When she didn't respond, he rolled his eyes in disgust, and suddenly she was angry, too. "It's been hard, okay? The physical training nearly killed me. And it wasn't exactly *easy* to let someone shave my head. I had to watch everything I did and said, so I wouldn't be exposed and thrown in *prison* for being a woman in Military."

"I just . . . this is too much, Aris. I can't believe you're here. That you're a . . ." His eyes went again to her head, "A soldier."

She couldn't stand the way he was looking at her. "Don't you get it? I did this for you, Calix! You said we couldn't Promise if we were so far apart. I thought you'd be *glad*—" She shook her head, disgusted with herself. And with him. "I was so stupid."

His eyes widened. "For me? Aris, that *is* stupid. I would never have asked—expected . . ."

"You're right," Aris said. "I shouldn't have done it, not for you. But for other reasons? Absolutely. Even if it meant leaving Lux. Even if it means being incarcerated. It was worth it." She swallowed, realizing she meant it, even after the horror of the last mission. "I've saved people. And the ones I couldn't save . . . I'm a good flyer, Calix. I've made a difference. Can't you at least *try* to understand?"

She wanted to tell him about the night she flew through the storm, how she'd impressed Major Vidar with her skills. She wished he would hold her in his arms as she told him of the little girl, that poor murdered family. Galec. Lieutenants Wolfe and Talon. Everything that had happened, she wanted to share it with him. With someone. She didn't want to have to carry it alone.

"You want me to understand?" His sharp-edged voice sliced through her thoughts. "You broke the law, Aris. You might be sent to jail! How could you mess with your future like that? *Our* future? And you lied to me, to everyone! The Aris I knew wouldn't have lied. She wouldn't have done this."

The words may as well have been knives.

Aris stood up, hands balled into fists. "You should be proud that I did." Tears were falling now; she didn't bother wiping them away. "Maybe even impressed. Hell, how about grateful!"

"Grateful?"

"I didn't let you go, Calix. I *fought* for you, to be here with you. And you can't even tell me you're happy to see me!" How could she have been so wrong about him? About everything? How could he look at her like that, as if she were a stranger?

"What do you want me to say?" He shifted his gaze to the floor.

"What do you *think*, Calix?" She wanted to punch a hole in the wall. After months as a soldier, her impulse was to hit, tear down, damage. She wanted to push him. Use her fists to make him understand.

His eyes burned when they met hers. "Oh, I'll tell you what I think. You're not going to like it, but I'll tell you. I think *you're* the one who doesn't understand." He stood and paced the room, his face flushed. "All this time, the one thing that kept me going was knowing you didn't have to see the things I've seen. That I could trust that you were safe, waiting for me, while I dealt with this hell. Don't you get how it comforted me, knowing you were in Panthea, away from this mess?" He stopped moving and stared at her, the anger fading from his eyes. "And now you tell me you've been in danger this whole time. That I could have lost you and not even known?" His voice cracked.

Guilt doused her anger, leaving her shaking and ashamed. Not for what she'd done, but for not finding a way to tell him. "I'm sorry," she said, "I wish I'd found you sooner. If we'd gotten to work together more, you'd know I don't need protecting. I'm stronger than you think."

His eyes were sad when he said, "But you shouldn't have to be strong. I'm supposed to be there for you. I'm supposed to take care of you."

Tentatively, she stepped closer and reached for him. "We can take care of each other. Those things you've seen—that I've seen —we'll carry them together."

With a shuddering sigh, he buried his face in her neck. "I can't believe you're really here, Aris. I've missed you so much."

She sagged against him, exhausted. Overwhelmed. In that moment, all she wanted to do was forget. Forget the last few months and go back to that night on the beach and be her old self again. "I missed you, too," she whispered against his chest.

His arms tightened around her and his lips found hers.

It was the kiss she'd imagined, yearned for in the months they'd been apart. It was salty with her tears, and it was desperate and deep. Calix's hands grasped her waist and pulled her closer, and her arms snaked around his neck, and she kissed him so hard she felt sure her lips would bruise.

He pushed against her, twisting until the back of her legs banged against his bed. And then they were falling onto the hard mattress, limbs tangled.

But when his hands brushed the bare skin of her back beneath her tunic, an odd shiver ran through her. Calix stopped kissing her, or she stopped—she wasn't sure.

"Are you okay?" He looked down at her, his weight pinning her to the bed.

She smiled, a little shakily, and tried to drown in his green eyes. It had always been so easy before. "Of course. Just a little overwhelmed." She pushed him until he was laying on his back and then snuggled up against his chest. She'd waited so long to feel his arms around her, hear his heart beat loud and steady against her ear.

He ran a hand along her head, the habit of brushing her hair back so ingrained he couldn't seem to help himself. When his fingers skimmed her neck, she winced. His eyes widened.

"You're hurt."

"Just a little bump. It's fine."

He sat up, turning her so he could inspect the wound. "It's not fine. This needs tending."

"Calix, really. Relax. It's okay." She drew away from his probing hands. The gentle touch was making her head ache all over again.

"No, it's not." He climbed off the bed and reached out a hand to pull her up. "Come on. I'll take care of you," he said. Just like he always did.

CHAPTER FIFTY-TWO

IT WAS WELL PAST DINNER WHEN THEY VENTURED TO THE large windowless cafeteria. Field menders worked odd hours, so they were permitted to avail themselves of the kitchen as needed. Calix scrounged a couple of packets of stew from a wall of gleaming silver foodsavers and heated them up in the high-speed warmer. They carried their bowls to one of the long white tables in the empty room.

Aris blew on the stew and watched as tendrils of steam curled between them. She smiled, shyly, when she caught him looking at her.

"It *is* good to see you," he said. "I miss your hair, though."

Self-conscious, she pulled the scarf tighter around her bald head, fingers catching on the edges of the bandage at the back of her neck. "It didn't bother me so much, when the person staring back at me in the mirror was a man. But it's odd now, to be myself and still have this."

He smiled. "It'll grow out. You'll be your old self in no time."

She choked on a mouthful of stew.

"Are you okay?" he asked, half-standing, as if he meant to lean over and pound her on the back.

Aris waved him off. "Fine. Sorry." She coughed. "Just swallowed wrong."

He sat back on the bench and picked up his spoon, watching her carefully. "You sure?"

She nodded and turned her attention to the food. For a while, they ate in silence.

But it wasn't a comfortable silence. She kept filling it with unvoiced worries and fears. She kept looking at his face, trying to see the Calix she remembered. Trying to forget that moment in the cave with Major Vidar.

You just need to get to know each other again. Talk to him. She could practically hear Dysis's voice, coaching her. "So," she said, clearing her throat. "Remember that move I told you about? The double backflip freeze?" He nodded. "I did it the first time they let me fly. It was amazing."

"I should have known you wouldn't really give up flying," he said ruefully. "You in Panthea . . . I should have guessed."

"I was in Panthea for a while. That's where I got the diatous veil, from this terrifying woman with a snake tattoo on her *head*. For the whole month I was there I couldn't fly. It was blighting awful."

"It's a wonder you survived," he replied, grinning.

"There was this one mission," she said, eyes brightening at the thought of Illia. "I had to take an injured flyer to Revening— she was a woman, too—and I thought I was going pass out, the way her leg was broken, all twisted, but—"

"Stop, Aris. Please," he interrupted, shaking his head. "I don't want to know. I can't imagine you out there, in danger. I don't want to. Please."

Her hand stilled with a bite of stew halfway to her mouth. "Okay, well . . . tell me about you then," she said. "How has it been here? You've sounded so tired in your comms. Has it been really bad—" but before she'd finished the question, he was shaking his head again.

"Let's not talk about the war." He reached across the table to touch her hand. "Anything but that."

What else is there to talk about?

"I think we should Promise," he said.

Her eyes flew to his face. "You do?"

"Well, yeah. If that's what you need to feel comfortable back in Lux without me, then it's worth it to do it now. I don't want you out here, risking your life just to be with me. I want you to be safe."

A Promise. It was exactly what she'd been hoping for when she started all of this. Well, not *exactly*. She'd imagined the asking would be more romantic, not so practical. And he wanted her to go home, give up her unit, her flying. She wanted the opposite. She needed to get back out there.

Except that she couldn't. She wasn't Aristos anymore.

Dysis's last words echoed in her mind: "I'll be looking back for as long as I live. But it doesn't change who I am."

Can I really go back? Be the old Aris again? She met Calix's eyes. He looked so different; it wasn't just the new thinness of his face, the tired hollows under his eyes. It wasn't the shaved head, or his skin, paler now without their daily walks on the beach. It was his expression, which reflected a change deep beneath the skin.

"Specialist Haan." Major Vidar's voice echoed across the cafeteria.

She stood up automatically and turned to face him, where he had paused just inside the doorway. "Sir?"

"I need you."

For a split second she wasn't sure what he meant, and her heart gave a sudden, unwelcome thud.

"We have a new, very important, mission. It must be executed tonight."

"But, sir. My veil." She glanced down at Calix, who was frozen in his seat.

"It doesn't matter. There's someone we have to find. And it has to be now." Already Vidar was turning toward the doorway, his body coiled with repressed energy.

"Who, sir? Did Jax give you information?" She walked toward him, searching his face. His urgency was contagious; she could feel her own muscles tensing.

He lowered his voice, so only she could hear him. "We have to save the Ward of Ruslana."

Her mouth dropped open. "The . . . Ward? But she's fine. She just spoke on the news today. I saw it when I was waiting to see Jax."

His face hardened. "Another statement on how she's renewed trade with Safara? Supplying them with money and guns in the war?" His eyes were cold. "Whoever that woman is, she's not the Ward."

Aris didn't understand what he was saying. "Who else could she be?"

"Lieutenant Latza saw a woman at the prison, someone being kept separate from the other prisoners. Her face was bandaged but her voice was clear."

Aris opened her mouth to ask another question, but Vidar went on. "That device you had—I think the technology was used to replace Galena Vadim."

"But sir, how do you know she didn't just change her mind?"

"I know it's not her."

"With all due respect—"

Vidar stalked closer, until he towered over her. In the bright light of the cafeteria his eyes gleamed. "Come with me."

With a quick, confused look at Calix, she said, "I'll be right back," and followed Major Vidar out of the room.

He didn't stop until he'd reached an empty office in the administrative wing of the building and locked the door behind them.

"Sir? I don't—"

The look in his eyes silenced her.

"I know that woman isn't the Ward of Ruslana," he said, "because Galena Vadim is my mother."

CHAPTER FIFTY-THREE

"Your *what*?" Aris's voice exploded in the small room, and she clapped a hand over her own mouth, shocked at the noise.

Major Vidar sighed impatiently. "My real name is Milek Vadim. I am part of a secret coalition of Ruslanan soldiers my mother placed within the Atalantan Military to help train and support them in their efforts to withstand Safara's advance. There are groups of us in nearly every unit. Wolfe and Daakon are my fellow operatives. Well, Wolfe was." He paused, and Aris tried to keep the memory of the last time she'd seen the Lieutenant from her mind.

"Mother never told any of her advisors about the program. She couldn't outright offer support to Atalanta. She and I organized it and communicated through special comms we set for predetermined times."

He paced as he spoke, and she could only watch. Major Vidar was from Ruslana? He was the son of Ward Vadim? If she looked closely enough, she could see a vague resemblance.

"Four months ago, right before the World Council, I logged into the approved frequency, but she never responded. I haven't heard from her since she was 'released' from the clinic. I thought perhaps she was being coerced into changing her policies, or grief over my father had affected her. But then you told me about the diatous veil."

Aris gasped as a new realization hit her. "Your father . . ."

His face tightened. "I couldn't go home for his burning. I thought maybe it was a trap, a way to draw me out." He closed his eyes for a moment, then continued, "Mother never contacted me directly. It was as if she suddenly didn't know how to reach me. For the past four months, I've been searching for an explanation. For some reason why she would go against every belief and value she held dear and support Balias."

"And you think the Safarans kidnapped her?" She couldn't believe he was sharing so much information with her. Shouldn't he be telling someone important, like Commander Nyx?

"Jax said the woman's eyes matched mine and she had a small, older scar on her throat. He saw it as she fell. It's my mother, I'm sure of it. They must have stolen or purchased the Atalantan veiling technology." His expression was grim. Determined. "We need to save her."

"As she fell?" Aris's heart pounded in her ears. This wasn't just some search and rescue mission, a couple of stranded soldiers. This was the leader of a dominion. If what Major Vidar —Vadim—said was true, the political implications were unthinkable.

"They shot her. Lieutenant Latza saw her go down. He couldn't tell if it was a solagun or tranq. In the chaos, he managed to escape."

"So, she could be . . ." She swallowed.

"We're going to get her." His voice was hard. "No one knows my connection to Ward Vadim, and I can't take the time to get authorization. You're the best flyer I've got, and I trust you. It's just you and me on this one." He stepped toward the door, and she went to follow him. *He really doesn't care that I'm a girl. He knows I can do this.*

"I have to say goodbye to Calix," she said.

"Fine, but hurry. We leave tonight."

"No." The word echoed in the cavernous room.

Calix was still in the cafeteria, sitting at the same table, her bowl of stew cooled to a gelatinous mess across from him.

"No?" she repeated, shocked.

"No," he said again, standing up. He held out a hand to her. "You can't go on another mission tonight. It's too dangerous. And besides, it isn't your job anymore."

"But it *is* my job. I have to go." She reached for his hand, but he dropped it before their fingers touched.

"Aris, no. If someone sees you impersonating a soldier, you'll be arrested! I won't allow you to go." He set his lips in a stubborn line.

Her heart splintered. "You won't allow me to go? What makes you think it's up to you?"

"I thought you did all this for me," he said, looking taken aback. "We're going to Promise. You have what you wanted. Isn't that enough?"

"No." The word burst from her lips. Even she was surprised at its force. She wished being with him *was* enough. It had been, once. But it wasn't anymore. Hadn't been, for a long time. "I'm sorry, Calix, but this is so much bigger than us. Can't you see that? This mission is important, and Major Vidar needs me. I have to help."

"So, that's it? You're just going to leave?"

Aris willed him to understand. "I have to go. This is my placement, my selection, in every way that matters. This is who I am."

She glanced at the Major, uncomfortable with his presence. He had stayed near the door and was acting, at least, like he wasn't listening. Turning back to Calix, she stepped closer, grabbing his hands. She waited until he met her eyes. "Say you'll be waiting for me when I get back. That we can figure this out."

For a long moment he said nothing, just studied her face as if memorizing it. Noting the differences, maybe, as she'd done with his. "I can't," he said finally, looking utterly lost. "I'm sorry, Aris. I know you want me to understand, but I don't think I can. You're not the same person . . . I don't know you anymore."

Aris dropped his hands and stepped away. A wave of ice cracked and shivered into place within her, burning where it pierced her heart. "You were right, back in Lux," she said, backing up. Her eyes never left his face. "We did change."

CHAPTER FIFTY-FOUR

"Lieutenant Latza was involved in a high-level surveillance mission when he was captured," Major Vidar said as he walked quickly down the hall. "The prison where he was held is just over the border in Safara, well defended. It's impossible to find by heat signature; thermal recognition is blocked. And if you're close enough to get a visual, they've already shot you down. But I've got the direct coordinates, so that will help."

"How are we going to get in, if they'll shoot us down as soon as they see us?" Aris hurried to keep up.

The Major slowed as they approached a blank door at the end of the hall. Inside, she found herself in a warehouse-like room with shelves stacked ceiling high. "We're going to bring them a prisoner."

She opened her mouth to ask him what he meant, but he was hurrying down one of the aisles, a scrap of silco in his hand. When he found the item he wanted, he carried it back to the front of the room. Inside the chrome storage container was a Safaran officer's uniform, boots, and weapon. Before she had time to look away, he'd stripped and was dressing in the dark gray pants and mottled gray-and-black jacket. There was even a helmet, sleek and black.

She waited for him to take a uniform for her out of the box, but with a sinking feeling she realized that wasn't going to happen. "You want me to be the prisoner."

He raised his eyes to hers and nodded, and she saw through the hard-edged Military shell he wore. "Calix was right," he said softly, "You don't have to do this. I know you're not used to these kinds of missions. And I'm not your officer anymore, Aris. You do have a choice. You know that, right?"

"I'm really only good at flying. Don't you want someone more experienced?" she asked, mind still whirling. "Someone you can count on?"

Major Vidar stepped closer. "*You* are the only person I can count on. Wolfe is gone, and Daakon is back in Spiro. And with the veil tech out there . . . I can't trust that anyone is who they seem." He gave her shoulder a quick squeeze. "Except for you. I know exactly who you are."

The words brought her to the brink of tears. *At least someone does.* She couldn't bring herself to speak. For a moment they stood in the entrance of that echoing room, in silence, their eyes locked. "I know what I'm asking," he added. "And what it could cost you. This is your choice."

Her choice.

Go back to Calix. Go back to being weak, helpless Aris and hope no one ever found out where she'd been for the past four months. Or stay here, with Major Vidar, as a flyer. A soldier. And maybe save a Ward's life.

It was a choice she'd already made, she realized. Not earlier, when she'd left Calix in the cafeteria. But months ago.

She took a deep breath. "I'm with you, Major Vidar—I mean Major Vadim. Tell me what you need me to do."

He spared her a small smile and grabbed her hand. "To start, you can call me Milek. Come on."

They wove through the racks of boxes until they found another that matched the numbers on Milek's list. This one held women's clothes: a dark green tunic, flowing pants, and a pair of soft, silk slippers. Another box yielded a shoulder-length black wig. Milek stood by the door while she hid behind a shelf to change.

"Done," she said, meeting him at the door. She tried to keep her hands relaxed at her sides, but the wig itched.

Milek smiled a little and reached out to readjust the fall of fake hair against her neck. "It's strange to see you like this, dressed like a woman."

She rolled her eyes. This getup was as much a disguise as her veil had been. "What's next?"

Milek swiped the passcard to open the door. "Time to see Lieutenant Latza."

Jax was asleep when they entered his room, but as soon as the door swished closed, his eyes opened. "Ah. Visitors."

"Up for a little information sharing?" Milek asked.

Jax nodded, glancing curiously at Milek's Safaran uniform. Aris perched on the chair next to Milek's.

Jax smiled at her. "Like the new look."

Before Aris could respond, Milek said, "We need to get into that prison. Immediately."

Jax turned his attention to Milek, his expression turning serious. "They'll shoot you down as soon as they see you."

"We'll be flying a Safaran wingjet in." Milek cocked his head toward Aris. "I'm taking them a prisoner."

"Ah." Jax nodded. "In that case, you have a chance. Foxfire is the unit that most often brings in civilian prisoners. Under Commander Eska, I believe. That's a name you should be able to use with relative impunity. I've heard he's a beast."

"What's the layout like? Do you know where the Ward was held?"

Jax shook his head. "No, unfortunately. Most prisoners are kept in a central holding room, called the pen. We only left it for washroom breaks once every three hours, alternating men and women. And 'interrogations.'" He brushed his fingertips against a nasty purple bruise on his cheek. "Those were held in cells down a long hallway. Two turns: left out of the room, then the second right. That's all I could glean of the layout. My guess is she must be in one of the interrogation cells. She was never put in the pen with the rest of us. And when she ran into the room during her escape attempt, she came from the left hallway."

"Do they interrogate all new prisoners?" Milek asked.

Jax nodded. "Upon arrival, all prisoners are processed. Which just means beaten in a private room, far as I can tell. You should be able to get to the interrogation cells easily."

"Surveillance?" Milek drummed his fingers on his knees. His impatience was a nearly physical force pushing against Aris.

"Cameras in all the halls, but not the cells. Never saw any guards stationed in the hallways. Once the alarm is sounded, you'll probably have a minute or two before they come after you." Jax scratched his arm, a thoughtful look passing across his face. "Might get a minute or two more since you're going in at night. They don't have as many guards on duty overnight. If you could cause some kind of distraction in the pen, that'd also buy you time."

"Are the guards armed with tranqs or solaguns?"

Jax scowled. "Both. And they've no qualms about going the deadlier route."

"What about access to the individual interrogation cells? How do they manage it?" Milek glanced at Aris, as if checking to make sure she was still there. She gave him a small nod. She wasn't going anywhere.

"The cell doors are locked with handprint sensors," Jax replied. "But because so many soldiers deliver prisoners, each guard has a backup passcard they can distribute to visitors. The card codes are changed every day, though, so the one I stole on my way out won't work. You'll have to snag one from a guard."

"What about our exit strategy?" Aris asked. "Once we get in and find Ward Vadim, how do we get her out?"

Milek glanced at her with a gleam in his eye. "That's where you come in."

CHAPTER FIFTY-FIVE

ARIS LANDED THE SAFARAN WINGJET WHEN THEY WERE STILL A distance from the prison. For a moment, they sat in the darkness of the wingjet, arms touching.

"You know what to do?" he asked.

"Yes, sir." She didn't look at him. Instead she stared out into the shadows of the forest and tried to keep her breathing steady.

"Alright, then."

She popped the shield and they got out, meeting on his side of the jet. The moon glowed above them, turning the thin scar along his cheek silver. For once, he didn't look like he was sneering; the perpetually quirked lip had a sweetness to it that made her want to smile back, even though she was dizzy with nerves.

"Are you sure?" His voice had lost its authoritative edge, and she could see the son, not the soldier, in his eyes.

"She's your mother, Milek. We have to try to save her." She held out her hands, wrists together.

He took her hands but, instead of binding them, he threaded his fingers with hers and drew her closer. If her heart, overtaxed as it was by the stress of their mission, had been able to beat faster, it would have. He shifted, bringing one hand up to touch her cheek. His pale face swallowed the dark, until the whole world was gone and all she could see was the soft glow of his eyes. He bent and kissed her, the lightest pressure against her lips.

Before she had time to close her eyes—or think—he drew back.

"Thank you. You are incredibly brave."

Then, as she tried to quiet her breathing, he bound her wrists with a length of twine. She wanted to speak, tell him the truth—that she was terrified. But the words wouldn't come. And it didn't matter. She'd do this, terrified or not, because it was her job. Because Milek was counting on her.

He bent down, and when he stood, he rubbed a thumb gently along her cheek, leaving a streak of mud. He did the same at her waist and along her neck. And then he tore her tunic.

The ripping noise of the fabric made her shudder. All the while his face was searching hers and his eyes were kind. But the signs of a simulated struggle still gave her goosebumps, and her stomach churned. The thought of a Safaran doing something like what Milek was staging, the thought of rough hands tearing at her clothes . . .

"Aris." His voice interrupted her dark imaginings. He held up a long, thin rod. "You remember how to use a sythin?"

"Yes." That was one lesson she'd never forget.

"If you need to incapacitate someone quickly and quietly, use this."

She nodded.

"Stand still." His fingers slid up her side, their warmth and the coolness of the sythin shocking against her skin. He tucked the weapon up under her breastband, beneath her arm. "Can you reach it?"

Her bound hands easily found the end of the sythin, where it pressed against the bottom edge of her ribs. "I've got it. No problem."

"Good. Now, when we get there, I'll have to be different. Maybe a little rough. They have to believe you're my captive. I'll say things . . . just don't listen, okay? Remember the mission."

"I understand."

Even as the words left her mouth, his face changed. The lines settled, the sneer at the corner of his mouth returned. He straightened his shoulders, and she realized he was again becoming the soldier, the secret operative who had infiltrated the Atalantan Military. He was no longer Milek, Galena Vadim's son. He was Major Vidar.

In turn, Aris took a deep breath and tried to channel Aristos . . . tried to remember that she was an Atalantan soldier, not the battered village girl she looked like. *You can do this.*

Milek helped her into the passenger seat of the wingjet and ran to the other side, flinging himself into the flyer's seat.

"You ready?" he asked one last time.

"Yes, sir."

Milek flew them toward the prison. His takeoff wasn't as smooth as she could have done, but he was an adequate flyer. When he spoke into the headset, calling the prison to let them know he was arriving with a new prisoner, Aris closed her eyes.

With a deep breath, she prepared to meet the enemy.

"Found her wandering the woods on my patrol," Milek said, his voice harsh, as he dragged Aris from the jet. He smiled at the two soldiers standing beside the wing, one tall and heavyset, the other shorter and thin. "Think she might be a spy. Is there someplace I can interrogate her?" She kept her eyes on the ground and made a show of trying to shove away from him. "In private?" He pulled her closer, up against his side.

At Milek's request, the soldiers stared knowingly at the torn fabric of her tunic.

"Of course. This way," the shorter of the soldiers said. He was slight, thin-lipped, and had a way of whipping his head back and forth as he walked that reminded Aris of a lizard. He led them toward a squat building that ran along the edge of the landing pad. Bright floodlights illuminated a sea of black wingjets, but the world beyond the tarmac was eaten by the night.

"What unit did you say you were with?" The fat soldier kept glancing back at her, his eyes a little too bright.

"Foxfire, with Commander Eska," Milek said, repeating the intel Jax had given them. He yanked her along as she pretended to resist. It wasn't hard; her brain was telling her to run, to get as far away from here as she possibly could.

"Commander Eska?" The short, lizard-like one paused. "I thought he was recalled to Haben."

The blood froze in her veins. *Holy hell, this is it . . .*

Milek laughed. "And yet the nightmares continue."

The big soldier finally took his eyes from Aris to glance at Milek. "Is it true he made someone eat donkey brains for two weeks because he missed morning formation?"

Milek shook his head. "Wasn't donkey brains."

"So, what was it then?" Lizard cocked his head.

With a jerk on Aris's arm to get her moving, Milek smirked. "Let's just say none of us ever missed formation again."

The soldiers asked no more questions as they walked into the building, but Lizard's slithering smile and the way he flicked his eyes from Milek's face to hers made Aris nervous.

They walked through the large main room Jax had told them about; pallets lined the walls and tables crowded the center. She saw men, even a few women and children, curled up on the hard pads. They were obviously trying to sleep, though the light was shining bright as day from giant panels in the ceiling.

Milek drifted toward the wall. He gave her arm two quick squeezes, their signal. Then he stumbled on the edge of a sleeping mat, going down on one knee. She was the only one who saw the tiny ball—a gas grenade—he tucked under the mat. Pretending to escape, Aris wrenched her arm free and made for the door they'd come in. Milek lunged for her, pulling her to a stop. "You tripped me, you snake! What could you possibly have hoped to accomplish? You'll pay for that."

Their guides shared a look as Milek hauled her back to them.

"Better get you two to interrogation," Lizard said, turning his gaze on her.

The soldiers led them past several other guards and through a door at the far end of the room. Aris watched Lizard's face from the corner of her eye. Any moment he was going to raise the alarm. She could *feel* his distrust. His suspicion. He nodded to a guard and she started to raise her head, panicked, to meet Milek's eyes, but he squeezed her arm tighter in warning.

The hallway was also brightly lit, with blank white walls and no windows. Lizard turned left.

Perfect.

"Just down here," Lizard said, his eyes glittering. Second hallway on the right, exactly as Jax said. The soldier swiped his hand across the wall about halfway down, and a door slid open. He walked into the room first, followed by Milek, who released her as he stepped inside.

The fat soldier took the opportunity to grab her arm himself. She let out a little whimper for effect. Then, as she crossed the threshold, she elbowed him in the gut, breaking his hold, and punched the panel to close the door.

When she turned around, the soldiers were on the floor in a pile. Milek stood over them, a sythin in hand.

"Nice work." She stared at the unconscious men. She couldn't look away from Lizard's thin face, worried that his eyes would open . . . that he'd look back at her and smile his slippery, knowing smirk. "How long do we have?"

"Not long. As soon as we leave the room without our escorts, we'll be on the clock. The gas grenade will go any minute. That will cause some confusion, maybe buy us another few minutes." He rifled through Lizard's pockets and fished out a backup pass-card. "This should work on the locks." He handed it to her, pulling the twine off her wrists as he did.

Milek handed her Lizard's solagun and grabbed the other for himself. "You go, start to the left. I'll work my way back toward the pen. I should be able to slow down whoever responds when the alarm is sounded. Unlock each door, but remember, the prisoners in these rooms may not be alone. You'll have to take down the interrogators. We're looking for a woman with bandages or a wounded face. Call her Galena . . . she'll respond if it's her."

"Yes, sir."

"If you find her, head back toward the pen." He spared her a small glance. "Be safe."

"You too." Aris's heart pounded against her ribcage like a wild animal trying to escape. "What will happen to the other prisoners?"

"As soon as we're safely away, we'll call in the coordinates to the nearest stationpoint. They'll send a unit to retrieve the others."

Aris nodded toward the soldiers on the ground. "And what about them? What if they wake up?"

Milek's voice was grim. "They won't."

As she slipped from the room, she heard the hiss of the solagun behind her.

CHAPTER FIFTY-SIX

ARIS RAN A FEW STEPS TO THE NEXT DOOR, HER SLIPPERED feet soaking up the cold of the carbonate floor. The pointed end of the sythin dug into her waist every time she moved. She held the solagun up in one hand and the passcard in the other, her eyes scanning the hall. At any moment she expected someone to round a corner and come after her.

She opened every door in the corridor, but all of the rooms were empty. Blank walls, unoccupied beds with neat piles of folded linens at their feet. Metal chairs bolted to the floor. The windows had all been painted over, white and featureless. In the absolute silence, every noise she made sounded too loud.

With every door that opened to an empty room, her stomach sank further. Jax had seen Galena go down . . . she'd been shot. Maybe they'd taken her to a mender in a different wing of the building.

Or maybe she was already dead.

When Aris opened the door at the end of the long hall, she bit back a surprised scream. A guard was standing in the middle of the room, his fist drawn back to hit the frail, gaunt-faced man at his feet. At the hiss of the door, the guard turned. Before he could yell, Aris grimaced and sent a burst of solagun fire at his chest. He dropped slowly, knees crumpling. She backed out of the door, eyes locked on the prisoner. His face was swollen and purple with bruises.

She didn't wait to see if he picked himself up and followed her.

She reached the end of the hall, turned the corner, and started on the next set of doors, her eyes constantly flitting along the corridor, ears straining for the slightest sound, praying she wouldn't have to shoot anyone else. Her hands were starting to shake.

In the distance came a faint roar and a scream. The gas grenade.

She was about to reach the end of the hall and was hoping Milek had better luck when she heard the muffled echo of a woman's scream. Aris slowed, creeping along the wall.

There. That door, fourth one on the left. The sounds were coming from in there.

Aris tightened her grip on the solagun.

She swiped the card and the door slid open. The instant the seal was broken, the full brunt of the screaming washed over her.

All she could see was writhing legs beneath a blood-stained sheet and the great bulk of a man in a white tunic standing over the bed.

"Stop!" She held her solagun up, ready to shoot. Her heart hammered in her chest but her hands were steadier than she expected. She kept her eyes focused on the man's broad back, away from the blood.

Before she had time to pull the trigger, he leapt, arm outstretched, and knocked the solagun out of her hands. He sliced his other arm through the air and her face erupted in pain. He followed with his fist, knocking her into the wall. She slid to the floor, cradling her face in her hands. It felt as if her skin had been held over an open flame. Eyes watering, she tried to move, but he gripped her throat and pulled her to her feet.

"What is the meaning of this?" he hissed, his white teeth gleaming.

Aris couldn't answer, couldn't breathe. She threw an arm up, trying to break his hold. No luck. Her fingers scratched at his wrist, but the hard muscles of his forearm may as well have been steel beams.

She tried to cough, tried to drag air into her lungs, to no avail. Dark spots bloomed in front of her eyes. Aris kicked the man as hard as she could. He grunted but his fingers remained locked around her throat.

"Who are you?" He pounded her head into the wall. He didn't loosen his hold enough for her to answer. With his other hand, he held something toward her face; its end shot blue flame. He brought it closer, as if he wanted to write on her skin. Just the thought made the line of fire on her cheek burn hotter.

She was going to die.

With the last vestiges of consciousness, she slid her hand up under her shirt. If she could—

There was a screeching rattle of a chain. The man turned his head. For a split second his hand slackened on her throat, and she sucked in half a breath.

Her fingers closed on the sythin. She pulled it free from her breastband, her thumb finding the button. Her torturer turned back to her, eyes widening at the weapon in her hand. His fingers squeezed harder, as if he wanted rip out her throat with his bare hand.

And then her arm drove the sythin into his stomach. For a moment he stared at her; then his mouth opened, and he dropped like a stone.

She tumbled to the ground, half on top of him, and bent forward, coughing. Her throat burned.

As she scrambled to her feet, she looked up and fought a horrified scream when she saw the red, scarred face of the woman looking back at her from the bed. When their eyes met, the woman began to cry.

"Galena Vadim? Ward of Ruslana?" Aris whispered, the words scraping along her injured throat.

The woman nodded, weeping.

"I'm Aris." She stumbled to the bed, the sythin still held

tightly in her hand. Galena's arms were shackled. Aris fiddled with the restraints, her fingers clumsy. With a clang, they finally snapped open. "Milek and I came to find you."

Galena threw her arms around Aris, knocking her back a step. "Milek is *here*?" When Aris nodded, the woman squeezed her tighter. "You blessed girl."

Aris resettled her wig, which was draped half across her face.

"We have to hurry." The words were barely audible. The pain of speaking made her want to scream, but that would only make it worse.

Aris bent to retrieve her solagun and stood over the man. She had to end him. It was safer that way. Still—she steeled herself to pull the trigger.

A hand touched her arm.

"Don't." Galena looked down at the man, her red-rimmed, ice-blue eyes full of hate.

"He'll come after us when he wakes."

"You can't kill him now." Galena's voice was shaking. "I will have him brought before the World Council for the crimes he has committed. His secrets will not be allowed to die with him."

Aris glanced at the Ward and saw she was deadly serious. She lowered the solagun but stabbed him again with the sythin, this time in the neck. She *really* didn't want him following them. Then she grabbed Galena's arm. "Let's go."

They burst into the hall; it was empty, but she could hear noise in the direction she'd come from. The guards.

She had to get to Milek.

She ran, helping Galena along. The older woman's face was red and oozing, her legs frail. She stumbled frequently, but kept moving.

Someone shouted behind them. Aris spun and shot her solagun toward the noise. One soldier went down; another kept after them. The two women flung themselves around the corner of the corridor. Up ahead, Milek was holding off three soldiers. He shot one in the stomach.

"Milek!" she tried to yell. He must have heard her, because he brought the other two soldiers down, fast and deadly as lightning, then turned to her.

Aris had almost reached him when an immense *thud* sent her flying.

She slid along the floor to his feet, her shoulder exploding in pain.

"What—" Her brain wouldn't work. And her legs weren't any better. Sounds ricocheted above her—shouting, the hiss of solaguns—but she couldn't keep track of the noise. She couldn't keep track of anything.

"Gods, she's been shot," someone cried.

"Come on, Aris!" That was Milek. She knew his voice.

Strong hands gripped her under the arms and pulled her to her feet. Her arm went around his neck, and she was stumbling down a long white hallway.

They burst into the large open room with the prisoners. The room was filled with smoke and chaos. Milek skidded to a halt at the far wall. She slammed against him. There was no door, no way out.

"What . . . ?" she whispered.

Milek smacked two explosives against the wall, then hauled her back toward a line of guards bearing down on them. Galena's eyes met hers, but all Aris could see was the burning of her skin, the red—

A guard shot off another flash of solagun fire, but Milek dragged her down to the floor just in time. She wanted to close her eyes, rest for a moment, just a moment.

Then the world exploded.

Milek shoved her and Galena through the smoking hole in the wall. She felt the concussion of another blast behind her, but she couldn't turn to see. She stumbled.

"Can you fly?" a voice shouted in her ears.

Could she fly? Flying was *all* she could do, all she was. If Aris couldn't fly, she was nothing.

She nodded.

Arms shoved her into the cabin of a wingjet. Her hands were

on the controls. She felt the pedals beneath her bare feet. She should have boots on. Where were her boots?

The warmth of another body filled the seat beside her. The shield closed.

Noise exploded in front of her. Silhouetted in the bright lights, an army stood. Solagun fire flashed.

"Now, Aris!" Milek yelled.

The wingjet rose, perfectly vertical, and then she shot forward, into the clump of men. Dull thuds echoed along the bottom of the jet. Distant screams. She flicked her hand and the jet twisted, gaining speed and height until they were spinning up and into the night.

For a while, flashes and booms exploded beneath her, and she spun and dipped and whirled. Through the dark, through the silence, she danced.

Eventually, the light died, and then it was just the black.

She glanced at the nav map; a forest spread before them, ridges of trees and barren land reaching up toward her. The squiggles of land mass went hazy, fading slowly in and out.

"Milek," she whispered, her hands loosening their grip on the controls. "You need to take over . . . I'm . . . I'm . . ."

I'm nothing, she thought as the darkness claimed her.

CHAPTER FIFTY-SEVEN

ARIS WAS IN A WHITE ROOM, AND THE CEILING WAS GLOWING, and Galena's torturer was standing over her, smiling. *Oh Gods.* She screamed, struggling wildly to escape, but her arms were trapped beneath the bright white sheets, and the lights above her glowed.

The man held his silver tool up to her face, drew it gently down her cheek so she could feel the cold metal against her skin. Her scream froze in her throat. She couldn't breathe.

His smile widened as the tip of the weapon shot blue flame.

Everything went black.

And then she was blinking and gasping into the light of another blank room. A stranger sat beside her, stroking her hand.

"Where am I?" Her face burned, and her throat was raw.

"Quiet now. You're at Revening. You're safe," the mender said. Only he wasn't a stranger after all. She recognized his delicate face and graceful hands.

"Zaro."

"Try not to speak. Your throat was damaged in the crash."

"The crash?"

Zaro squeezed her hand, eyes narrowing in warning. "Yes, the crash. During your routine trip to Feln Stationpoint."

Aris blinked. Was she still dreaming? None of that made any sense. She'd been nowhere *near* Feln.

"Where's Milek?" she asked urgently.

Zaro sighed. "Major Vadim is in Ruslana, with the Ward. He waited a few days, to make sure you were well. But he had to go. You've been unconscious for some time."

"That's enough," a gruff voice said.

Aris shifted her head, wincing at the pain in her throat. Commander Nyx stood behind Zaro. Without another word, the mender stood, spared Aris a small smile, and left the room.

Aris tensed automatically; she'd never seen Commander without snapping to attention. It felt *wrong* to just lie there, to not acknowledge his presence in some way. "Sir," she whispered.

Commander Nyx didn't sit. He placed a digitablet on her lap. "I'm going to need your signature before we leave."

Aris raised her brows in question.

The Commander scowled. "It's a statement saying that you have been working as a consultant for the Military sector through the Enviro office in Panthea. You were en route to Feln for a meeting when your wingjet crashed. If you deviate from this story in the press or in public in any way, you will be detained. Do you understand?"

"But it's not true." Aris shook her head and felt a twinge of pain in her shoulder. "I was part of the mission to save Ward Vadim."

"Not officially. If you'd been Aristos, I'd be giving you a commendation right now. But as Aris, a woman, I have to bury your role in the rescue and deny any rumor of your involvement."

Panic unfurled in her chest. "But I don't have to be a woman. Only Major Vadim and Calix know. I can still be Aristos. Dianthe can make me another veil. Please—"

"When Major Vadim returned to Revening with you and the Ward, your true identity was exposed. Your crew and some of the menders recognized you. We were able to keep it from the media, but not the other soldiers on point. I'm sorry, Haan. As far as the Military is concerned, Aristos is dead." Commander Nyx tapped the digitablet with one thick finger. "Now, you will sign this."

Aris tried to keep her face blank, tried to be the soldier, but she couldn't hold back the tears. They ran down her cheeks, stinging in some places, until her whole face was on fire. She *wasn't* a soldier anymore. And, with Commander Nyx's story, it'd be like she never had been. "Does Milek know?" she whispered. Surely he wouldn't let this happen if he did?

The Commander didn't answer.

Aris could hardly breathe. "Am I—does this mean I'm going to jail?"

The lines of his face remained unforgiving. "We received authorization to remove your Military brand." *Like a criminal.* "For now, you'll be going home, but if you reveal your involvement in Military or Ward Vadim's rescue, you will be prosecuted. Do you understand?"

"But I helped save Ward Vadim." Aris hadn't expected to stay Aristos forever, but she didn't realize she'd just be *erased*, her actions forgotten. "I was a good flyer. I helped people. Why do I have to lie?"

"Because there are no women in Military." For a split second, Commander Nyx's eyes softened. "And there never will be."

CHAPTER FIFTY-EIGHT

IT WAS HAPPENING AGAIN. ARIS WAS IN THE WHITE ROOM, trapped beneath the sheets, and the blue fire was getting closer. Only this time it was held by one of the blank-faced Safaran soldiers she'd killed. His uniform was burnt away by solagun fire, his skin blackened and rotting. He smiled; he would enjoy exacting his revenge.

She struggled to get away, but strong hands held her down, shook her, and somewhere she heard a woman scream.

"Aris, Aris!" a voice from her childhood called to her.

She fought against the hands, fought against the sheets. The soldier was holding her down, and his eyes were so cold and black and *flat* they looked like doll's eyes. Blank and inhuman.

She screamed again.

And then she was free, ripped from that barren white room and into her father's arms. Her face burned, her throat was raw, and all she could do was gasp and cough as he held her, whispering her name over and over in her ear.

"I'm okay," she murmured, staring over his shoulder at the half-open shades of her bedroom windows. The milky glow of Lux's pathways painted the floor with silver. This was her bedroom. She was home.

Her father didn't answer her, didn't let go, and she realized he was crying.

"Father, I'm fine." She wiped the tears from his cheek, wishing it were true. "It's okay. Really."

He leaned away from her, squeezing her shoulders once before letting go. There was so much pain in his face, etched in the furrow between his brows, the sagging skin beneath his eyes. It killed her. But he didn't say anything, just kissed her forehead and left the room, his shoulders hunched and his steps dragging.

She swallowed; her throat still throbbed.

She slipped out of bed and pulled on black leggings and a short exercise tunic. The dim light coming through her windows was changing to the grayish gold of dawn.

After padding to the washroom, she splashed cool water on her face and stared at herself in the mirror, as she did each morning, hoping that by some magic her reflection had changed.

It never did.

Aris ran a tentative finger across the angry red rope of scar that began at her temple and slashed across the bridge of her nose to the opposite corner of her lips. There was no way to hide it, to hide from it. It had been weeks, and still the scar burned red.

Her hair had grown to a sleek dark cap; a little while longer and she'd have curls. She still caught herself running her hand across her head, surprised to feel soft hair, rather than smooth skin or the hitch of stubble.

She drew the neckline of her tunic up and tried to cover the fading yellow bruises that circled her neck. Zaro said her voice would never sound exactly as it had . . . the man had done lasting damage to her vocal chords when he'd tried to rip her throat out. Some days Aris pulled down the corner of her tunic to stare at the small red scar on her shoulder, where the solagun blast had burned clean through, but today she didn't. It was just another reminder.

The only way she'd survive was to try to forget.

She turned away from the mirror and walked through the

house, her feet quiet against the tile. The door to her parents' bedroom was shut; her father had probably gone back to bed. She slipped from the house without a sound.

It didn't take her long to descend the steep path to the beach. By the time the sun had risen above the village, she had run for miles, her bare feet sinking rhythmically into the sand. Already, the air that streamed against her face was warm and moist with humidity.

She knew her father didn't mean to look at her the way he did, like she had died and was her own ghost, haunting him. But that didn't make it easier to bear.

When she had arrived at her parents' door, Commander Nyx made Gus and Krissa sign confidentiality agreements like the one she had signed. But he'd let her tell them the truth, or most of it anyway, that she'd been part of a search and rescue unit, disguised as Aristos. She wasn't allowed to mention the Ward of Ruslana.

Her father had been so angry. "You mother and I thought you'd disowned us, that we'd never see you again. But this is so much worse. How could you do such a thing?"

And she had tried to explain. "I wanted to be with Calix," she'd said, her voice still a hoarse whisper. "And then . . . that didn't even matter anymore. I was happy as a flyer, Father. It fit. Like it was what I was supposed to do."

But everything she said just made his face go redder. "You could have been killed, and for what? A stupid crush? Some misplaced act of rebellion?"

"It wasn't about rebelling!" she responded, her own face heating up. "It was about doing the right thing. I saved lives, don't you get that? What I did was *important*."

"You think fighting in this war is important? Even the Ward of Ruslana is urging us to work with Safara. If we'd just give them what they want—"

Aris slammed a hand on the counter, rattling dishes and making her mother gasp. Her voice low, dangerous, she growled, "You don't know what you're talking about. You have no idea what Safara is capable of, how close they are to destroying this dominion. Stop talking about things you don't understand!"

Her father's jaw had dropped.

She had stomped away, slammed her bedroom door . . . and felt the thick swell of shame threaten to drown her. She'd never spoken to him that way before. She'd never been a violent person, never wanted to punch walls or slam doors. But she'd been Aristos for too long.

Aristos wanted to tell Gus the whole truth, that he wasn't just a flyer, but the flyer who'd helped save Ward Vadim. Only no one knew that Ward Vadim had needed saving. There'd been nothing on the news; Aris had no idea if the true Ward had resumed her place yet or not.

Aristos wanted to spar with Dysis, wanted to punch and weave and parry until he was too tired to think, too exhausted to care.

But *Aris* couldn't do those things. So she ran instead. The irony. She never would have thought it possible, but running was the only thing that gave her any sense of freedom now. She pumped her arms harder, pushed herself faster as she flew along the beach.

And still her worries paced her, refusing to be left behind.

Calix had turned his back on her. Milek had disappeared. And she was a girl again. No longer a member of the Atalantan Military. No longer a flyer.

She had nothing.

She *was* nothing.

Every few days, Krissa pushed her to dust the groves, saying it would ease Gus's mind. But Aris couldn't fly anymore, not even to dust. Not even for her father.

The nightmares wouldn't let her.

WHEN ARIS RETURNED to the house, her parents were in the great room watching the news vid with their breakfast. She could hear the murmur of the monitor in the distance, but no one called hello or came to meet her when the front door slid closed. She moved around the kitchen, fixing a cup of strong tea and rummaging in the foodsaver for leftover bread and cheese from dinner the night before.

Through the main arch, she could see a corner of the monitor and her mother's knee. "Anyone need anything?" she called, on impulse.

"We're fine, doll," came her mother's voice in response.

Aris bit off a chunk of bread, hoping that today her stomach would settle, today would be the day the nightmares wouldn't follow her, when she heard the sound of something shattering.

Dropping the piece of bread, she ran to the main room.

Shards of glass glittered on the floor at her father's feet, and a dark puddle of tea was spreading across the cream tile. But no one was looking at it or moving to clean up the mess.

Aris glanced at the monitor, the reporter's voice jangling incoherently in her ears. She gasped.

The Ward of Ruslana—the fake Ward Vadim, Aris could tell, face devoid of any scarring—stood at a podium before the Council Building, but she wasn't speaking because a host of soldiers in Ruslanan blue were swarming the stage. Behind her, Ward Nekos, his wife, Bett, and Ward Balias stood frozen. A number of other dignitaries were screeching in fear and struggling to escape into the audience of reporters.

"Pardon me," the fake Ward was saying, obviously flustered. "There seems to be some sort of situation." At first she seemed to think they were there to protect her. Even Ward Nekos stepped forward, surveying the crowd for danger. But then one of the men drew Ward Vadim's arms behind her back and clapped restraints on her wrists. "Now *wait a minute*," she said, her voice still amplified by the microspeaker on her lemon-yellow dress.

Aris watched, eyes wide.

"What the blighting hell is going on?" Gus asked, the worry

thick in his voice. The puddle of tea was still spreading around his feet.

Another woman walked onto the stage, helped by a tall man with a thin scar that drew his lip into a sneer. Milek. Her heart lurched.

"Watch, Father." Aris sank into a chair, eyes glued to the screen.

"People of Ruslana, you have been deceived," the woman said, her microspeaker throwing her voice over the murmurs of the crowd. She turned to face the camera. It zoomed in on her red, disfigured face.

Krissa gasped.

"This woman is not who you believe her to be." The woman with the wounded face walked to stand beside the Ward. "I am the real Galena Vadim, and as you can see, someone has gone to great pains to ensure that you never discovered this truth."

The camera panned out, and Aris could see Milek again, his face grim with determination as he moved to flank the woman pretending to be his mother. She didn't even seem to recognize him. The whispered exclamations and questions from reporters threatened to drown out what was happening on stage.

"This is ridiculous! How can you—I am just appalled. Where is my security?" The woman who looked like Galena sputtered and yelled, her voice carrying over the murmuring crowd. The real Galena reached up to the back of her double's neck and released the device Aris knew she would find there.

Immediately, the woman's features shimmered, melted, and reorganized themselves. She still looked a lot like Galena once had, but her nose was longer, her lips thinner, her cheeks gaunt. The crowd gasped.

There was a clatter and a thud as Ward Nekos's wife threw herself forward, knocking over the podium in the process. She stood nose to nose with the real Galena. The camera zoomed in on her; she didn't flinch, even that close to the Ward's ravaged face. "How did you get free?" Bett hissed, moving as if to grab

Ward Vadim's arm. The crowd had quieted, and the micros-peakers picked up every word.

Milek stepped forward and put himself between them.

"Why, Bett?" Ward Vadim asked.

Bett held on to her anger for a second longer and then, grad-ually, it bled from her face, leaving her eyes hollow. She buried her hands in the brilliant orange fabric of her dress. "It was for the good of the dominion. I'm sorry, Galena," she whispered. "I'm sorry, but it was the only way."

The crowd in front of the stage was silent, and Aris had the strange sense that she'd walked in on the rehearsal for a play. She wondered how long the cameras would be allowed to record the drama, when someone would remember that the world was watching.

Ward Nekos stepped in front of his wife. "What have you done?"

A shout cut through Bett's reply. The fake Galena was fighting her restraints, trying to get away. Milek took Bett's arm and nodded to Ward Vadim, then he and his soldiers led the captive women off the stage.

In a whisper, a reporter's voice recounted the events that had unfolded: "It seems there was a plot to replace the Ward of Ruslana with a double using some kind of device. It's unclear to what purpose, but one can gather it had something to do with the war. As we're watching now it appears Ward Nekos's wife was involved as she's being led away . . ."

Ward Vadim again spoke over the crowd. "As the rightful Ward of Ruslana, I would like to announce a few policy changes, effective immediately." She turned to stare at Ward Balias, who was standing still as a statue at the corner of the stage, that strange smile of his fixed in place. "First, I am reinstating all military and economic sanctions on the dominion of Safara."

The crowd didn't make a sound.

"Second, I am establishing a tribunal. I hereby formally charge Safaran operative, code name Elom, with war crimes against the Ward of Ruslana."

In her mind's eye, Aris saw the man's black, pitiless eyes as he clutched at her throat. She swallowed, her hands shaking. *Elom.* Now she knew his name.

"And finally," the Ward said, taking a deep breath, "I would like to pledge to Atalanta whatever Ruslanan military and economic support is necessary to defend the dominion, now and forever, from Safara."

The news agents erupted with shouted questions.

Krissa tapped the panel on the table beside her chair, and the screen went blank. For a moment, the room hummed with silence.

Gus turned to Aris, as if somehow he thought she would have the answers. "What you said about Safara destroying us. Do you know something about this?"

She stared at him, her chest tight. She couldn't stop herself from telling him the truth, not this time. "I helped save her. The real Ward. I helped Milek save her."

His face was pale, his skin papery and creased with wrinkles. He looked so much older now than she remembered. Confusion and anguish warred in his eyes.

He opened his mouth. "I . . ."

"I'll get a towel for that spill," she said, and she fled the room.

Chapter Fifty-Nine

"I'T'S SO SAD FOR THE WARD, DON'T YOU THINK? THAT SHE'S so ugly now? I mean, obviously she can still do her job and everything, but if I were her I'd have to get it fixed or something. I wouldn't want everyone staring, and you know they're going to stare. She's a public figure for Gods' sake!" Echo tossed her enormous cloud of hair and took a sip of her drink, and Aris was grateful for the moment of silence.

Echo's newest ring, Bynne, sat next to Aris. He was tall and solid, with thick black hair and terrible hand-eye coordination. Aris had already saved her glass from his wandering elbow twice. She was confident she could take him in hand-to-hand . . . he was big but clumsy, and she'd learned to dodge pretty well.

Aris shifted again on the stool, hoping no one would notice her fidget. She was wearing a dress for the first time since she'd returned home, and she kept forgetting to keep her knees together and ankles crossed.

"Oh, I don't know. I think there's a strange kind of symmetry to the scars," Phae said. Her silver dress and glitter-streaked black hair shimmered in the low light of the bar. "Once they heal completely, the pattern could be quite beautiful." She leaned closer to Rakk, her eyes soft. He smiled back, his expression more relaxed than Aris had seen since he was sent away.

Echo's laughter tinkled out over the table. "Scars, *beautiful?* Come on." And then she gasped, just as Aris felt a sharp movement beside her. Aris glanced at Phae and guessed she'd probably kicked her, because Echo hastened to add, "But not *all* scars are ugly, I mean, there are plenty . . . um . . . tasteful—"

Aris knew Phae hadn't been objecting on her account. She couldn't bring herself to look too closely at Rakk; the pattern of his burns reminded her of the last time she'd seen Galec. "Why don't we just say 'scars have character' and move on?" Aris suggested, and Echo nodded eagerly. The table lapsed into awkward silence.

The Toad was relatively quiet. The band hadn't started yet, and their group was wedged into a corner away from the dance floor.

Rakk leaned across Phae. "So, Aris," he said, his voice serious. "In your consulting trips, did you find that things were getting worse or better? When I was in Bieza, fighting was almost daily. Was it—"

"She doesn't want to talk about it, Rakk," Phae interrupted. "Leave her alone."

Aris wanted him to finish his question; she *did* want to talk about it. All of it. The truth. Even if it meant getting sent to jail. Because maybe if she told someone what had really happened, how she felt, she wouldn't be so terrified of falling asleep at night. Maybe she'd be able to put the past to rest.

But she couldn't.

So she smiled and leaned into Phae's side. "Thanks," she said, pretending they were still friends, that there wasn't an ocean of silence and secrets and disappointment between them. Pretending that she really had worked in Panthea and missed Phae's wedding for one of her consulting trips. "I don't know much about the war, anyway. I was far from the front lines."

"It's a shame, how the Ward's wife sold that veiling tech and all, just to try to help Atalanta, and how it all backfired on her." Bynne stared at his glass. "She thought what she did would make

Safara end the war . . . and now she'll face a tribunal. Poor Ward Nekos."

"Poor Ward Vadim," Aris grunted.

Everyone glanced at her, and she realized she'd forgotten herself. She said the words again, louder and higher. As a girl would say them.

But she couldn't help wondering what joke Otto would make, or what Dysis would say. And Galec . . . She swallowed and kept her eyes down.

"I got a comm from Calix the other day," Rakk said, clearly trying to jumpstart the conversation again. But at the mention of Calix, Aris's heart clenched. She didn't have to look up to know the girls were exchanging looks. They knew she and Calix weren't speaking anymore, though they didn't know why. Oblivious, Rakk went on. "He said the fighting's been a bit quieter where he is. But they're seeing more refugees."

"We'll see an influx soon, I suspect," Bynne said.

Aris couldn't help but remember past nights at the Toad, when Calix and Rakk had talked like Bynne and Rakk were doing now. When she'd been content to just lean back and listen, Calix's arm around her. She didn't fit anymore. Not with what she'd been through, and not without Calix.

When the band began to play, Echo squealed and scampered to the dance floor, hauling Bynne with her. Rakk and Phae followed, trying to draw Aris with them, but she smiled and shook her head. She didn't feel like dancing. With a vague, fond smile at her friends, she slipped away.

<hr>

SITTING at the mouth of the cave on the beach, Aris watched the endless waves of the ocean sparkle in the moonlight. She could watch the water for hours, the eternal and hypnotic ebb and flow. Her eyes caught on a shadowy fanax floating in the wind, dipping and diving through darkness.

Calix had said she didn't need to be a fanax, that being small and agile was her greatest strength. And Milek had called her brave.

She dreamed about him sometimes, but he was never in her nightmares. She wished she'd been able to see him, to say goodbye.

She stared at the black line where sky met water. The truth—her truth—was like that horizon; it stretched on forever in her mind, flat and unbroken.

She wasn't Aristos and never would be again.

But she wasn't Aris either. Not the Aris who stayed in Lux, who let Calix and everyone else take care of her. She didn't know where she'd go, what she'd do, but she couldn't stay here.

She stood, her eyes drinking in the sight of the ocean, the delicate dance of the fanax above the waves. Calix or not, flyer or not . . . Lux was no longer where she belonged.

Chapter Sixty

Pyralis looked up when Galena entered the room, her blue eyes as bright and wary as ever. She stopped when she reached the wall of glass and kept her face turned toward the forest, away from him.

"Ward Vadim," he murmured, moving to stand behind her. He could see her reflection, the angry red weals that marred her pale skin. But her eyes were just the same.

"So it was Bett," she said. She reached up, placed a palm against the glass.

The respectful distance between them was too much. He wanted to be closer, to take her in his arms. He wanted to draw her hand into his, pull her against his chest and kiss her wounded cheeks.

Instead, he sighed. "The operative, Elom, promised her that Safara would withdraw if they received the diatous veil technology. If the sanctions were removed. I believe . . ." He paused. "I believe she thought she was acting in the best interests of Atalanta."

"How did she procure the technology? How did she even *know* about it?"

"One of her Tech placements, years ago. She went back, ordered a device on my authority." Anger tightened his words.

Galena was silent for a moment. "Have you questioned Ward Balias?"

"He continues to disavow all knowledge of the plot. I've not yet been able to find evidence of his involvement."

She made a small, skeptical noise in the back of her throat. "And Josef? Bett was aware he would be assassinated?"

"She says Elom promised her no one would get hurt." Pyralis swallowed, eyes drawn again to Galena's reflection.

She whirled to face him, her lips twisted into a grimace. "And do you believe her, Pyralis?" she asked, her voice hard even as she so casually spoke his name.

He reached out and took her hand. Her fingers were cool, smooth . . . small in his. Softly, he replied, "It doesn't matter. Whatever her motives, whatever she was promised . . . she betrayed this dominion. She betrayed me, and she put you willfully in danger. No punishment is great enough for her crimes."

Bett had begged him, when she confessed. Begged him to have mercy, to believe that she was trying to save Atalanta. She'd screamed at him, told him he didn't understand how he'd driven her, dogged her with his weariness, his despair. She was watching her dominion burn, and she had to do *something*.

In the end, though, it wasn't up to him. The tribunal would decide her fate. She would go on trial like any other citizen.

And he would never look at her again without seeing Galena's burned face. No matter what the tribunal decided, Bett would be the Ward's wife no longer. Breaking the union would be difficult; it would take years and a lot of money, but there was no other course. Not for him.

"Did you know? Did you guess?" Galena whispered. She hadn't freed her hand from his, hadn't pulled away.

Pyralis drew her a step closer. "I wanted to believe it wasn't you. It didn't seem possible that you would align yourself with Ward Balias, that you could look at me with such . . . neutral disinterest. And you—she—never mentioned Milek. It all seemed too strange and uncharacteristic." He released her hand and moved to his chair, bounced a fist on its back. "But I couldn't be certain. After everything . . . the way I knew you felt about me. I betrayed you. I did wonder if perhaps this wasn't, well . . ." He turned to glance at her. "Your revenge."

Galena drew herself to her full height, letting the sunlight shine against her damaged face. "Whatever I felt for you, Pyralis, I would never have put our dominions in danger."

Pyralis leaned against the chair, remembering how proud and distant she'd been when he'd asked her for help. Even then, she had been willing. And what had he done when she'd fallen ill? When she'd acted strange and gone against their agreement? Nothing. He'd been willing to believe the worst of her.

"I should have known. I should have done more to discover the truth, to find you." When he continued, his voice was bitter. "Josef would have done more."

Galena sighed and inclined her head to stare at her clasped hands. "Perhaps. He was a good man. He deserved more in this life."

"Galena—"

She put a hand up. "Don't. I have no wish to trade regrets. There is something else we need to discuss."

He raised a brow. "And that is?"

"There are rumors spreading that a female soldier was instrumental in my rescue."

"We can easily remedy that. We'll release a statement that a civilian girl was extracted at the same—"

"No." Galena cut him off. "That is *not* how we fix this."

CHAPTER SIXTY-ONE

WHEN ARIS GOT BACK FROM HER MORNING RUN, KRISSA WAS standing in the kitchen, staring blankly at the floor.

"Shouldn't you be at work?" Aris asked.

Krissa looked up and heaved a great sigh. Her smooth skin was red from crying. "You're going to *leave* us again, aren't you? And *just* when we got you back."

"What are you talking about?" Aris had only just decided she couldn't stay; how did her mother know?

"I heard it on the news, about them repealing the ban. They're going to allow *women* in Military—"

"*What?*" Aris leaned against the wall, knees suddenly weak. "What did you say?" She must have been mistaken. There was no way—

Krissa sniffed. "Surely you heard? Ward Nekos announced it this morning."

"I—I don't understand." Aris swallowed, her mind blank. Women in Military . . . but . . .

"Well, it's a bit more complicated than that, of course. He said women won't be *selected* for Military, but he explained about the dominion's secret experiment. What *you* were a part of, I'm assuming." Krissa wiped under her eyes and pinched her cheeks, pulling herself together as she continued. "He said that any

298

women currently serving will be allowed to do so without disguising themselves as men. And *next* year they'll allow female volunteers."

Aris slumped against the wall. This couldn't be happening. The Commander said women would never be a real part of Military.

Krissa noticed Aris's reaction and put an arm across her shoulders. "My *doll*, you really didn't know?"

Aris shook her head and stared up at the ceiling. She didn't want to start crying. "No, I didn't know."

"Ward Nekos said that a female operative was instrumental in saving the Ward of Ruslana, and *that's* why 'the brave women currently serving Atalanta should be recognized and allowed to serve as themselves.' He was talking about you, wasn't he?"

Aris shrugged and stepped away from her mother's arm. "They made me leave. I don't think they'll let me go back."

Krissa sighed. "You're not happy here. I can see it. Even your father can see it. You miss it."

Aris clenched her fists and fought the tears back with an effort. "I do, sometimes. But—"

"You should try. *Make* them take you back." Krissa raised her chin. "You're a hero."

The tears spilled. A hero? That's how her mother saw her?

"Flying is who you *are*, Aris. I didn't—I didn't see it until you stopped." Krissa started crying again, noisy sobs into her hands.

Aris kissed her mother's soft, damp cheek. "Don't cry. It'll all be okay. *I'll* be okay." She prayed the words weren't just another lie.

"5 Cleo, the River," the driver said.

Aris paid him and slipped from the terran. She stared at the great chrome door, let her eyes follow the building's façade upward until it disappeared into the darkness. She took a deep breath and rubbed her arms briskly, even though she wasn't cold.

The same old man stood in the lobby; he showed no spark of recognition when she whispered her name. As he put through the call, she was struck with sudden doubt. What if Dianthe refused to see her? But in a few moments, the man nodded and pointed to the lift.

When the lift finally stopped and Aris stepped into the corridor, Dianthe was waiting.

Aris walked stiffly forward, clenching her fists and raising her chin, because what she really wanted to do was run down the hall and throw herself into the woman's arms.

"So. You've come back," Dianthe said when Aris reached her.

Aris stared at the blood-red snake and forced back the tears. "I came to apologize."

Dianthe pointed through the door and waited for Aris to walk before her into the apartment. It hadn't changed; the great purple chair still squatted in the center of the room, and the lights of the city still glittered cold and remote through the window.

Dianthe poured two glasses of amber liquid. Leaning against the table, she held one out. "Now what is it you want to apologize for?"

Aris reached for the glass and took a small sip. The drink burned down her throat like Elom's fire. She coughed. Finally, when she could breathe again, she rasped, "I'm sorry I couldn't make it. I let you down."

"Is that what you think you did?"

Aris shrugged and looked down at herself, at her pale pink dress and delicate leather sandals. "I broke your only rule. I exposed the truth about Aristos. I failed."

Dianthe moved, cat-like, and suddenly her long fingers were wrapped around Aris's bare arm. She led her to the bench by the window and drew her down so they were sitting next to each other, their backs to the view. For the first time Aris could remember, Dianthe's touch was gentle. "Aris, how can you think you failed? You're the *reason* the ban on women in Military was repealed. You saved the Ward of Ruslana."

Aris's eyes flew to Dianthe's face. "How do you know that?"

Her lip quirked. "I know a lot of things. Don't you remember?"

"They told me I could be 'detained' if I say anything about what I did. Who I really was." The words tasted bitter as they left her mouth. Aris's eyes fell to her lap. "Nothing seems to fit anymore. I can't be Aristos, but I don't think I'm Aris either. I don't know *who* I am." She was lost.

Dianthe grabbed her knee. "You are a woman who gave up everything to defend her dominion. You are a flyer."

Aris shook her head, the faces of her nightmares flickering behind her eyes. "Not anymore."

"Do not *ever* undervalue your gift for donkey-headed persistence, my girl," Dianthe said gruffly. "You were your own person before you became Aristos, and whoever you become now," she let go of Aris's knee, "you're strong enough to be her too."

THE NEXT MORNING, Aris forced herself onto her family's landing pad. Her legs shook so badly she could hardly move, but Dianthe's words, her faith, pushed Aris forward.

By the time she'd clambered into the wingjet and settled her hands on the controls, black spots were dancing before her eyes and a cold sweat chilled the back of her neck.

You are strong enough. You can do this.

She reached out to tap the nav panel and tried to ignore the churning and cramping in her stomach. This was where she *belonged*, blight it. A few nightmares and a rocky landing or two weren't enough to keep her from the freedom of open sky. Hadn't she flown through violent storms? Enemy fire? And she'd survived it all.

Today was a beautiful day, with no Safaran soldiers trying to kill her. No dangerous missions. It was just a little dance.

This should be easy.

She took a deep breath and tried to get her shaking hands under control.

But it was no use.

What is wrong with me?

The hum of the wingjet shivered under her skin with the heat of Elom's flame, and the three soldiers she'd killed stared at her from every shadow. Her body began shuddering so violently she had to close her eyes and hold her breath, afraid she was about to break apart.

Shaking, pale, exhausted from the effort, she slipped down the side of the jet and fell against the white-hot landing pad.

She let herself lie there for a moment, knowing if she stood she'd be sick.

Eventually Aris hauled herself up and stumbled to her room. When her hands and legs stopped trembling, she grabbed a bag from her trunk and threw it on the bed. Slowly, she drew clothes from her delicate white dresser and stuffed them into the bag, pausing only to breathe through a series of stomach cramps that nearly bent her double. She didn't stop until the bag was packed and waiting by the door.

She stood in the doorway, staring down at it.

Everything she'd ever wanted had been hard. Learning to walk again after the fever, becoming a soldier to find Calix. Helping to save the Ward. But she'd never given up, never backed away from a challenge.

Aris straightened her shoulders.

And I won't this time either.

Every day she would try. No matter how bad the nightmares got. No matter how sick she felt. Every day she would climb into her wingjet and try to fly.

And when she could, when the dead soldiers slept and Elom's hands held no power over her, then she would take this bag and fly away.

She would volunteer. As herself this time.

Calix, It's true, what you said. I am not the Aris you knew, not the girl you left on the beach so long ago. Back then, I flew to please only myself. I didn't know what I was capable of. I thought I was content to stay in Lux, to be your little hummingbird and forget the rest of the world.

But I was wrong. I can't be content with that and neither can you. There's a war raging, and we both have the skills to help. It's my duty just as much as it is yours. I am sorry I lied to you. But I'm not sorry I did what I did. I know you value the rules, but sometimes . . . sometimes breaking them is the right thing to do.

I hope we'll see each other again someday. That maybe someday you'll want to find out who I am now, who this Aris is. I think, Calix, if you let yourself, you might like her. I do.

ACKNOWLEDGMENTS

This book has been a true labor of love, spanning ten-plus years now. From submitting to publishers, to self-publishing, to selling it to a digital-first imprint, to going out of print, to bringing it back to the world with Snowy Wings Publishing, this book and I have been on a JOURNEY. There have been countless people at all the different stages of this book's life who have helped, encouraged, supported, and inspired me.

I want to thank Regina Wamba for the beautiful cover, Intisar Khanani for teaching me the Kickstarter ropes and being a sweet and supportive friend, Victoria Alessandri for the incredible character art, Virginia McClain for the graphics, and Jessica Khoury for the incredible map. Pam Gruber, my agent, for helping me get the rights back. And all of my incredible Kickstarter backers, who made the special edition possible.

But, of course, this book had a life before. So I'm going to share my previous acknowledgements as well, because we would never have gotten to this point without the following people:

Heartfelt thanks to my incredibly insightful editors Lanie Davis and Eliza Swift at Alloy Entertainment, and the rest of the team, including Les Morgenstein, Josh Bank, Sara Shandler, Kristin Marang, Romy Golan, Matthew Bloomgarden, Hayley Wagreich, and Natalie Sousa.

Thank you to the team at Amazon, Caroline Carr and Philip Patrick, for beginning the program with Alloy and being so enthusiastic about *Rebel Wing*'s inclusion in it.

Thank you to Rachel Marks and Rebecca Friedman.

Before all these fabulous folks at Alloy, Amazon, and RF

Literary changed my life, *Rebel Wing* was *Shattered Veil*, a book I loved with all of my heart, a book that I just couldn't give up on. Here are the people who wouldn't let me:

Thank you to my earliest (some might say bravest) readers: Héloïse, Mandy, Norma, Rachel, Dawn, Morgan, Rebekah, Michelle, Laura, and Cory. You guys rock my socks. To Fatima Petersen, for inspiring Aris's gorgeous hair. To Theresa and Deward Ray, for providing a comfortable place to write and the most delicious brain fuel. I am now a cupcake addict because of you. To Wendy Schmalz and Catherine Frank, for all of your enthusiasm and support for this book. To Julia Blum, for believing that Aris—and I—had an important story to tell. To my wonderful final-round betas—David Pandolfe, Bethany Dellinger, JJ, and Bernadette Hearne.

Thank you to Victoria Schmitz at Crimson Tide Editorial for the free editorial assessment and your enthusiasm for *Shattered Veil*. To Regina Wamba, for being a total rockstar. You are everything that is awesome and amazing. Ali Cross, thank you for your kick-butt formatting skills and even bigger talent for being an awesome friend.

Huge thanks to my amazing critique partners Shari Arnold, Susanne Winnacker, and Jennifer Walkup—I feel so privileged to work with you and call you my friends. Thank you, also, to my critters in Winston-Salem (miss you guys!), Kass Morgan, Jessica Spotswood, Stephanie Perkins, and to all the other authors who've interacted with me, inspired me, supported me, and generally been fabulous, including the Bookanistas, Indelibles, S3G, Twitter author friends, RDU Nanos, and more. The YA community is powerful, affirming, and inclusive—and I'm so proud and grateful to be a part of it.

Thank you to the Blanton and Hall clan for welcoming me with such open arms, and for your enthusiastic support of my writing. To my parents for embracing my early nerdiness and sending me to all those writing camps. You were on to something there! (And thanks, Mom, for making all your friends read my books.) To Betsy and Suzanne, for being such strong, positive female role models, and for being so supportive of my writing. It means so much.

To Jody Escaravage: You are the most amazingly generous, loyal, supportive friend. Aris is as strong and capable as she is because of you . . . and if you promise not to tell anyone, I'll admit the same is true for me. Also, big hugs to Felix. (Someday you can show him his name in print.)

To all of my wonderful readers, thank you for taking a chance on me. You're the reason I keep writing.

To the courageous women and men serving in the Armed Forces—especially those who made the sacrifice of hiding who they were to fight for this country during the years of "don't ask, don't tell"—you have my gratitude and utmost respect.

To my children, Oliver and Mena: thank you for cheering me on, supporting me, and making my life so much fuller and more fun than I could have ever imagined. I love you so much.

And, finally, to Andy: this book wouldn't exist without you. Thank you for your support and military insight. We've been through a lot together—deployments, moves, and plenty of surprises—and I wouldn't trade a moment of it. I love you.

About the Author

Tracy Banghart is the author of many young adult books, including the Grace and Fury series, *A Season of Sinister Dreams*, and *Perfect Girl*. She also writes picture books, including *Love Like Chocolate*. She has a BA in English from Davidson College and an MA in Publishing from Oxford Brookes University. She is an enthusiastic journal writer, traveler, Girl Scout leader, Army wife, knitter, stained-glass artist, and mom to two kiddos and three pets. Follow @tracythewriter on Instagram or visit her at www.tracybanghart.com.

www.ingramcontent.com/pod-product-compliance
Lightning Source LLC
Chambersburg PA
CBHW061638190726
48289CB00006B/1653